"What's the matter, Russell? Afraid you might like me in spite of yourself?"

It was already too late for that. Kiley Russell faced him. "Don't misunderstand. I think we can work together just fine, but let's keep things strictly business."

"All right."

"Which means we probably shouldn't be dancing."

Collier released her arm. "Gotcha."

Ignoring the sinking feeling in her stomach. Kiley watched as he turned and made his way through the crowd toward the bar. Good. Now there would be no misunderstandings, no more dancing, no more touching.

Her gaze traced the broad line of his shoulders, the slightly ragged edge of his dark hair as she recalled the seductive feel of his hard body against hers.

Who was she kidding?

What she felt for him was hotter and more dangerous than mere "like."

Dear Reader,

June brings you six high-octane reads from Silhouette Intimate Moments, just in time for summer. First up, Ingrid Weaver enthralls readers with *Loving the Lone Wolf* (#1369), which is part of her revenge-ridden PAYBACK miniseries, Here, a street thug turned multimillionaire on a mission falls for the enemy's girlfriend and learns that looks can be deceiving! Crank up your air-conditioning as Debra Cowan's miniseries THE HOT ZONE will definitely raise temperatures with its firefighter characters. The second book, *Melting Point* (#1370), has a detective heroine and firefighting hero discovering more than one way to put out a fire as they track a serial killer.

Caridad Piñeiro lures us back to her haunting miniseries, THE CALLING. In *Danger Calls* (#1371), a beautiful doctor loses herself in her work, until a heady passion creates delicious chaos while throwing her onto a dangerous path. You'll want to curl up with Linda Winstead Jones's latest book, *One Major Distraction* (#1372), from her miniseries LAST CHANCE HEROES, in which a marine poses as a teacher to find a killer and falls for none other than the fetching school cook…who hides one whopper of a secret.

When a SWAT hero butts heads with a plucky reporter, a passionate interlude is sure to follow in Diana Duncan's *Truth or Consequences* (#1373), the next book in her fast-paced miniseries FOREVER IN A DAY. In *Deadly Reunion* (#1374), by Lauren Nichols, our heroine thinks her life is comfortable. But of course, mayhem ensues as her ex-husband—a man she's never stopped loving—returns to solve a murder and clear his name…and she's going to help him.

This month is all about finding love against the odds and those adventures lurking around the corner. So as you lounge in your favorite chair, lose yourself in one of these gems from Silhouette Intimate Moments!

Sincerely,

Patience Smith
Associate Senior Editor

Please address questions and book requests to:
Silhouette Reader Service
U.S.: 3010 Walden Ave., P.O. Box 1325, Buffalo, NY 14269
Canadian: P.O. Box 609, Fort Erie, Ont. L2A 5X3

MELTING POINT

DEBRA COWAN

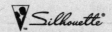

INTIMATE MOMENTS™

Published by Silhouette Books

America's Publisher of Contemporary Romance

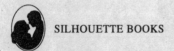 SILHOUETTE BOOKS

ISBN 0-373-27440-8

MELTING POINT

Copyright © 2005 by Debra S. Cowan

This edition published by arrangement with Harlequin Books S.A.

® and TM are trademarks of Harlequin Books S.A., used under license.
Trademarks indicated with ® are registered in the United States Patent
and Trademark Office, the Canadian Trade Marks Office and in other
countries.

Visit Silhouette Books at www.eHarlequin.com

Printed in U.S.A.

Books by Debra Cowan

Silhouette Intimate Moments

Dare To Remember #774
The Rescue of Jenna West #858
One Silent Night #899
Special Report #1045
"Cover Me!"
Still the One #1127
Burning Love #1236
Melting Point #1370

*The Hot Zone

DEBRA COWAN

Like many writers, Debra made up stories in her head as a child. Her B.A. in English was obtained with the intention of following family tradition and becoming a schoolteacher, but after she wrote her first novel, there was no looking back. After years of working another job in addition to writing, she now devotes herself full-time to penning both historical and contemporary romances. An avid history buff, Debra enjoys traveling. She has visited places as diverse as Europe and Honduras, where she and her husband served as part of a medical mission team. Born in the foothills of the Kiamichi Mountains, Debra still lives in her native Oklahoma with her husband and their two beagles, Maggie and Domino.

Debra invites her readers to contact her at P.O. Box 30123, Coffee Creek Station, Edmond, OK 73003-0003 or via e-mail at her Web site at: www.debracowan.net.

This book is dedicated to firefighters.

ACKNOWLEDGMENTS

My deepest gratitude to David Wiist,
retired Chief of Fire Prevention, Edmond, OK,
a true gentleman who patiently answers countless
questions; to Jack Goldhorn, PIO, Norfolk Fire Rescue,
Norfolk, VA, whose enthusiasm always makes me smile.
Both of you go beyond the call to help me with accuracy.
Any errors are mine. To Linda Goodnight, nurse, writer
and friend, and her wonderful son, Dr. Travis Goodnight.
Finally to my agent, Pattie Steele-Perkins.
Thanks for never giving up.

Chapter 1

A gunshot exploded in the frigid night, the sound cutting sharply through the thunking of the hydrant valve and the water gushing through the fire hose. In full turnout gear, Presley firefighter Collier McClain threw himself to the ground. A few yards in front of him, at the door of the burning warehouse, Dan Lazano wobbled and fell. The nozzle flopped. Collier automatically moved his hand up the line to gain control and shouted, "Mayday! Firefighter down!"

Keeping the nozzle on and water streaming into the building, he belly-crawled forward. Light from the flames illuminated Lazano's steel-soled boot. Collier wet down the surrounding space, making a "safe area" for him and the injured man as the two-man Rapid Intervention Team from the Presley Fire Department followed the hose line straight to him.

The moon was a bloodless white, the January air brittle. Black smoke and hot water wrapped around Collier like a thermal blanket, burning his neck. He sprayed water on the safe area until Pitts and Foster reached Lazano, then he pushed the lever forward to turn off the nozzle.

As two other firefighters dragged in another line already shooting water, Collier moved out behind Lazano and the rescue crew. Pitts and Foster, firefighters and medics, dragged the injured man into the grass, yards away from the building. While they began administering basic life support, Collier yanked off his helmet and Nomex hood, his heart hammering in his throat.

"Damn," Pitts yelled. "He's gone."

Collier followed the other man's gaze and saw a dark wetness spreading over Lazano's chest through a ragged hole in his turnout coat.

"McClain, is that Lazano?"

Through the stomp of feet and hiss of water and grunts of effort, he recognized Captain Sandusky's voice and nodded. He stared down in disbelief at the black stickiness on his glove. Blood?

"What happened?"

Collier shook his head.

Sandusky knelt, reaching toward the downed man. "Is he out?"

"He's dead." Collier's gaze locked with his captain's.

The other man blinked, alarm rising in his voice. "Where did that gunshot come from?"

Collier jerked a thumb over his shoulder. Pitts and Foster looked away, their throats working.

"This is four." The captain's tortured words mirrored Collier's thoughts.

Since October, three other firefighters had been murdered. Tonight's victim and one other were from Station House Two.

Sandusky flipped on his flashlight, then cursed. "I'll call the police. Your new boss, too."

Collier stood there stunned, only one thought circling through his head. If he'd been first on the nozzle tonight, as he usually was, *as he had tried to be,* he would be the one lying dead in the grass.

* * *

A firefighter had been killed at a fire scene. Not by smoke or burns but by a gun. Murdered.

Detective Kiley Russell wished she didn't have experience with anything like this, but she did. All of three months' worth. Lieutenant Hager had paged her tonight because of the other firefighter murders she had been working since October. His grim announcement of another victim had balled a cold knot of dread in her gut. Serial killer. A sniper.

The first victim had been killed during a fire call at the gymnasium of Presley's oldest high school. The second victim had been murdered five weeks later at a motel he'd checked into with a mystery woman. Number three, the only female, had been shot in her home garage.

Somebody was after the firefighters in this Oklahoma City suburb.

Kiley gathered her mass of wild red hair into a ponytail, stuffed her feet into sneakers and grabbed her heaviest coat out of the hall closet. Moving out of the house, she clipped her badge and holstered Taurus onto the waistband of her jeans. The new year was starting off with a bang. Literally.

January cold pressed the air like a thick layer of batting. As Kiley maneuvered her late-model Mustang through the streets of Presley, she called her sister's cell phone and left a message so Kristin would know Kiley would miss their weekly Saturday breakfast just a few hours from now.

She headed for the south side of town and Benson Street, an industrial area that housed several warehouses. The fire was at Rehn's Coffee Warehouse.

By the time she arrived, patrol officers had blocked off the area. Red and blue lights flashed from the police cruisers book-ending the scene. She showed her badge to the uniformed officer posted at this end of the street, then parked beside the ambulance crouched in front of the curb with its back doors open, its empty gurney raised and waiting.

Scanning the massive building, Kiley stepped out of her car and pulled on her fleece-lined gloves. The blaze appeared to be out. Large scene lights, attached to two fire trucks, shone on the warehouse. Gray-brown smoke swirled into clouds. A concrete drive, wide enough to accommodate two semi trucks side by side, led up to a heavy metal door. Docking doors and offices opened into a large parking lot on the side.

Shards of glass glittered in the dusky white light put off by bulbs shining from under the eaves of the flat-topped building. Black sooty water ran down the concrete drive and into the streets, sloshing over the tops of her tennis shoes.

Kiley's breath frosted the air. Thank goodness this wasn't a residential area and there were no bystanders. Three fire engines, one ladder truck and one rescue unit lined the curb in front of the warehouse. Stations One, Two and Four, she observed. More than one Presley station house responded to fire calls, mainly to ensure enough manpower. House fires typically had two stations responding as well as the station that housed the rescue truck. The size of this warehouse had probably warranted the response of three stations. Tonight's victim was the second one from Station Two. Did that mean anything?

Three black-and-whites, two trucks from local utility companies and the M.E.'s wagon crowded the width of the street. Two vans sporting local news logos pulled up to the barricade blocking traffic behind her. Kiley moved around the rear of her car and stopped at the curb to give her name and rank to the cop logging in personnel with his clipboard. A sharp wind pulled tendrils of her hair across her face, and she shoved them back.

Having checked in, she started up the flat drive, sidestepping deflated canvas hoses. Firefighters moved around the scene, the short browned grass now soggy and black. A length of yellow crime-scene tape stretched down the left side of the drive, across the entrance and up to the back corner of the shipping dock. Although she expected to find nothing, she sent two officers to search the area and the area across the street for the gun.

There were no windows in the front of the building, but there were several on the side, a few panes now shattered and saber-toothed in the darkness. A male firefighter stood in the center of the football-field-size drive, aiming a video camera at the scene. Kiley had recently learned that the Presley Fire Department videotaped eighty percent of their scenes, especially if they appeared suspicious.

About seventy-five yards from the door, a lone fireman knelt on the ground next to a body. Other firefighters gathered around him.

"Detective!"

Kiley turned to see Captain Martin Sandusky from Station Two.

"Here. You'll need to put on some boots." The barrel-chested man, sweating despite the freezing temperature, caught up to her. "That way you won't have to worry about any hot spots or sharp objects."

Debris littered the grass and the cracked concrete drive. From what Kiley could tell, the trash appeared to be mostly ash, glass and fiberglass insulation, but nails, screws and pieces of metal could easily be scattered as well.

"Thanks." She took the steel-soled rubber boots and pulled them on over her tennis shoes, then walked with the captain up to the circle of firefighters.

Frigid air stung her cheeks and nose. She burrowed deeper into the lining of her coat. Presley was small enough that all police, including the detectives, worked solo except in fire death cases. Procedure between Presley's police and fire departments stated that when PFD had a dead body at a fire scene, they contained the blaze then stopped and called Homicide. Tonight, the victim was again one of their own.

"What can you tell me so far?" she asked the captain.

"We rolled up. Lazano and McClain both headed for the nozzle. I thought McClain had it until I heard a boom and saw Lazano being dragged over by the rescue crew."

So, Collier McClain was working tonight. Peachy. "How severe was the fire?"

"It was going great guns when we arrived and powered up as soon as Lazano got the door open, but it was out in less than twenty minutes. It was a sniper shot again, came from behind us across the street."

What was going on with this lunatic? As she approached the tight circle of firefighters with their captain, the five men and two women eased back enough that Kiley could see the body.

Captain Sandusky cleared his throat, drawing the gazes of the firefighters except the one guarding the victim. "Guys, here's Detective Russell."

They greeted her with solemn nods. She'd come to know most of them over the past three months.

"Where's Investigator Spencer?" someone asked.

"She's on her way." Kiley took in the soot-streaked yellow hats, the wet, grimy turnout gear, smoke and tear-reddened eyes on all the firefighters, but her attention homed in on the man lying motionless at their feet.

Still wearing turnout gear, the man's handsome face and dark eyebrows were unmarred from smoke. The glinting darkness of blood on his chest had Kiley swallowing hard.

"I'm sorry," she murmured. "Who moved the body?"

"We did." Two firefighters raised their hands.

"Pitts and Foster," Sandusky supplied. "They're our Rapid Intervention Team tonight."

"We retrieved him and started working on him," one of them said.

"It's standard procedure." The kneeling fireman raised his head and looked at her.

The air seeped out of her lungs. After Sandusky's mentioning that Collier McClain was here, she had expected to see him, but she hadn't been prepared.

In this light, his eye color was impossible to discern, but Kiley remembered the stormy green that was now glazed with shock. That wasn't all she remembered.

She'd spent the past four weeks trying to forget the Christmas party at the Fraternal Order of Police club. That knee-melting dance. His nerve-tingling drawl. Why did he have to be *here?*

He gestured to the body crumpled on the frosty grass. "Lazano had on all his protective gear, but they had to get him out of the danger zone, see the extent of his injuries. There was no way of knowing if the building was going to come down, if the fire was going to swallow us up."

She glanced over her shoulder at the warehouse, ignoring the sudden hitch in her pulse. Collier looked ragged, but he was as darkly compelling as ever. The concrete building was streaked with black, and glass littered the east edge of the driveway. "Looks like the fire was contained pretty quickly."

"It was," the captain put in, staring down at Lazano's body.

"I'm sorry about your man, Captain. I'll be able to piece the scene back together with firefighter statements and those from your RIT."

"Good."

She refocused her attention on Collier. His helmet rested beside him.

"Here comes Investigator Spencer now," someone said.

"I'll see how she wants to handle this." Kiley broke away

from the others and went to meet Presley's fire investigator, needing a moment to gather her composure.

After that dance at the Christmas party, she had asked her sister what she knew about Collier McClain. Kristin had told her that he had broken his engagement about eighteen months ago and since that time he had dated and dumped half the women on the city's payroll. Hearing about Collier's playboy reputation had immediately thrown up the walls Kiley had built while growing up with a man just like that.

She had dated a lot in her thirty-one years, but she'd made it a rule to never date guys like Collier, guys she had come to refer to as "hit-and-runs." Thanks to her father, Kiley knew to keep a distance from men whose relationships didn't last as long as it took to spell the word. Whatever reaction she'd had to the rangy firefighter during their dance had been nipped in the bud. She needed to shake it off and get her head in the game.

Kiley had been working with Terra August Spencer since the first firefighter murder in October. Even if it hadn't been city policy, Kiley needed the expertise of a fire cop. The clue to solving these murders might be something found at a fire scene. So far, all their leads had fizzled out, which frustrated them both.

They had four firefighters who had been murdered—*shot*. Two of them during calls and two who had been killed while off duty.

The willowy fire investigator moved with the slowness of her advanced pregnancy. Kiley knew from their recent work together that Terra Spencer was due in a month's time. She gave the other woman a smile of recognition. "How are you feeling?"

Terra grimaced. "Like a blimp. And I'm moving about as fast as a turtle. Sorry y'all have to wait on me."

"No problem."

Concern darkened her green eyes. "Who's down?"

"Dan Lazano."

"I didn't know him very well," Terra murmured. "What can you tell me?"

Just as she started to fill the other woman in on what she knew so far, the investigator's cell phone rang.

Terra reached into her pocket and flipped open the phone. "Hi, honey." She looked at Kiley and held up a finger as she stepped a few feet away, reassuring the person on the other end.

Probably her gorgeous husband, Kiley surmised. Terra had married Presley detective, Jack Spencer, a couple of years ago. She'd been glowing ever since. The impending birth of their child made her radiant.

Kiley felt a twinge of envy. She'd kissed plenty of frogs during her thirty-one years on this planet, but never her Mr. Right. She wasn't sure what she wanted in a man, but she knew what she didn't want. Her gaze slid grudgingly to Collier McClain. She knew *exactly* what she didn't want.

"Sorry about that." Terra walked back over to her, sliding her cell phone into the pocket of her heavy coat. "The closer the due date gets, the more Jack checks on me. Now, what's happened?"

Kiley smiled, giving the woman her full attention as she answered.

When she finished, the other woman shook her head, horror streaking across her face. "I guess we haven't had any luck finding the weapon?"

"I've got a couple of uniforms searching the area, but there's nothing yet."

Terra gave a start and patted her stomach with an apologetic look. "The baby doesn't like being dragged out of bed."

Kiley grinned. "Neither do I."

"I guess we'd better begin. Maybe we'll turn up something here."

"Maybe so." Kiley shared the fire investigator's frustration over the cold trail of leads on their other homicides.

As they moved toward the group of waiting firefighters, Terra said, "I'll go ahead and do the walk-around with the guys then meet you back here. Once we determine the structure is secure, you and I can go inside and begin our investigation there."

"All right. I'll start interviewing witnesses." And she would start with Collier McClain.

Presley had seen a serial arsonist before, but not a serial killer. A little over two years ago, a cameraman for one of the local news channels had started setting fires to get Terra's attention, then murdered anyone who he perceived as distracting her attention from him.

Kiley had been promoted to detective ten months ago and in October had happened to catch the call involving the firefighter who'd been shot in the back as he ran into a fire at Presley High School's gym.

Terra lifted the camera around her neck to snap pictures of the building and surrounding area. Two firefighters unloaded portable floodlights from Terra's SUV and set them up inside the warehouse. The daylight-strength power of the scene lights outside brightened the area.

When the other woman started toward the building, Kiley walked over to the body again. The group of firefighters had scattered. Dan Lazano's facial features were recognizable. Since he had been wearing all his protective gear, there were no visible burns on what she could see of his body.

Ken Mason, the Oklahoma County coroner, knelt beside the body.

"What do you think, Doc?"

"No soot around or in the nose or mouth, no burns at all. Like Sandusky said, Lazano never made it into the building. The only injury I've noted so far is the gunshot wound. It's a through-and-through."

In through the back, out through the chest. "Thanks." She

turned, searching for Collier McClain and saw him near the warehouse's front door talking with Terra.

The man was rangy, strong and built with the lean lines of a baseball pitcher. His hawkish features were sharp in the unstinting white light from the megawatt bulbs illuminating the scene. He wasn't her type at all, which was exactly why she'd danced with him. And why her over-the-top physical reaction had rocked her. Might as well get this over with.

Taking a deep breath, she started toward him. He left Investigator Spencer to meet her halfway.

"I need to ask you some questions," she said quietly.

"All right." He looked tired and dazed.

"Tell me what happened. Or what you remember."

He dragged a hand down his face, his turnout coat wet, his breath curling in the cold air. "I went for the nozzle."

"Was that usually your spot?"

"Whoever got there first, but yeah, it was usually me."

"Go on."

"I was off the truck and ahead of Lazano when this stupid cat tripped me. By the time I got around the dumb thing, Dan had the nozzle and was on his way into the building."

"And you were how far behind him?"

He shook his head. "I don't know. Four, five steps. He was at the door."

Collier had long legs; his stride was easily over a yard. "And then what?"

"He started in, then I heard the gunshot."

"You knew right off what it was?"

"I reacted more from reflex at first. We've all been jumpy since Miller's murder," he said grimly.

Gary Miller was the first firefighter who'd been killed by the sniper three months ago. "Then you went for Lazano?"

"Yes." He stared over his shoulder at the warehouse. "The padlock was cut. We didn't have to use force to open the door."

She followed his gaze to the door, now open. Terra's flood-lights illuminated the inside of the big concrete cave.

So the sniper had time to aim for the best shot while Lazano took those two heartbeats to open the door. Kiley scribbled the note in her notebook. "How long before you heard the shot?"

"I'd guess maybe two seconds, three. It was quick."

"Did you work the scene where Miller was killed?"

"No, but I was there."

"Why?"

He shrugged. "I heard the call and went by. Turned out they needed another pair of hands so I stayed for a while. Don't you cops do that?"

Yes, they did. "Do you remember seeing anyone hanging around that night? Anyone you might've noticed here, as well?"

"No." He thought for a moment. "There may have been people walking or driving by tonight, but I didn't see a thing besides that stupid cat."

"Okay." Kiley glanced over at the victim, now being transferred into a body bag. "How long did you know Dan Lazano?"

"Twelve years. We went through firefighter academy together, then he was assigned to Station Two about five years ago."

A tightness in his voice made Kiley switch her focus to him. "Were you friends?"

In the glaring, smoke-hazed air, she thought she saw his mouth tighten. "Not really."

Was there resentment under his words? "Enemies?"

"Not exactly. We had a tug-of-war going on over the nozzle."

"About who would get it first?"

He nodded.

"Know anyone who would want to hurt him?"

Collier's gaze bored right through her. "No, but you'll probably hear different."

"Okay," she said expectantly. At five-nine, Kiley didn't have to look up to very many men, but she did with the six-foot-plus firefighter. A tiny sliver of awareness shimmied up her spine. What was it about this man? She dismissed the giddiness he put in her stomach, but allowed herself to search his eyes. She saw a rawness there before he shuttered them against her. What was he not telling her?

Oh, yeah, she was really getting somewhere with this guy. "McClain—"

"Lazano and I were friends once." He glanced away, clearly reluctant to talk.

"It's better if I hear it from you."

He stepped closer, the odor of smoke swirling around her. "He and my fiancée were—" He broke off and dragged a hand down his smoke-buffed face. "I found them together."

She drew in a sharp breath. That was brutal. Now she understood the emotion that had flashed through his eyes, and her chest tightened. She really didn't want to continue this line of questioning, but she had to do her job. "So you had a reason to hate him."

"But not kill him."

"Your fiancée cheated on you with one of your friends." Kiley could only imagine the pain. "If my ex took up with one of my friends, I couldn't find it that easy to forgive."

"Not forgiving is a long way from murder, Detective."

"Not to some people." Just because Collier had broken his engagement didn't mean he wasn't still in love with his ex. And maybe angry and hurt enough to kill the man who'd betrayed their friendship.

Anything was possible and he could've hired a sniper and been here to fight the fire, but Kiley had a good sense of people. Collier McClain didn't seem to be the kind of man who would hire someone else to take care of his problems. He would do it himself, face-to-face. The fact that he could've easily been the one killed tonight also helped in settling her questions about his involvement. Once she checked his alibis for the nights of the other murders, she could probably mark him off her suspect list officially.

A glance over her shoulder showed Terra stepping inside the warehouse, but Kiley had more questions. She looked back at her witness. "I may need to talk to you again later."

"I'll be around." He tucked his helmet under his arm and tunneled a hand through his short, wet hair.

Annoyed at the way his cool voice knotted her nerves, she moved over to Pitts and Foster, the safety crew who had been sent by Captain Sandusky to talk to her.

She needed to put aside her personal feelings. The memory of that dance, the feel of Collier's large hand curled warmly on her hip, the hard length of his body against hers. She had a job to do and she would focus on that. Looking for commonalities between the victims had Kiley asking the same questions she had asked at the other three murder scenes.

Did tonight's victim socialize off duty with any of the others? Did he go to the same doctor or church with the other victims? High school or college? Had he been involved in a side business with any of the victims? Again all answers were no.

About thirty minutes later, she joined Terra outside the front door of the warehouse where the fire investigator again stood talking to Collier McClain. Three firefighters had backed up his story about the cat as well as vouching for him on the other nights in question.

And the firefighters she'd interviewed had confirmed that he and Lazano did have an ongoing rivalry regarding who would get the nozzle first.

"The structure is secure enough for us to go inside," Terra said when Kiley reached her. "It's lucky the next warehouse is at least three hundred feet away or this whole side of the street might've gone up."

It appeared this fire, like the others, had been set to lure the firefighters here and kill one of them, but they needed proof. "Did you see anything that hinted at arson?"

"Not yet. The window was blown out from the inside, probably from heat, but that doesn't mean we're looking at arson." She glanced at Kiley's feet. "Good, you have on some of our boots. You need a helmet, too."

"Is there falling debris?"

"We want to be prepared."

Kiley took a helmet from the firefighter who held one out at Terra's request and slid it onto her head.

Collier McClain stood silently to the side. He had cleaned the ash from his face, but there was strain around his gray-green eyes and the same guardedness she hoped he saw in her eyes. She shut off further thoughts of him and followed Terra inside the cavernous concrete and metal building. It smelled of burned coffee, wet ash and the searing odor of charred insulation and chemicals. Light glanced off white burlap bags of coffee stacked on row after row of wooden pallets.

Strong light streamed from the portable floodlamps, and Kiley stopped, taking a quick look around the soaked floor, wet wooden pallets stacked with now-sopping white bags of coffee.

"I bagged the padlock so we can check it for prints."

Startled to hear McClain's voice, Kiley spun. "What are you doing?"

He frowned. "Going through the building."

"Why?"

"He's my new fire investigator," Terra said absently. "You know he's been working with me on his days off. For about the last year and a half."

"Yes, but he fought this fire." She looked away from his level gaze, wishing she'd had a little warning about his more significant involvement in the investigation. She'd known their working together would happen eventually, but she wasn't ready. "How can he investigate and work the scene as a firefighter?"

"It's happened before. Besides, this is his last shift. When he reports to work on Monday, it will be for me."

Kiley knew displeasure and sheer panic showed on her face.

"What's going on, Kiley?" Terra looked slightly irritated.

"I...just didn't expect him to also investigate."

"Is *he* a suspect?" Collier asked tightly.

"No." Curling her hands into fists at her sides, her gaze shot to Terra. "This isn't a conflict of interest?"

"No." The other woman glanced at Collier then back at Kiley.

"Can you handle it, Detective?" His smoke-roughened voice challenged her.

She wasn't about to let him see how off balance she really felt. She flashed a smile at Terra. "Let's go. I'll try to keep up."

"Whew, good. I'm going on maternity leave in two weeks. I want Collier to know everything I know about this scene."

"Is he going to take over this case?" Had she just squeaked?

"Unless we clear it before I have this baby, and I don't foresee that. So, you'll have to partner up."

Kiley gave a forced smile, avoiding Collier's gaze.

"Let's get started, then," Terra said.

The three of them began a slow walk, sloshing through dark water, with Collier beside Terra and Kiley slightly behind. Her eyes narrowed on his broad shoulders. Collier McClain wasn't just Presley's newest fire investigator, and her partner for the time being. He was the one man she'd sworn to avoid like the Ebola virus.

Chapter 2

Collier had wanted to be first on the nozzle tonight, but nothing about this call had gone the way he'd wanted. Not what had happened to Lazano. And not seeing Kiley Russell.

Collier hadn't allowed himself to think about her since that Christmas party at the FOP club. Then tonight, on the second day of the new year, she'd burst in front of him like a firecracker.

In the month since meeting her, he hadn't forgotten the curve of her hip beneath his palm as they'd danced. Or the warm, spicy fragrance of fresh woman and body heat.

Kiley Russell wasn't conventionally beautiful like Gwen, but he wasn't the only man who couldn't take his eyes off her. Her tangle of red hair hinted at a wildness that was banked in her eyes. Creamy skin and rosy cheeks gave her a fresh-faced appeal that invited people to like her even though Collier sensed that if she decided to seduce a man, those stunning blue-green eyes could knock him clear into next week.

What really had Collier's internal alarm screaming was the

memory of Detective Russell's laugh. Low and smoky, the sound had grabbed at something deep inside, telling him that his attraction to her was more than physical. He'd managed to bury all that over the holidays, but seeing her now brought the memories bubbling to the surface. Memories he had no intention of giving free rein.

In the year and a half since he'd called off his engagement to Gwen, Collier hadn't regretted his new no-strings policy with women. He didn't like that Kiley Russell was the first woman to make him think about breaking it. Liked even less that his thoughts were on her instead of the crime scene in which they stood.

"Since we can't take measurements of the body's original position," Terra said, "we'll have to rely on the Rapid Intervention Team and any other eyewitness accounts to determine where Lazano fell."

Kiley stepped up, pointing to a spot in front of the open doorway. "The RIT put Lazano here."

"That's right. And so did the attack crew who took over for me and Lazano." Collier turned, his gaze skipping over the puddles of black water on Benson Street. "The shot came from behind. Probably from that warehouse across the street."

Kiley made a note in her notebook.

Standing on the edge of the bright light thrown by the portable floodlamps, Collier walked to the bloodstain barely visible on the wet concrete and dictated the location into Terra's handheld tape recorder.

"I'm surprised all the blood wasn't washed away," Kiley observed, following the other woman into the warehouse. "I guess it would be too much to hope we might get some prints off this door? I'm guessing the firefighters probably blasted them off with their hoses."

"We're trained to put out the fire, which means we can't really worry about preserving evidence," Collier said from behind her. "To put out a blaze, you've got to chop holes in the roof, tear down walls, kick out windows plus soak everything in thousands of gallons of water. Even so, we're trained not to get carried away with our water streams. We douse the flames and make sure they don't rekindle. And we typically use a wide spray pattern, like a fog. If that doesn't work, we have to use a small spray, so a straight stream could've destroyed that evidence."

"You're both assuming there were prints to begin with," Terra said as they paused shoulder to shoulder in a small huddle.

Kiley slid a look at Collier. "What about the heat? Would it compromise a fingerprint?"

"Prints can be tricky. Most people believe fire destroys all evidence, but that's not true. It would take hot, hot temperatures to distort or destroy a print. From the condition of the wood pallets, I don't think the fire burned long enough to get that hot. The door is barely discolored." He pointed over his head to a steel beam with dark streaks. "None of the steel up there is melted, though it is discolored and marked. The melting point for steel is 2500 degrees."

"So a twenty-minute fire wouldn't normally be hot enough or long burning enough to melt the I-beams?"

"Not unless there were flammable liquids or explosives, something to help it along."

"What accelerant do you think was used?"

"Maybe none. That's something we need to find out." He studied the steel beams supporting the apex of the roof. "It doesn't appear the fire got hot enough or high enough back here to melt the steel."

"Just some of the aluminum walls." Terra pointed to some damaged sheeting.

Kiley scribbled in her notebook. "So what does that tell you?"

Terra looked at Collier expectantly, so he said, "That the fire temperature on the walls was less than 660 degrees and that whatever reached the ceiling probably burned less than a thousand."

The detective nodded and made another note.

"First, we'll try to confirm or eliminate arson," Terra explained over her shoulder.

Collier added, "Part of that process will be checking the electrical wiring."

Kiley resettled her helmet. "So, all we know at this point is that Dan Lazano was murdered."

"Right," Collier said. "It was definitely not suicide." Suicide was one manner of death that had to be eliminated in the course of an investigation. Given he was an eye witness, Collier could do that with confidence. He still couldn't believe Lazano was dead. And how close he had come to being a victim himself.

"I'm sure you've both already taken note that this is our second victim from Station Two." Terra stopped a few feet away, her pretty features grim. "It's the first time that's happened."

"Since the first two firefighters worked out of different stations," Collier said, "the connection is not that the victims worked out of the same house. I'll be interested to see if any of our previous interviews turn up on the list again."

"Let's get busy," Terra interrupted, "and see what we can find."

"Lead the way," Kiley said.

To ward off the smoke headache already pulsing at the base of his skull, Collier downed several ibuprofen without water and passed a few to her. She took them and slid them into her pocket. He mentally shrugged. Maybe she didn't get smoke headaches from tromping around fire scenes.

He flexed his hands inside the pair of stiff gloves Terra had loaned him. At Russell's request, his well-used gloves, stained with Lazano's blood, were now bagged as evidence outside with another cop. The three of them worked their way from the least amount of damage to the worst.

Terra snapped pictures from several angles and Collier dictated information about their position and observations into her recorder. In his other hand, he carried a shovel and her tackle box. They stopped frequently, shoveling ashes and debris, searching for evidence.

Over the past eighteen months, he'd built his own tool kit, which included every kind of tool from pliers and tape measures to hacksaws and hammers. For evidence gathering, he carried sterile paint cans, paper and plastic bags and a couple of small jars for liquids. Since he'd been on his last firefighting shift tonight and his new job wasn't supposed to officially begin until Monday, he was without his kit.

Lazano's murder had moved up Collier's start date…and teamed him with a woman he would rather avoid. As a fire investigator, he had the authority to interview and interrogate but not to arrest or serve warrants like Russell did. Because of the policy between the Presley Fire Department and Police Department, he would have to work with Detective Russell until one of them proved the death was an accident or murder. They already knew Lazano's death hadn't been a suicide and didn't believe there was anything accidental about it, so it appeared he would be working with the redhead until they closed these murder cases. Just dandy.

The physical reaction he'd had to Russell during that dance had been warning enough, but combined with the insistent curiosity he felt about her, he had backed way off. And he intended to stay that way.

"I have to hand it to y'all," Kiley said from behind him. "The amount of patience this takes is incredible."

Collier shared a look with Terra. She'd had to remind him more than once that investigations took time and patience. He'd had to learn to curb his firefighter's attack mentality and to carefully, thoroughly, follow the crime trail one step at a time.

He'd wanted to work fire investigations for more than two

years, which was why he had readily agreed to apprentice with Terra for no pay. Besides putting him in a good position to nab the promotion to fire investigator when another spot with her office opened up, he'd also taken on the additional and demanding hours as a way to forget about Gwen. And he had.

Another fire investigator hadn't been approved and budgeted until a few months ago. He'd taken the test, passed his independent assessment and been interviewed by Terra along with another candidate. She had offered the job to him, and the other man had found a job shortly thereafter with Oklahoma City's fire marshal.

Kiley trailed him through the center of the warehouse, wet grime sucking at her boots. "I remember Terra saying that arsonists typically set fires either for revenge, attention or to hide evidence of another crime. In this case it looks like the fires are being set as bait to attract the firefighters to the scene and kill them."

Collier turned to her. "I agree."

"I guess we should consider insurance fraud. If only to show we eliminated that motive."

"Warehouses are always prime marks for fire insurance fraud," he admitted.

"It's possible that one person set the fire for insurance money and that another person murdered Lazano," Terra offered, rubbing at her lower back again. "But this is too much like the other murders. I think our arsonist and sniper are the same person. And I think we're dealing with an emotional fire setter as opposed to a pathological one."

"What's the difference?" Kiley asked.

"An emotional fire setter strikes out of revenge or hate," Terra said. "A pathological torch gets off just by setting fires."

Kiley glanced around the warehouse. "Since we're dealing with a serial killer who's using the blaze to bait firefighters, we have an emotional fire setter."

"It appears that way." Collier dragged a hand down his face. "So while arson definitely plays a role, we should be looking for someone who has more motive to kill than burn."

"I think you're right." His boss looked as grim as he felt.

Kiley adjusted the too-large helmet on her head. "I'll check on the warehouse's insurance policy, anyway, just to cover our bases."

As they worked their way to the worst burn area, the fire's origin, Collier documented every step with photos and sketches.

On the east side of the interior, Terra halted in front of him and sniffed the air. "I don't smell any accelerant. No gasoline, no kerosene, nothing."

Collier couldn't smell any, either. Scenting accelerants was a natural ability Terra had that he didn't, but she had said that didn't matter. What would make him a good fire investigator wasn't what he could smell, but what he observed.

Scanning the coffee pallet and metal wall directly in front of him for the "low point" or point of origin, his gaze settled on a blackened circle on the concrete.

Both women walked up beside him. Collier kept his focus on the spot in front of him, concentrating on determining if this fire was arson. Why would a fire start here? There was no heat source, so he could eliminate that the blaze had been accidental. He pointed to a small mound of charred material in the middle of the blackened circle. "This pile of rags is the point of origin. Looks like it may be towels."

"Let's take a look at burn patterns on the pallets and coffee bags that burned, the leftover debris here and on the floor, ground, ceiling," Terra said.

After carefully bagging a fist-size amount of the remaining cloth, he used a small sterile paint can to hold a sample of the charred wooden pallet. Terra took photos of the places where the samples had come from, while Collier indicated the same on the drawing of the fire-sketch layout he'd started for the warehouse.

To be thorough, he also sealed a handful of coffee beans, but he didn't expect to find that they had absorbed any accelerant. He studied the charred pallet and a ten-inch stretch of black going up the metal wall beside it. He ran a quick test with the portable "sniffer," a small boxlike instrument that detected carbons like those usually left behind in gasoline or flammable liquids.

Glancing up at Terra, he was aware of Kiley in his peripheral vision. "The readout is negative for any kind of gas or flammable liquids. Right now it looks like the fire started with a match and a bundle of towels."

"I don't think the arsonist tried to hide it, either," his new boss said. "Probably lit this bunch of cloth then waited for the fire alarm to trip."

"They had probably already scoped out their position across the street." Kiley glanced toward the front of the building. "And the fire was set close enough to the door for a quick exit."

"Another sign of arson." Collier's stomach tightened at the cold calculation indicated by the scenario they were starting to piece together. Calculation that could've killed *him* this time.

Between that and the redhead behind him, his nerves were stretched taut. He shut the tackle box and rose. "From the obvious placement of the towels, I don't think the arsonist cares if we figure out how the fire started. The hardest blazes to determine are the ones with a single match and a little thought."

"All the fires have basically been set in the same way and a rifle used in all four of them." Terra braced a hand at the small of her back.

"The first fire at the high school gym and this one tonight were started before the shootings," Kiley observed. "But the fires at the motel and in the victim's garage were set *after* the victims were killed. Just to get the firefighters to respond?"

"I'd say yes."

"Lisa Embry and now Lazano give us two vics from the same station. Miller was with Station Three and Huffman with Four."

"Going through the first three victims' shifts at their respective station houses gave us the calls they had in common." Collier put a new roll of film into his camera. "We'll check to see if Lazano's work schedule coincides with theirs."

"All the murders have occurred within the first week of the month so we should cross-reference those dates with the rescue call dates." Kiley flipped a page in her notebook. "We still haven't found anything in the first victim's background to suggest someone would want to kill him. As for the second victim, we haven't found the blond woman witnesses say Rex Huffman was last seen with at that motel."

"What about Lisa Embry's ex?" The third victim and her husband had gone through a nasty divorce and custody battle. He had ended up with the house and joint custody of the kids.

Kiley's jaw firmed. "We should talk to him again, ask him where he was tonight."

Terra picked up the thread. "Kiley and I will continue to work our way down the list of people who have died in fires within the last six months to a year. Or fatalities that occurred when any of these murdered firefighters were on the scene. The killer could be someone who blames the firefighters for the death of a loved one."

"In the meantime, these guys are a bull's-eye every time they respond to a call." Collier couldn't keep the rage out of his voice. "Just like Russian roulette."

And he could've been one of the victims tonight. The cold knot coiling in his gut was more than nerves. It was a sobering sense of mortality that he hadn't felt in a lot of years.

"We'll find this murdering scumbag, Collier," Terra reassured.

Kiley nodded, watching him with a fierce determination in her eyes and an understanding that made him pause. She pulled her gaze away to stare at the remains of the pallet, wrinkling her nose. "I like coffee, but not that roasted."

Her remark served to ease the heaviness that had settled over them. Collier smiled and noticed Terra did, too.

"So, how does it work?" Kiley asked. "The towels catch fire, it spreads to a pallet then the coffee bags?"

"Yes," he answered.

"What about a security alarm? The first patrol officer on the scene said only the fire alarm went off. Why didn't the security alarm sound?"

"Are we sure they have one?" Collier asked.

"Good question."

"I imagine they do," he said, "but we need to make sure. The windows that were shattered were blown outward from heat, not inward as if smashed by someone trying to break in."

Admiration flared in her eyes. "You've picked up a lot, seeing as how you've only been able to work with the fire investigator on your days off."

"After a year and a half," Terra said, "those days add up. I'm lucky that he wanted the job badly enough to do it."

"And come Monday, I'll even get paid for it." Collier rolled his shoulders against the tautness stretching across his muscles. Russell had a way of looking at him that made him feel as if she were peeling off thin layers of himself that he didn't want peeled.

He turned away, training his flashlight on the wall of melted aluminum sheeting. He took out his screwdriver and folded back a piece of the warped metal, checking underneath for electrical wires. Even though they believed they'd found the cause of the fire, he would make sure there had been no electrical glitches.

He would like it a lot better if Kiley Russell would move to the other end of the building. Or better yet, leave.

He could feel her behind him and itched to watch her, see how she operated. But he had a job to do and he wasn't about to screw it up. Especially for a woman.

Kiley had spent the two days since the murder conducting interviews. She, Terra and Collier had split up after the walk-through with the agreement to call each other if they got a lead. Otherwise they would meet at the fire investigator's office on Monday morning to view the video of the fire scene.

Early Sunday evening, Collier left a message on Kiley's cell phone while she was asking the owner of Rehn's warehouse some follow-up questions. He had found something on the videotape of Lazano's fire scene he thought she and Terra should see.

About an hour after he left the message, she pulled up in front of a quaint rock house and double-checked the address the department secretary had given her. Yes, this charming thirties-style cottage next to an historically registered house was his.

An unfamiliar black Corvette sat at the curb between Mc-Clain's house and his neighbor's. Terra's red SUV wasn't here, and Kiley considered waiting in the car until the other fire investigator arrived. She didn't relish the idea of being alone with Collier, not now and not in two weeks when Terra went on maternity leave. But staying out here was silly. This was all about the case, and judging from his cool professionalism at the scene the other night, it would stay that way.

She flipped off the ignition, palmed the keys and stepped out of her car. The fat snowflakes that had begun falling while she spoke to the warehouse owner clung to her hair and cheeks as she walked to Collier's front door.

Whatever McClain had found must be good. For a man whose normal speaking voice was a slow-hands drawl, his words had been crisp and urgent. She wondered if he ever got that hot and bothered over a woman.

Her interviews with the firefighters from Station Two had unearthed some interesting and impressive information about the man who had taken up more of Kiley's thoughts than she liked. He was a third-generation firefighter and great at his job. He was someone you'd want to lead you into a blaze or watch your back. And until eighteen months ago, he had been engaged to Gwen Hadley, a wealthy, gorgeous blonde Kiley had seen in Oklahoma City's society pages.

Thanks to Collier, she already knew why he'd broken off the engagement, but his brother firefighters had felt the need to tell her, as well. Her sister, whose job as secretary to the city attorney put her in a position to hear most scuttlebutt, added some bits that Collier and his friends hadn't shared.

She didn't blame him for keeping the details to himself. He hadn't just walked in on his fiancée and his friend kissing. A half-naked Gwen had been wrapped around a half-naked Dan Lazano, and Collier had caught them in the act. The shock and cruelty of such a betrayal made Kiley's chest hurt.

Standing on his small, protected porch, she stabbed at the doorbell. The night was clear and cold. She shivered under her lined uniform coat.

"Hello?"

A masculine voice sounded behind her, and she whirled. "McClain, you move quieter than anyone—"

She broke off as the man stepped into the wedge of pale-yellow light. He was tall and handsome and *not* Collier McClain.

A glance back at the large black numbers to the right of the door post confirmed that this was the address she'd been given. "I'm looking for Collier McClain."

"Just my luck." The man gave her a flirty smile, startling her with dimples in the exact place she'd seen on Collier. His dark brown hair was mussed, the sleeves of his plaid flannel shirt rolled up. "I'm his brother, Walker."

"Hello." She pulled her badge from her coat pocket and showed it to him. "I'm Detective Russell with the Presley PD."

Amusement glinted in his eyes. "Is this about work or do I need to get him a lawyer?"

She grinned. "It's about work."

"He's inside. C'mon in." He turned, jamming his hands into the front pockets of his well-worn jeans and hunching his broad shoulders against the cold.

She stepped off the porch and followed him down the sidewalk to the garage. He was as long-legged as his brother. "Do you live here, too?"

"No. I'm helping him put down the floor."

Ah, that explained the grimy knees of his jeans, and probably the 'Vette. She followed Walker through the garage, struck by the spotless interior. There wasn't a speck of dirt anywhere on the gray painted concrete floor. A shiny white and chrome pickup was the lone vehicle. A row of cabinets lined the wall in front of her, and tools hung in a precise line to the left of where she entered. "I didn't know McClain had a brother," she said.

"And a sister." Walker opened a door in the garage and ushered her inside the house. "How long have you known him?"

The question was mild enough, but Kiley read curiosity in the man's eyes. Now she could see they were the same dusky green as his brother's. "Not long. We're working some cases together."

"So you're not here to arrest him?" Laughter marked his words.

"I could probably be persuaded."

He chuckled as she followed him through a cozy, charming kitchen done in clean white tile and navy stripes. On closer inspection she discovered that what she thought was wallpaper was actually paint. He must have a great decorator.

Modern appliances belied the decades-old charm of the

stone house, and window blinds rode up to reveal a winter-brown landscaped backyard. They passed a small room housing the washer and dryer. An old redbone hound with more gray than red on its face lay in front of the dryer. As she walked past, it looked up sleepily, then closed its eyes again.

They walked through a small formal dining room, which her mom would've loved, and into a cozy living area where a fire burned in a stone fireplace. Taupe carpet provided a warm counterpoint to the navy-and-burgundy-plaid sofa and two navy leather recliners.

Walker McClain turned to her. "Can I get you something to drink? He'll be right out."

"No, thanks, I'm fine." If Collier was in such an all-fired hurry to show her what he'd found, where was he? "This house is great."

"He's remodeling the whole thing. We put down a new floor in the entryway this afternoon. That's why I couldn't let you in the front door. Would you like to see it?"

"Sure."

They walked back to the small dining room and crossed to the arched opening in the opposite wall. The entryway's dark red brick was laid in a meticulous herringbone pattern. "Wow. He did this himself?"

Walker's eyes twinkled. "Well, he helped *me* do it."

"Hardly," Collier said dryly behind them. "You don't know herringbone from a chicken bone."

"Whoever did it, it's beautiful." She turned, and her words nearly slid back down her throat.

Sweet Saint Christopher. With his bare, muscular chest and low-slung jeans, Collier looked like Mr. July on the city's firefighter calendar sold to raise money for the new community center. He *was* Mr. July, she realized with a start. *Man, oh, man.*

There was something to be said for all the hose dragging and lifting and chopping that firefighters did.

"Sorry to have made you wait, Detective." His gaze did a slow sweep of her body as he rubbed a towel over his dark, wet head.

"No problem." He wasn't wearing socks or shoes, and something about his bare feet made her toes curl. "Your brother kept me entertained."

Light from an overhead fixture slid across his golden chest. His shoulders and biceps were large, the muscles cut with definition. She'd felt that massive chest before, but she had never seen it. It probably would've been better if she hadn't.

She cleared her throat. "You had something you wanted to show me?"

His brother arched a brow. "Like your *etchings?* I thought you had better lines."

Kiley laughed, but a flush warmed her entire body.

Collier grinned good-naturedly. "Don't you have somewhere to be, bro?"

"Yeah, yeah."

Collier swiped the towel across his chest then draped it over one shoulder. Muscles across his belly flexed with the movement, and the same unwelcome anticipation she'd felt during their dance rose up inside her.

She seriously had to stop looking at him. "Your house is great."

"Thanks."

She nodded. He really needed to put on a shirt. Was that a scar just below his navel, peeking over the waistband of his jeans?

From the corner of her eye, she caught a smile on Walker's face and glanced over.

He slapped Collier on the shoulder. "I'm outta here. Looks like you two have business. Call me when you're ready to do the hallway floor." He turned to Kiley, amusement and open curiosity sparkling in his eyes. "Detective, it was nice to meet you. Maybe I'll see you around sometime."

"Maybe so," she murmured. Doubtful, she thought.

He stepped over to his brother and said in a low voice, "Why can't you ever leave any for the rest of us?"

"We're working together," Collier muttered. "That's it."

Oh, yes, Kiley thought. That was *so* it.

Walker disappeared around the corner with a tuneless whistle. Collier led the way back to the living room. She followed, hearing the garage door close, signaling the departure of his brother.

"Sorry I had to ask you to come here. I'm expecting a delivery from the home store. This'll be the third time they've tried to get my order straight, and I want to make sure it's right."

"No problem."

"You got here fast."

"Your message sounded important." She dragged her gaze away from the flex of sinew and muscle, her thoughts going to his disgustingly active and very well-known dating life. Which had no bearing on this case at all. "I'm ready any time you are."

"Nice to know, Detective." His voice lowered suggestively.

She arched a brow. "How long before *you're* ready, McClain?"

"Let me grab a shirt."

Please. "Okay."

The back view had to be as good as the front so she refused to watch him leave the room. He returned wearing a red T-shirt stamped with PFD in faded white letters. The sleeves snugged around hard, sculpted biceps, and she admitted to a little disappointment that his chest was covered.

He glanced at his watch. "I thought Terra would have called me back by now."

"I don't mind waiting until she arrives to watch the video."

"She's probably on her way. Can I take your coat?"

She shrugged out of it and watched as he hung it in a small closet behind them.

He moved past her to the recliner closest to the sofa and curled his big hands over the back of the chair.

"I—" she started.

"Terra," he said at the same time. He gave her a crooked smile. "You first."

"I tried to interview Sherry Vail yesterday, but she's still away on a business trip." The former Presley firefighter had been dismissed in disgrace and told she would never work as a firefighter again. After the murder of victim number two, Rex Huffman, Terra and Kiley had learned about a sexual harassment complaint Vail had filed against him, so they'd talked to her back in November.

"When she was fired five months ago, she took a job with a company that sells parts and accessories for firefighting equipment. I think she has to go out of town quite a bit."

Kiley tucked her hair behind her ear. "I recall that Lazano was one of those called to testify against her at her disciplinary hearing."

"Yes, just like the other three victims."

The blonde had ample motive to hate the firefighters from her old station house. Kiley knew the woman's termination had been justified. Vail had been lazy, frequently absent, undependable at a fire and at different times had filed sexual harassment complaints against two male firefighters who pissed her off.

Collier ran a hand across his nape. "I agree she should still be on our list."

"I'll keep trying until I connect with her." Kiley stuck her hands in the back pockets of her jeans. "What were you about to say before I started?"

"Terra told me that the two of you interviewed the coffee

warehouse manager and all the employees. The manager said there was a working alarm system."

"Yes." Kiley pushed up the sleeves of her dark green sweater, fighting the urge to pace. She could smell the fresh soapy warmth of his skin and couldn't stop wondering about the line of puckered flesh that disappeared beneath his waist-band. She needed to focus. "Their system is computerized, so we were able to get an activity printout from the security company. The alarm was activated last night at closing, just after eleven o'clock, then bypassed at eleven-thirty. They have a backup battery for situations like that, but it was disabled, too."

"So, we're talking about someone who knows the warehouse schedule and also how to deal with security systems."

"Right. And maybe someone who knows electricity in general. Not just some cat burglar who can jimmy open a door."

"Were any prints lifted from the alarm box?"

"No, no prints anywhere."

"You're not still blaming that on the firefighters?"

"No."

"Good."

"I checked into the warehouse across the street, the one where you thought the shot came from. It's for a lightbulb manufacturer. I looked around on the roof and had some uniforms search around the building, but we didn't find anything."

Collier nodded.

"We're running the names of the victims who died during the rescue calls alongside the names of employees of the warehouse to see if we can find any connection." She paused. "Changing the subject, I heard from some of the firefighters that Lazano used to be involved with our third victim, Lisa Embry."

"Yeah. That was a while back."

"The man sure got around. How long ago were they together?"

Collier thought for a minute. "Probably close to five years ago. She was married for four years, and her affair with Lazano ended before she even met her husband. Ex-husband," he amended. "Lisa and Alan divorced at the end of last summer."

"I just heard from more than one source that Alan Embry is a possessive, jealous man and harassed Lisa mercilessly until some of you guys paid him a visit."

"That's true." Collier folded his arms over his chest. "Our whole shift threatened to hurt him if he didn't back off. I wasn't in on it, but I would've been if I hadn't been at the training center. Embry was really scaring Lisa, actually stalking her. He thought she had hooked up again with Lazano and he made her life miserable. Phone hang ups at all hours of the night, pictures of her undressing slid under her door or stuck in her mailbox. Threats. One time he flattened all her tires, and she couldn't get to school to pick up her sick kid."

"So it's not a stretch to imagine this guy could've killed her in her garage and killed Lazano tonight."

"No, and he was plenty hot about the guys paying him a visit. That could be motive for Miller's and Huffman's murders."

Kiley nodded. "In our interviews with him right after Lisa's murder, Alan said he had never owned a gun and didn't know how to shoot."

"No one's disputed that so far." Collier shoved a hand through his hair. "So I'd say we still consider that he hired the murderer."

"I agree. Since he works for the city as an electrician, he'd certainly have the know-how to screw with a security system. He could get into the building, start a fire and let the sniper do the rest."

"Yeah, talking to him is definitely on our to-do list."

"I tried to see him yesterday, but he wasn't at home or work." Kiley's next step was talking to McClain's ex-fiancée, but she didn't want him around for that, since his name would likely come up.

She was too aware of the fresh-showered scent of him, the underlying tension between them that went back to that dance at the Christmas party. "I'm anxious to see what you found on the video. Maybe we can watch it now, then again when Terra gets here?"

"All right." His quick agreement was the first sign she'd had that he might be just as antsy as she was. "You've seen the videos of the other fire murder scenes, right?"

"Yes." Kiley took a seat on the end of the sofa. Across from her, a burning log crackled in the fireplace, and warmth from the flames reached across the floor. The television sat on the adjacent wall, facing the end of the room where Collier stood. "I know y'all video most of your fires."

He nodded. "We use them to train others in investigation and also to keep the chain of evidence in our control. That way it can't be tampered with."

He eased down into the chair closest to her, then picked up the remote and turned on the television and VCR.

The picture flickered to life, and they watched grayish-brown smoke plume out of the side windows of the coffee warehouse. The camera picked up the occasional orange flame shooting through the smoky wall. A firefighter, unrecognizable because of his hood and helmet, rushed forward with the nozzle.

"That's Lazano," Collier said quietly.

A second firefighter appeared behind him in the frame. "You?"

"Yeah." Maybe a second later the sharp crack of a gunshot rang out. Lazano went down.

Collier hit the ground and vanished out of the frame. The shouted "Mayday! Firefighter down!" was muffled but audible. A pair of firefighters—the Rapid Intervention Team—

rushed into the picture, bending low then straightening to drag Lazano away from the flames. Another two-man team rushed toward the building with a hose gushing water. There were no more pictures of Collier and the victim.

For several minutes the camera stayed focused on the fire, catching the sounds of thundering water, yelling voices, sirens in the distance. Flames crackled and hissed in the background. The firefighters moved in smooth synchronization. After the blaze was out, the camera panned the perimeter of the building, down the west side of the driveway to the street and across three fire engines.

Kiley wondered what Collier was thinking. Despite what had happened between the two men, watching a brother firefighter die in front of him had to be hard.

He paused the tape. "Right there."

She leaned forward, studying the frame. "Ladder truck, hoses, hydrant, fireman."

"Since he isn't wearing a hood or a helmet, I can see his face. That guy isn't a firefighter. At least not from here."

"*What?*" Kiley dragged her hair over her shoulder with one hand as she scrutinized the screen.

"I know almost every firefighter in Presley, and I've never seen this guy."

"Really?" She got that little head rush she always did when she got a good lead.

"I went back over the tapes from the three previous fire scenes and I didn't see him in any of them. There's an unidentified male in the first tape, but Terra already tried to have that enhanced. The tech couldn't get a clear shot of the person."

"But we have a clear shot of this guy." Kiley rose, excited. "This is the first lead we've had on this murder, McClain. Good job."

"All I did was look at the video," he said wryly, stopping the tape.

"But you picked up on the man. I wouldn't have. That's why it's such a good idea to have guns and hoses working these cases together."

"Guns and hoses? You're a piece of work, Russell." He chuckled at her slang for cops and firefighters as he stood and started into the kitchen. "I'm going to call Terra again. You want something to drink?"

"Sure." She followed him. "We need to get a photograph made from the video. The police lab can do it if you don't have the equipment."

"That's where I'd take it, too." Grabbing a cordless phone from its spot on the wall, he punched in a number and waited for several seconds, then hung up. "Still no answer on her cell. I'll try her house."

There was no answer there, either.

"Maybe she and Jack are out to dinner." Kiley traced his steps to the refrigerator, leaning a hip against the counter that butted up to it. "We can show the picture to the other firefighters and anyone else at the scene."

He nodded, opened the fridge, bent down to grab a cola and handed it to her.

She leaned forward, taking the chilled can. "We'll need to check mug shots, too. And maybe the enlarged picture will show if the guy has a tattoo or any other distinguishing marks. If he does, we can have Crime Analysis check the field interview cards for any matching descriptions."

"I'll touch base with all the station houses and see if anyone has reported any stolen gear." Collier straightened and stepped away from the fridge at the same time she popped the top on her soda can. His elbow banged her forearm, jostling her drink.

They both grabbed for the can, their combined grips crushing the tin and spewing soda all over her front and down her arm.

Collier quickly reached behind her and tossed her a towel. "Sorry."

"No problem. I was in the way." She blotted the front of her sweater then the sleeve and her hand. Facing the sink, she set down the towel and her drink, then turned on the faucet and put her sticky hands under the water.

"You missed some."

"Where—" She broke off, jolted by the sudden feel of his big hand settling hotly on her hip. He reached toward her with the towel. With one knuckle, he angled her head and dabbed at the underside of her jaw.

She froze. They hadn't been this close since the FOP Christmas party. She could feel the heat of his body and his subtle woodsy scent drift into her lungs. His lean thigh brushed hers, but it was the hand on her hip that shocked all her nerve endings. His fingers splayed low on her back, right where her hip curved into her bottom. He'd held her the same way while they danced. The memory was so vivid she could almost feel the provocative friction of his body moving against hers.

"Got it." His voice curled around her with just an edge of seduction.

The low, sexy drawl was the same she'd heard that night, too. And her body did that same melt-in-the-center thing. The realization forced some energy through her dazed limbs. She turned off the faucet and plucked the towel out of his hand, drying her hands as she walked away. "Thanks."

No way was she going all soft around him. She didn't care how good he sounded. Or looked. Or felt.

Just then the phone rang. Collier crossed to the wall and picked it up. His side of the conversation consisted of "oh" and "yeah" and "okay." She tried to read his face and determine if he was talking about the case.

In a few moments he hung up, his features tight and grim. "That was Jack Spencer, Terra's husband. She's in the hospital."

Apprehension started a low drumbeat inside her. "Don't tell me."

"She's having her baby."

"Now?" Kiley squeaked.

"Now."

She saw the realization in his eyes the same time it hit her. Now only the two of them would be working this investigation.

"Oh, great," they said in unison.

Chapter 3

On Monday afternoon Collier left the fire investigator's office early to attend Dan Lazano's wake. Not just out of obligation to a fellow firefighter, but also because he had come darn close to being in that casket himself.

Lazano's parents hosted the gathering at their modest brick home in northwest Oklahoma City. Collier stepped through the front door and scanned the people overflowing from the spacious living room into the dining room. He managed to make his way through the throng of firefighters, paramedics and city officials to Tony and Simone Lazano and offer his condolences on the loss of their son.

Collier might have resented Dan for what he and Gwen had done, but he hadn't hated the guy. Not anymore, despite what Kiley Russell thought.

Thinking about his curvy new partner lit off a spark of irritation. Partnering up with her gnawed at him, but he figured it gnawed at her just as much. He'd seen that flare of panic in her eyes last night when he'd delivered the news about Terra having her baby before either of them had expected her to.

He wanted to believe it was the challenge of Kiley's back-off attitude that put a kick in his blood, but everything about her from that sexy tangle of red hair to those luscious long legs charged him up. If she were any other woman, he would take her to bed and get her out of his system, but the redhead set off high-powered warnings in his head, and he'd learned the hard way to listen.

If he'd paid attention to those doubts about Gwen, things between them would never have gone as far as they had. Or gotten so ugly.

At a table draped with a white cloth, on the far wall of the dining room, he filled a cup of coffee and turned, searching the crowd. Shelby Fox, a former station mate, raised her cup, and he nodded at the slender brunette. A flash of red hair behind her caught his attention, and his eyes narrowed as Detective Russell let herself in the front door, then spoke to an older gentleman standing nearby.

She sure didn't let any grass grow under her feet. No doubt she was here to work the crowd, see if she could learn anything about Lazano. The fact that she was doing her job shouldn't have irritated Collier, but it did. And when she shrugged out of her heavy black coat and revealed the simple black dress beneath, his irritation edged into something else. Something hot and reckless.

Her hair was down today but pulled away from her face, the thick mass brushing her shoulders. It was the dress that had his grip tightening on the delicate china cup. The soft-looking, midnight fabric skimmed over every curve, accentuating her full breasts and trim waist. The hem fell just below her knees, and the legs encased in sheer black hose were the best Collier had ever seen. He couldn't resist mentally following the line back up beneath her dress.

"Oh, hell," he muttered, gulping at his coffee, then wincing when he burned his tongue.

"Pretty hot stuff, McClain." Shelby Fox had made her way over and stood at his elbow.

"Huh?" There was no way she could've known he was looking at—lusting after—Kiley Russell.

She gave him an odd smile. "The coffee? I blistered my mouth a minute ago."

"Oh. Yeah." He'd already established he wanted Kiley Russell, but why did his chest always tighten when he saw her? Just like it had the night they'd danced at the Christmas party. He didn't know, and he was pretty sure he didn't want to figure it out.

"Word is you could've been the one to buy the farm instead of Lazano," Shelby said soberly.

"Yeah. It was too close."

"Glad you're okay."

"Thanks."

They sipped their hot drinks and spoke to other firefighters who stopped at the table for coffee or tea and sandwiches that had been cut into quarters.

Shelby reached across the table behind him and plopped a sugar cube into her cup. "How's your first day on the new job, Investigator McClain?"

"I've spent most of it doing paperwork for the Personnel Department."

The brunette shifted to make room for Jerry French, a veteran firefighter from Station One. "Anything on that warehouse fire yet, or any leads on Lazano's murder?" she asked.

"Not yet."

French jerked at his tie. "You got thrown right into the middle of a big humdinger, didn't you? You been up to the hospital yet to see Terra and her baby girl?"

"I went early this morning," Collier said. "But she was asleep and so was Jack. I'll try again later."

"Did she have to have a C-section?" Shelby asked. "One of the guys was talking about it."

Collier nodded. "I think it took her and Jack by surprise, but I heard everyone was doing well."

Talking about Terra reminded him of his new partner, but he didn't see Kiley anywhere. Where had she gone? That instant last night when he'd had his hand on her shot through his memory. As much as he hated it, he wasn't going to lie to himself about the electricity that arced between them. They struck sparks off each other, and he wanted to find out just how long they would burn, but he knew better than to explore it.

Something about Kiley warned him that she wouldn't be that easy to walk away from. And walking away from women was what he did ever since his engagement to Gwen Hadley had gone to hell. He'd bought into the true-love thing once, and he was done. For good.

The detective's wariness around him said she had learned the same hard lesson. He wasn't going to follow up on the slow sizzle that had started in his blood the minute he'd held her at that Christmas dance. And he instinctively knew she wouldn't, either.

They could work together and get the job done, then go their separate ways. Her slightly awkward manner the night before at his house was proof she wanted the same thing.

They were both professionals. Regardless of the searing current that seemed to zap him whenever he was within a foot of the red-haired detective, Collier intended to do his job. He wanted to make a good impression, especially on his first solo case. All he had to do was concentrate on the investigation, and that annoying awareness he felt around Kiley would disappear. Pretty soon he wouldn't feel anything different for her than he felt for any other co-worker.

"I didn't know if she'd be here or not," Shelby murmured.

Collier followed her gaze across the living room and saw Gwen, who spoke to Mr. and Mrs. Lazano before she melted into the crowd. "Why not?"

"She and Dan broke things off about two weeks ago."

He nodded. He'd heard about Dan and Gwen's breakup, but the other firefighters didn't often discuss the pair around him.

"Lazano couldn't take her drinking anymore," Shelby said.

Collier gave her a sharp look. "Had it gotten that bad?"

"That's what I heard."

He probed the crowded room for Kiley, wondering who she was talking to, if she had learned anything new about Lazano. His gaze shifted back to the corner he'd just scanned.

She stood there huddled next to a coat closet talking to Gwen. She hadn't told him she planned to interview his ex, but he could tell by the intent way she listened that interviewing was exactly what she was doing. And she'd left him out of the loop. No doubt his name had come up at least once. The whole idea of the two women talking about him made Collier queasy. He started for them, wondering who had identified Gwen to Kiley as his ex.

As he walked up, he heard Kiley say, "Thanks for your time. If I have any other questions, I'll be in touch."

"We'll probably both be in touch," he said as much for her benefit as Gwen's.

His ex pivoted to face him. "Oh, Collier. Hello."

Her greeting was subdued, as was her makeup and clothing. Subdued for Gwen, anyway. She was pale, her brown eyes red and swollen from crying. The black, long-sleeved sheath she wore could've been painted on her slender frame. Next to Kiley Russell's vibrant coloring and personality, his former fiancée seemed almost bland.

He had expected to feel at least a twinge of his old anger toward the blonde, but instead he felt sorry for her. She looked uncertain and troubled.

"Why would you need to talk to me, too?" she asked.

"I just transferred into the fire investigator's office."

"I didn't know." She stepped closer, her gaze locked on his.

He shifted back until his heel bumped the wall. "This is my first official case."

"I thought the police investigated mur—things like this." She dabbed at her eyes with a tissue.

"Since this was a murder at a fire scene, the police and fire departments work *together*." He gave Kiley a pointed look over Gwen's head.

His ex nodded, though Collier wasn't sure she really registered his words. Kiley stood quietly to the side, studying him with the intensity of a bird dog on point.

Gwen crumpled her tissue into a ball. "This is just awful, isn't it?"

"Yes."

She reached out and touched his arm. "Can we talk later?"

"About Lazano?"

"No."

The plea in her eyes said she wanted to talk about *them*, but they were finished. He'd never felt it with such finality. He didn't want to hurt her, but he wasn't interested. "If you think of anything else about Lazano, we need to know."

Gwen's face crumpled and tears welled in her eyes. "Collier, I'm so sorry. For everything."

"Hey, it's okay." Feeling caged, he pulled a handkerchief out of his suit coat and pressed it into her hand. "This is a bad day for everyone. Don't beat yourself up, Gwen."

He turned and caught Shelby's eye, motioning her over. "Let Shelby take you to your car."

Gwen studied him for a moment, resignation finally crossing her features. She turned to Kiley. "I hope I helped."

"You did. Thanks." Kiley smiled.

Collier watched as Shelby guided Gwen through the crowd

and toward the front door. From the corner of his eye, he caught Kiley moving away, too.

"Oh, no, you don't." He snagged her elbow and pulled her back.

"Watch it, McClain."

"*You* watch it," he said in a low voice, turning so he could block her escape with his body. "Leaving me out of the loop like that could be construed as breaking procedure. Why did you do it?"

"I'm in the clear on this." She pulled away from his hold, though she stayed with her back pressed against the wall. "I figured your name would come up when I talked to your ex. She was more likely to give me honest answers without you around."

Someone squeezed behind him, and he leaned closer to her, teased by her soft scent. "So what did Gwen tell you? And don't leave anything out."

"I think she's still hung up on you."

Collier rubbed the nape of his neck. "She's just confused. Why interview her here, anyway?"

"I tried to talk to her last night, but she only returned a few hours ago from a ski trip in Colorado. She agreed to talk to me here."

"So, she knew about Lazano's murder?"

"Her mom called and told her." Kiley watched him carefully.

"Did you ask her about the last time she saw him?"

"She said it was two weeks ago, the night they called it quits."

"You sound skeptical."

"I'm wondering if her memory's reliable. She told me she has a drinking problem."

"Yeah."

"What do you think?" Kiley pressed. "*Is* she reliable?"

"I don't know. She was at one time."

She paused, her blue-green eyes meeting his. "Were you ever going to tell me your ex-fiancée's name?"

"If you'd asked me, I would have." He hadn't wanted to tell her as much as he already had. "Does knowing who she is have anything to do with our investigation, Detective?" He lowered his voice, trying to rattle her. "Or are you asking for personal reasons?"

He was surprised to see a dull flush color her cheeks.

She shrugged. "Just connecting the dots."

"You obviously would've figured it out when you learned she was Lazano's ex, too."

"I realize his murder is even more personal to you than the others because of Miss Hadley. Are you going to have a problem working this case?"

"It's not like there's any choice." He wanted her to shut up about this whole thread of conversation. "Terra's out on maternity leave. It's you and me. The end."

"So you can put aside your personal feel—"

"Yes," he bit out. Collier's usually even temper spiked. "If there's a screw up, Russell, it won't be because of me."

She searched his eyes, then nodded. "Okay. Well, I want to check Gwen's alibi for the night Lazano was killed and make sure she was really in Colorado like she said."

"I can make some calls."

"I will."

"You can't cut me out of everything."

She eyed him coolly. "All right, you do it."

"Done." He wondered if things would always be so prickly with her. "On the way here, I stopped at each station house to show the picture of the fake firefighter."

"Wow, the lab got to that really fast."

He nodded. "Your copy is in my truck."

"Did anyone recognize the guy?"

"No. Station One did tell me that some of their gear turned up missing in late September."

"So that would coincide with when these fire murders

started. Too bad we can't find Mr. Fake in any of the earlier fire scene videos." She brushed her hair over her shoulder.

Just once he'd like to get his hands in those red curls. "I can give you that photo print before we leave."

"Great. Want to meet me outside in about fifteen minutes?"

"It's a date," he said.

"No—"

"Figure of speech, Russell. Don't get your hopes up."

Her eyes flashed. "You're safe, McClain. Completely safe."

He watched her walk away, totally hypnotized by the length of those legs and tried to remember why safe was what he wanted.

About seven-thirty the next evening, Kiley walked through the glass doors of Presley's two-story community center. She'd been ordered by Lt. Hager to attend tonight's dedication and grand unveiling of the new facility.

Though not fancy, the gray tiled floors were tasteful, as were the faux marble walls. The lobby stretched the length of the rectangular shaped building. Hallways on either side led to several rooms that would serve as meeting places for city employees as well as citizens' events. The upper floor provided more space. Four sets of doors ahead of her opened into the large all-purpose room being used for tonight's dedication.

After leaving her coat with a volunteer, she stepped through the nearest set of doors and took in the expansive area decorated with streamers and blue, white and gold balloons. A wooden stage centered at the opposite end of the room held a five-member band tuning their instruments. A cash bar was set up in the corner close to the stage.

The mayor, various city councilmen and women, and other city leaders strolled around. Kiley glimpsed the governor deep in conversation with Chief of Police Nick Smith. She spoke to

several police officers who had shown up because they'd gotten the same memo she had from Lt. Hager. As she moved
through the crowd, she recognized a few firefighters, too. All
the men were dressed in suits or uniforms. The women
sparkled in dressy, after-five attire. A tall blonde in a tight, black
sequined dress cut down to *there* caught Kiley's attention.

She had to look twice to make sure the woman wasn't
Gwen Hadley. The relief she felt reminded her of the earlier
meeting with Collier's former fiancée. Kiley typically didn't
feel out of her league with either men or women, but standing next to Gwen at that wake had made her feel invisible. The
woman had flawless skin and a flawless figure, but she obviously had her share of problems, too. Kiley felt more sure of
herself now, but she was still less steady than she liked around
Presley's newest fire investigator.

It was because of the emotion she'd seen in his eyes yesterday as he'd talked to his ex. The momentary flash of old
hurt on his face had tapped at something deep inside Kiley.
Gwen had made it clear she wanted to talk to Collier in private, but he had kindly refused. He'd probably been more kind
than Kiley would've been if their roles were reversed.

The image of a solicitous Collier McClain certainly didn't
match that of the footloose bachelor she had heard about or
seen at the Christmas dance. She told herself to forget about
that emotion in his eyes, but for a brief period, she'd glimpsed
the *man.* Not the fire investigator or the reputed Romeo, but
a man who'd been hurt by a woman. She pushed away the
thought. Emotions—his *and* hers—came a distant second to
the business she needed to conduct with Collier. And business
was all she cared about.

They had gotten no identification from the photo of the
fake fireman, and they had spent the morning looking at mug-
shots. No luck there, either. They had begun sending e-mails
and faxes to a list of surrounding prisons in Oklahoma, Texas

and Louisiana, asking if any of them had recently released an arsonist.

Kiley's afternoon had been taken up in court waiting to testify on a burglary arrest, and Collier had offered to finish sending the queries to the prisons. She hadn't heard from him since before lunch when he'd told her Gwen Hadley's alibi was solid. She wondered if he had learned anything new.

She expected he would be at tonight's dedication, representing the fire investigator's office in Terra's absence. After Kiley spoke to Chief Smith and exchanged a few words with Lt. Hager and his wife, she made her way to the cash bar and ordered a ginger ale.

Despite the freezing temperatures outdoors and the veed back of her dress, the crowd of people inside kept her more than warm. It didn't take long to spot Collier dancing in the center of the carpeted room. He wasn't the tallest man here, so why had her gaze gone straight to him as if reeled there?

She should go ask him if he had any new information, but she couldn't bring herself to stand near the stream of women who kept asking him to dance. In a dark suit with a crisp white shirt and muted red tie, he looked distinguished and commanding. He was clean shaven, the overhead light blunting the sharp angles of his jaw- and cheekbones, and still his appearance was rugged. She'd thought him blatantly male in his turnout gear, but the effect tonight was devastating. She could appreciate a gorgeous man even if she didn't want him.

Recalling the bare chest she'd seen at his house, she knew the broad shoulders beneath that jacket were every bit real and not an illusion created by good tailoring.

Kiley hated these types of events, where she had to dress to the nines and schmooze with city officials. She would much rather be talking to the residents of Presley, for whom this center had been built, but Collier looked at ease as he chatted with members of city government who danced past him.

Watching him move on and off the dance floor with obscene regularity, Kiley saw no trace of the wounded man from yesterday. Just the heartbreaker she'd heard about, the one she planned to avoid. As a high-tempo dance song ended, he escorted Shelby Fox off the floor, and the pair joined a group in a corner that included Kiley's sister, Kristin.

Deciding she'd rather talk to him in a crowd as opposed to alone, Kiley made her way toward the corner. She recognized Clay Jessup, the lanky cop who stood between her sister and Shelby, but the man to her sister's left was unfamiliar. Kristin's hair was the same dark gold as their mother's, with enough wave to coax it into whatever style she wanted. Tonight she wore it down and loose, just as Kiley did. The fluttery white blouse she had paired with Kiley's long black satin skirt was as dressy as the bronze knee-length dress Kiley had chosen.

More than one guy had asked Kristin to dance, but Kiley noted Collier hadn't. Probably because he'd been too busy dancing with everyone else.

She walked up to the edge of the group, and her sister smiled. "Hi, Ki."

"Hello."

Kristin pulled her into the circle. "Does everyone know my sister?"

"Hey, Russell." Clay Jessup smiled and Shelby waved.

Kiley and Clay had gone through the police academy together, and she knew Shelby because the woman was one of Clay's closest friends. Kristin introduced Trey Vance, a computer technician from her office.

Kiley felt Collier's gaze burning her skin and finally met his eyes. "Hello, McClain."

"Detective." His gaze skated over her body, and reaction clenched her belly.

Why, why, why did she have to feel *anything?* Determined

to ignore the drumming pull of awareness she felt, she started to move next to him and ask if they'd had any responses yet from the prisons. Someone tapped on the microphone situated on the small stage a few feet away, and she paused.

After a few seconds of screeching feedback, Mayor Griffin greeted everyone and encouraged applause for the band as its members left the stage for a break. The mayor then invited everyone's attention to the newly completed building and this spacious room, which would host community events such as senior citizen exercise classes or the citizens' police academy.

The shiny wooden stage steps were trimmed with the same blue-and-gray flecked carpet that covered the floor and complemented the blue walls. The large space, which could be partitioned off to make four rooms, sparkled with the shine of newness. After a few moments the mayor introduced everyone who had worked on the community center's planning committee.

When he introduced prominent criminal defense attorney Raye Ballinger, Trey Vance said, loud enough for their small circle, "I can't believe they let her serve on the committee. The best thing the 'Ball Basher' could do for Presley would be to leave."

Mayor Griffin turned the program over to Raye for her comments, and Kiley grimaced, unsure about what to expect from the woman. She'd had dealings with the dogged attorney in court.

Raye Ballinger was dressed to kill in a dramatic off-the-shoulder black-and-white gown with black elbow-length gloves. Her blond hair was piled atop her head; light caught the sparkling necklace and matching earrings she wore. From what Kiley had heard, the attorney earned enough to afford real diamonds.

"The city probably paid for those earrings and that necklace," Kristin said behind her.

"We're probably still paying." Trey's voice was low. "You know, her brother committed suicide several months back. Everyone expected her to sue the city, and sure enough, she instigated a lawsuit last month."

Raye Ballinger had also brought a suit against Presley about three years ago for a policeman who said he'd been fired unfairly. She had intimidated every witness she could, and Kiley had the scars to prove it. She hadn't folded under the lawyer's sharklike attack, but others had. The woman was relentless to the point of cruelty, and Kiley had never liked her.

It appeared no one in this small circle did, either. Raye had once ripped Kiley to shreds on the witness stand during a rape case. She hated to think what the woman might have done if they'd been alone.

"If that lawsuit gets to court, there's no justice," Clay Jessup said to Collier.

Kiley glanced over at the two men. "What happened with her brother?"

"Last spring—April, I think—we got a call about a house fire," Collier said. "Three stations responded and were able to get to the guy by using the ladder, but as they climbed down, he took a dive. It was Ballinger's brother."

"I remember." She thought back to the coverage, done to the point of saturation, by local television stations as well as Presley's and Oklahoma City's newspapers. "It was pretty awful."

"I guess the scene turned ugly," Jessup said. "Shelby said Ballinger went ballistic, blaming everyone around."

"She talked to the mayor right after it happened." Kristin tucked her hair behind her ear. "But no one heard anything else until she filed the lawsuit."

Collier shook his head. "I don't see that she has grounds. Jamie Ballinger tried to kill himself by torching that house, and when that didn't work, he jumped from the ladder. Everyone did their jobs. There was no negligence."

"Well," Clay said. "Skip Dickens was a known drunk with DUIs *on record,* and she got him reinstated, plus his back pay and a two-million-dollar settlement out of Presley."

His reminder about the policeman Raye Ballinger had represented came as the lawyer finished her remarks. Applause swelled throughout the large room.

Kiley watched as the woman stepped down from the stage and moved through the crowd, stopping here and there to speak to people. She had a reputation for disliking cops. Evidently, hose draggers were on her list, too.

Clay asked Kristin to dance and the pair moved to the center of the room. Trey and Shelby followed.

"Looks like we're alone at last," Collier drawled with a twinkle in his eye that said he knew he made Kiley jumpy.

She'd be darned if she let on that his "come getcha some" tone turned her nerves to jelly. Or caused a surge of energy to zip through her body. "I wanted to talk to you, anyway. Did you hear back from any of the prisons?"

"Not yet. I did finish e-mailing and faxing everyone on our list."

"Wow, you were busy today—"

"Hello, Detective Russell."

Her muscles tightened at the sound of the frigid, silky voice just behind her. What could Raye Ballinger possibly want? Kiley turned. "Hello, Counselor."

The attorney swept her long, red-nailed fingers through the air in an encompassing gesture. "We certainly appreciate you coming to the dedication."

"It's very nice. The residents will get a lot of use out of the center."

"We value all the support we get from the police department."

Kiley met the woman's hard blue eyes, unable to tell if the attorney was being sarcastic or not.

Raye shifted her gaze to the tall man in front of her. "And the fire department, too. I understand congratulations are in order, Collier. For your promotion to the fire investigator's office."

"Thank you." He slid a hand into the front pocket of his slacks and smiled easily at the barracuda.

Raye's ruby-slicked lips curved, and Kiley blinked at how the smile softened her eyes, making her appear almost shy. "Perhaps you'd whirl me around the dance floor once, Investigator?"

Well, well. It looked as if Fireman Flirty could bring out the human side of the disagreeable woman.

As smooth as French silk pie, Collier responded, "I'd be honored, Counselor, but I've already promised this dance to Detective Russell. Thank you, though."

"Some other time, then." Once again Raye was cool as she moved off.

Before Kiley could say "over my dead body," Collier's hand was at her back and he guided her onto the floor.

"I must've missed your promise to dance," she drawled, giving a little hop to avoid being stepped on. She had to catch his rhythm so she wouldn't trip.

"You were my closest out."

"Oh, please stop." She batted her eyelashes at him, exaggerating her best Southern accent. "You keep talkin' like that and I might melt into a puddle right at your feet."

He grinned. "Serve and protect. I thought that was your creed."

"I doubt you need either one, especially from a woman," she said smartly.

"Raye would've chewed me up and spit me out if you hadn't rescued me. Besides, now we have a chance to talk without being interrupted."

"I thought you said you didn't hear anything today."

"I didn't."

She tried to ignore the way her body melted against him as if starved for his. As they glided around another couple,

Collier's hand moved up her back, touching bare skin between the open vee of her dress. The warm press of his slightly callused flesh on hers caused her heart rate to hitch.

"But I did read the copies of your notes from all the fire murders. I'm planning to try and contact Alan Embry again in the morning. Do you want to go?"

"Absolutely." Her tone was ridiculously breathless, but maybe he would think it was caused by the dancing. An urge came over her to smooth her palm over his wide shoulder, but she resisted. Why couldn't she keep her mind on business? McClain didn't seem to have any problem doing so. "Maybe we can get somewhere with him."

"Maybe so. Since we've had no luck finding him at home, I'm hoping we can catch him at work, so let's try him first at the city's maintenance division."

At the husky tone in his voice, Kiley glanced up and found his gaze locked on her. Desire burned in his eyes, making them a deep green, and her body went soft, as it had when they danced at the Christmas party. Like it had last night. She should've let him take his chances with Raye Ballinger.

"I tested the towels we found at the warehouse." His voice was low, his breath brushing her temple. "Just as we thought, there was no accelerant. A match and some rags, exactly like the other fires."

"What does that tell you?" Kiley was amazed she could form a coherent sentence. Her movements shadowed his in a sensual rhythm. The sound of music and laughter and voices faded until she could hear only the rapid-fire beat of her heart and smell the dark woodsy scent she'd already come to recognize as Collier's. "Did the arsonist know what he was doing or just choose that method because it's easy?"

"Hard to say. If we're right about our theory that the fire was set only to draw firefighters to the scene, then this was the perfect way to do that. The towels and an ignition are enough to start the fire, then catch a pallet like those at the warehouse. Or start up the wall like the flames did at the high school gym. This method gives an arsonist plenty of time to get out and leave the scene before the firefighters arrive."

She knew she should step away, but the languorous sensation moving through her body overruled common sense. She struggled to keep her mind on the case. "How much about fire would a person need to know in order to plan something like that?"

"Some," Collier admitted, his gaze roaming over her face.

"Could a firefighter have started the blaze?"

"Sure, but so could someone with a lot less experience."

"So we still don't know what kind of person we're looking for."

"Not yet."

They danced breast to chest, hip to hip, and Kiley's body strained to get closer. His thumb stroked slowly across her bare back, and she ached to feel more of him. Her gaze moved to his lips, and she imagined kissing him, tasting him.

It hit her then, that skittish, jittery feeling she'd gotten the first time she'd danced in his arms. He might be her partner in this investigation, but he was bad news in any other way. She stepped out of his hold just seconds before the song ended.

"Hey, what—"

"Song's over," she said brightly, looking for an escape.

He glanced at the band, then back at her. "Couldn't wait, huh? I've never known a woman as jumpy as you are."

"No, I suppose you haven't." She started for the edge of the crowd. "It probably would've done you some good to be turned down occasionally."

"You have to be asked before you can turn someone down, Detective." Strong, hot fingers closed on her arm and he guided her through the crowd. "What is your problem?"

They reached the wall, and Kiley faced him. "I've heard about your reputation."

"Which is what?"

"That you should publish your own phone book to keep up with all the women you've dated."

His eyes darkened. "You shouldn't believe everything you hear."

"Look, you're not my type. That's all."

"What type is that? Or do you even have one?"

She glanced around, glad to see they weren't attracting attention. "It isn't a guy who charms a woman into bed, then walks away."

"I never make promises to any woman," he said tightly. "And I'm up-front about that."

"Bravo. It doesn't mean people aren't hurt."

His gaze narrowed on her face, and his hold on her arm gentled. "People like you?"

She didn't like the gut-deep, instant connection she suddenly felt to him, the flare of naked panic that he had recognized something in her that most people didn't.

His voice lowered in a way that made her feel he was touching her. All over. "What's the matter, Russell? Afraid you might like me in spite of yourself?"

It was already too late for that. "Don't misunderstand. I think we can work together just fine, but let's keep things strictly business."

"All right."

"Which means we probably shouldn't be dancing."

He released her arm. "Gotcha."

She nodded, relief mixing with disappointment. "So, I'll meet you in the morning at Embry's office?"

"Eight o'clock okay?"

"Yes."

"See you then."

Ignoring the sinking feeling in her stomach, she watched as he turned and made his way through the crowd toward the bar. Good. Now there would be no misunderstandings, no more dancing, no more touching.

Her gaze traced the broad line of his shoulders, the slightly ragged edge of his dark hair as she recalled the seductive feel of his hard body against hers. Who was she kidding? What she felt for him was hotter and more dangerous than mere "like." She wanted to jump his bones. And she just wasn't going to do that with Collier McClain.

Chapter 4

At eight o'clock the next morning, Collier pulled up to the building that housed the City of Presley Maintenance Division where Alan Embry should be starting his day. Russell was already in the parking lot, standing inside her open driver's-side door and writing something in a notebook on the roof of her red Mustang. Waiting on him.

There was no denying the adrenaline that shot through his system. She'd put him in the hot zone the first time he'd seen her, *every* time he'd seen her, and today was no different.

After last night he couldn't get around that. His impulse to dance with her in order to escape Raye Ballinger might have saved him a few minutes of aggravation, but it had left him with more than an hour of hot, hard want.

She wore dark slacks and a deep-purple sweater beneath a sleek, fur-lined black leather coat. The frigid air, hazy with the promise of more sleet, had color snapping in her cheeks and her eyes glowing like jewels. If he hadn't already known the pure blue-green color of her eyes, he would've been able to tell from feet away. The tousled mane of hair she'd worn loose last night was pulled back into a twist. It looked neat and professional, and he wanted to get his hands in her hair and mess it up.

He needed to get a grip and focus on the job.

Sleet had begun falling just after he'd arrived home last night. It had stopped before he'd rolled out of bed early this morning, and the streets and sidewalks were coated with a thin layer of ice, as was the parking lot.

As he carefully guided the fire investigator's Explorer into the space next to Kiley's car, she glanced up. They were on the south edge of the lot, which was bordered by a line of trees stripped bare of leaves, their spindly branches sheathed in glittering ice.

Killing the engine, he eased out of his truck and shut the door, testing the slickness of the asphalt. Frigid air stung his cheeks.

"Hey, McClain," she said cheerily with no sign of the tension that had been between them last night when he'd walked away from her. "Looks like you made it without slamming your truck into a curb."

"Hose draggers can drive in any weather, just like cops, Russell." He made his way gingerly to the rear bumper and took a few steps closer to her.

She grinned and bent to reach inside her car, coming up a second later to hand him a foam cup. "Coffee?"

"Thanks." He took it as she reached inside for her own cup. He remembered the look on her face when she told him she didn't like his type. Someone had hurt her. Who? He shouldn't want to know, shouldn't care, but he'd been wondering since last night. Since she'd stepped out of his arms before he'd been ready to end their dance.

"I've got to have something hot when it's this cold out. Do you want cream or sugar?"

"No, thanks."

"How about a doughnut or a bagel?"

"What are you, a mobile coffee service?" He leaned over and peered inside her car. "What else do you have in there?"

"Just a little supply of things. I have an apple. Would you like that?"

He shook his head. Collier wasn't a breakfast person, and was she really this bright-eyed and smiley so early in the morning?

She closed her car door and started with him across the slick surface.

He sipped his coffee as he glanced at the opposite side of the parking lot where city employees were already spreading salt and sand in an effort to prevent people from slipping on the ice. "Maybe by the time we're finished with Embry, they'll have reached our side of the lot. Then we'll be able to move a little more quickly. The weather guy said this stuff probably won't melt off the trees and power lines for another two or three days. It's not supposed to get above twenty degrees."

"Don't you kind of hate it when the ice melts? Right now everything is so pretty, with the sun shining through the icicles. See how the light glows on the branches? It's clean looking, peaceful."

He slid her a look. "Are you always this happy in the morning?" Until he had at least one cup of coffee, he wasn't even civil. "That could really get on my nerves, Russell."

She smiled. "I figure I've already got a head start on that."

She was definitely getting under his skin, but probably not in the way she thought.

They took careful half steps all the way to the front glass door, and Collier held it open as she stepped inside ahead of him. Her spicy scent drifted on the cold air, balling a knot in his gut.

Several feet inside the door, they approached a long counter that resembled those used by bank tellers. Residents who didn't like automated payments or complaints could come here to pay their bills or report a problem in person. Three women manned this customer-service area, and the space behind them was taken up with ten desks and clerks whose keyboards clicked nonstop.

Pennie Miles looked up. She smiled, reminding him why he'd thought about asking her out. "Hi, Collier."

"Hey, Pennie." He moved around Kiley and up to the counter where the petite brunette stood.

"I enjoyed our dance last night at the dedication," she said quietly.

"So did I. Maybe we can do it again sometime."

"Absolutely."

He grinned, feeling the detective's gaze boring into his back. "I'm here on business this morning. Need to see Alan Embry."

"He's in the call room giving his assignments for today." A thirtyish woman with long, black hair answered as she stepped up beside Pennie and aimed a sultry smile Collier's way. "It's down the first hall you passed when you came in. You sure do look familiar."

"That's what I was thinking." This from an attractive older woman with short graying hair who walked over to join them.

He smiled. "I think if we'd met before, I'd sure remember."

"Sheesh, I feel like I'm at a bar," Kiley muttered.

Before she could flash her badge, he asked the others, "Can you please point us in Embry's direction?"

Pennie gestured to her right toward a corridor off the foyer. "That way."

"Thanks. See y'all later."

The brunette leaned over the counter. "The room is at the end of the hall. You can't miss it."

Collier lifted a hand as he and Kiley walked back toward the front of the building.

"I'd be more than happy to take you down there," one of them called. "I don't mind."

"We've got it. Thanks." The detective fell in behind him, saying under her breath, "Well, that only took three times longer than it should have."

"On a schedule, Russell?"

"Obviously not the same one as you."

He grinned. Several feet away from the door marked Call Room, he stopped. "Once we get him alone, how should we play this? You go first or me?"

She thought for a minute. "I've interviewed him before with Terra, and he didn't take too well to either of us asking him questions. Maybe you should take the lead. That way you can ask him some of the same things I already have, and we can compare notes."

"Okay. Since we don't have any proof he murdered anyone, we've got a lot of territory to cover. Jump in if you think of any questions I'm missing."

"Maybe he'll slip up, give us something we can prove is a lie."

He leaned around her to peer through the strip of glass in the heavy wooden door, his arm brushing her shoulder. She stepped back a fraction, just enough to let him know she didn't want him in her space.

"He's in there," Collier said quietly.

"Good."

They didn't have to wait long. A few minutes later the door opened and more than a dozen men, all dressed in the gray coveralls that served as their uniform, ambled out.

Collier caught Embry's eye, who paused and hung back as the other employees streamed around him. Collier hadn't seen Alan since Lisa's funeral last month. He'd shaved his head and gotten an earring. The thick arms and neck told Collier that the man still lifted weights.

The man shot an irritated look at Kiley before turning to Collier. "What are you doing here, McClain?"

"I've just transferred to the Fire Investigator's Office." He hitched a thumb over his shoulder toward Kiley. "This is—"

"I know who she is."

In his midforties, Embry's face looked as flatly cold and threatening as some inmates Collier had seen. "We need to ask you a few questions."

Kiley eased up beside him. "But first I need to read you your rights."

Embry's head jerked toward her. "Why?"

"Standard procedure." Collier knew from his notes that Terra and Kiley had done the same thing before their previous interview. "We're just asking questions, that's all."

Embry frowned as she began reciting the man his rights. Collier hoped this didn't make Embry clam up, but Russell was smart to Mirandize the guy. They didn't want any technicalities he could use to get off later if he turned out to be their arsonist and murderer.

"I've already answered a bunch of questions from *her*." Embry stabbed a finger toward Kiley.

"This is regarding a different case."

"This isn't about Lisa's murder?" he asked uneasily.

"Another firefighter was murdered on Friday night," Kiley put in quietly.

"Yeah, Dan Lazano. I heard. What does that have to do with me?"

Aware of two co-workers talking down the hall, Collier pointed. "Would you like to go back into the call room?"

"Why?"

"Strictly for privacy. We have several questions."

The man's hazel gaze sliced accusingly to Kiley. "I don't need privacy. I haven't done anything."

"Okay." Collier shrugged. "We heard you had a problem with Lazano, that you thought he was seeing your wife again."

"She's—she was my *ex*-wife. Lisa was involved with him

before she and I met. She broke it off before then, too. You know that."

"Just getting my ducks in a row."

"If she and Lazano were seeing each other again, I didn't know anything about it."

Collier eyed the other man for a moment, keeping his tone easy. "We know that Lazano was one of the men in the group of those who paid you a visit about your harassing Lisa."

"He wasn't the only one." Embry's face hardened.

"The other two male firefighters who were killed were also part of that group," Kiley said evenly.

"Are you saying I'm a suspect?" Alan snarled.

Collier agreed that Kiley's call about him taking the interview was a good one. Embry probably would have already shut her down.

"Where were you just before midnight on Friday?" she asked.

The other man's eyes narrowed to slits. "I was with my girlfriend."

"What's her name?"

"Angie Bearden."

"So you're not seeing—" Kiley glanced down at the notebook she held "—Neva Sasser anymore?"

"No."

"What's Angie's address?" Collier asked. "Where does she work?"

Embry gave the information grudgingly, and Kiley jotted it down as Collier continued, "We've tried to get in touch with you a couple of times since the night Lazano was killed. Where have you been?"

"I took my kids to their grandparents for New Year's Eve and we stayed a few days. In St. Louis. Today's my first day back at work."

"Was Angie Bearden with you?"

"Yes."

Embry's brief hesitation before answering had Collier deciding that this alibi would be one of the first things they checked. "Did you have problems with any of the other murdered firefighters?"

"What kind of problems?"

"Grudges, say maybe for the visit they paid you when you and Lisa were divorcing?"

"No."

"None at all?" Kiley asked.

He glared at her. "Well, I didn't like them butting in, but I moved on from it."

"When was the last time you saw your ex?"

"I guess about two weeks before she died," Embry said thinly. "The kids wanted to meet her at church so I drove them there."

Collier watched the guy's face. "Did you two argue about anything?"

"No, I didn't even talk to her. Just let the kids off at the door."

"When was the last time you did talk to her?"

"It was on the phone. Probably a couple of days later."

Kiley seemed fine about Collier conducting the interview, so he continued, "How long have y'all been divorced?"

"Five or six months now."

"How long were you married?"

"Four years," Alan said impatiently. "You already know this, McClain."

He shrugged. "I still need to ask."

Kiley spoke from beside him. "Did Lisa ever mention being afraid of anyone? Any enemies she had? Threats she may have received?"

"No. What does this have to do with Lazano?"

"Just trying to see if there are any connections we need to check out." Kiley gave Collier a look that seemed to be urging him to do something.

"Do you own any guns, Alan?"

"No. I told *her* that last time, too. What's the deal? You have to go behind her and make sure she gets stuff right?"

Kiley's face didn't change, but Collier felt her stiffen and saw her nudge back her coat so the gun at her waist was visible. "No," he said firmly. "This is a joint investigation. You know Presley's FD and PD work together on cases when a victim dies at a fire scene."

"Yeah."

"Do you know anything about guns?"

"Only which end fires the bullet."

Collier nodded as he slid his notebook into the pocket of his camel cashmere overcoat. "Okay, that's all for now. Stay available, all right?"

Embry didn't answer, just gave them both a hard look as he shoved his way into the men's room behind them.

Collier waited until he and Kiley were halfway down the corridor. "What do you think?"

"It should be easy enough to check his alibi with the girlfriend. We should also talk to his neighbors. See if they noticed when and if he was gone around New Year's Eve."

"We'll check his phone records, too, and see if he talked to Lisa when he says he did. Did you get any kind of vibe from him?"

She moved ahead of him, glancing back. "Not really. I don't like him much, but I think that's more to do with his personality than my suspicions about him. He reminds me of—"

"Who?"

"Doesn't matter." She glanced at him. "He's changed a lot of things about his appearance since Terra and I spoke to him after Lisa's funeral."

"You mean, like shaving his head?"

"And getting an earring. He's lost weight, too. You can definitely tell he's back in the dating scene. I've seen lots of men, married and single, who make drastic changes in their appearance like that because they're with a new woman."

"You sound pretty sure of yourself."

"I'm betting the new girlfriend is twenty-two or twenty-three, blond and…blessed. We'll both have a better feel for him after we talk to her."

He nodded, rubbing his nape. The interview had gone better than he'd expected. When Russell suggested he take the lead, he'd anticipated that lasting all of two, maybe three questions. But she'd let him do most of it, speaking up only to ask the more pointed questions and making herself a target for more of Embry's antagonism. Collier admired that.

As they reached the front door, she stopped so suddenly that he nearly stumbled over her. "Hey! What gives?"

She turned with a huge grin on her face, eyes dancing as she jerked a thumb over her shoulder. "Nice shot."

His gaze went to the door and he growled, "Who put that up?"

This year's firefighter calendar was taped to the door, open to the month of July and him, shirtless in boots and bunker pants with his suspenders dangling.

"We couldn't resist, Collier," Pennie called as she leaned over the counter to see him. "It's not every day we get a bona-fide calendar boy in here."

He gave them a mock glare and pushed open the door. "Don't y'all have any work to do?"

They laughed in answer. Shaking his head, he stepped outside, a cold wetness burning his cheeks. It was sleeting again.

Kiley eased up next to him. "I thought you looked familiar," she mimicked the words of the older woman inside.

He threw her a look. "Don't start."

She grinned. "I'm sure you got plenty of grief from the hose draggers who didn't participate."

"Yeah. I wouldn't have agreed if it weren't for charity. I

had to look at that picture for a solid month plastered on the front of everyone's lockers and in the shower."

She laughed, the smoky sound grabbing him right in the gut just like it had the first time he'd heard it at the Christmas party. "Hmm, there's an idea."

"Don't even think about it, Russell. I guarantee payback and it will not be pretty."

She whipped a pen out of her coat pocket and waggled it under his nose. "Can I get your autograph, Mr. July?"

"Sure." He plucked the pen from her. "Where would you like it?"

"Have you done this before?" she asked in amazement.

"A few times. Women seem to like it if I sign their—" his gaze dropped to her breasts, lingered before returning to her face "—underwear."

She laughed. "In your dreams."

He couldn't help a grin. "Since you're shy, it doesn't have to be there." He took her hand, turning her palm up and signing his name with a flourish.

"Hey!" She tugged at his hold, slipping on the ice and sliding into him.

"Whoa." He grabbed her shoulders, but she'd already knocked him off balance. He couldn't stop her fall. Or his.

They hit the icy asphalt hard, and he grunted from the impact. They spun toward the curb. Kiley landed on top of him and rolled off, skidding another few feet. He ended up on his back and she on her stomach.

She squealed. "This is freezing!"

He tried to stand, but his feet kept going out from under him. By the time he scooted over to the curb and managed to plant himself on the frozen grass, he was laughing. So was she. She got to her hands and knees, making it about a foot in his direction before she sprawled facedown on the ice. She muttered something, then went completely still.

Concern streaked through him. "Hey, you all right?"

"Yes," she said in a strangled voice.

"You sure? You look funny, like—"

"I just ripped my pants, okay!"

"Are you kidding?"

"No."

He tried, but he couldn't hold back a laugh. She glared. "How about giving me a hand, calendar boy, instead of cracking up over there?"

"That offer to autograph your underwear still stands. This could be fate."

"I don't think so!" Her lips twitched.

He stretched out a hand to her. She couldn't quite reach so she pushed herself to her knees and skimmed across the slick surface toward him. "My coat is going to be ruined."

She was laughing as he grabbed her hand. Her momentum plus the glass-slick asphalt spun her around, and he lost his hold on her. He snagged an ankle, feeling something bulky and hard as he pulled her the rest of the way to him.

"You wearing a gun under those pants?"

"Yes, ankle holster." Her hip bumped into the curb, and she came to a stop sprawled between his legs, blinking up at him.

"Hmm, I was wondering how to get you in this position, Kiley Russell."

"Shut up and help me."

He got a firm hold high on her arm and tugged. She scrambled over his thigh and plopped down beside him, breathing hard.

Sudden images popped into his head of her breathing hard against him for a completely different reason.

"Unbelievable." Her smile was warm and open, and her eyes sparkled with energy.

He grinned, reaching out to touch a kinky strand of fiery hair that had come loose. "Your hair's messed up."

"Just like the rest of me," she panted, pushing tendrils out of her face. "I can't believe these slacks are torn." She laughed. "I hope no one saw that fall. It really hurts my image as an officer of the law."

Collier looked around. "I think your tough-chick reputation is safe. You sure you're okay?"

"Yes."

She was still breathing hard, and Collier found his attention fixed on her mouth. Sleet drizzled over them. His backside was freezing, his face chilled, but none of that did anything to cool his blood. All his senses were focused on her spicy scent mixing with the wintry air, the pale gloss of color on her lips. He wanted to taste her. Had wanted to since dancing with her at that Christmas party. Had wanted to last night, he admitted.

She looked at him then and went very still. She had to be able to read the want on his face. It thundered through him, growing more reckless and demanding by the second. Somehow he managed to rein in the wild hammering of his blood. When he touched her, all he did was graze a finger across her chin.

She drew back, giving a nervous laugh. "Wh-what are you doing?"

"It's a little red, probably from when you fell."

"Oh." She reached up and touched the spot, her gaze locked on his as if it were impossible for her to look away.

Raw, searing hunger ripped through him. That one brief touch was enough to make him recall the feel of her baby-soft skin beneath his palm last night. The way that backless dress had traced every curve, set off legs that went on forever. Finally his brain kicked in. He cleared his throat. "Want to change before we interview Angie Bearden?"

"Yes," she answered quickly, the raggedness of her voice causing him to clench his fists to keep from reaching for her.

He carefully got to his feet, dragging the heel of his shoe across the ice to reach the grass below. He helped her up, letting go of her as soon as he felt she was steady. "Think we can make it to our vehicles without a repeat of that performance?"

"I hope so," she said smartly, looking down at herself. "I don't want to ruin any more clothes."

He grinned, the rush in his blood slowly ebbing. From her car she called to confirm Angie Bearden had gone into work today. She had, so he and Kiley agreed to meet in northwest Oklahoma City at the woman's place of employment.

Collier was glad for the break away from Kiley Russell. He had kept himself from kissing her, though it had taken more effort than he'd expected. The woman fired his rocket, but she wasn't the fast-ride, hot-sex and no-strings type of woman he'd set his sights on after Gwen had ripped his heart to pieces. Kiley would want a commitment, and the last one he'd made had sent him down in a burst of flames.

He couldn't afford to be distracted by her, professionally *or* personally. She'd been the one to put on the brakes last night after that dance, but he planned to keep riding them as long as they worked together.

Chapter 5

Just after five-thirty that evening, Kiley strode through the front doors of Presley Medical Center carrying a small gift bag for Terra's baby. Needing to update Collier on a couple of things about the case, she had left him a voice mail on his cell phone and a message with his secretary, Darla. If she hadn't heard from him by the time she finished her visit with Terra, she'd call him again.

After their interview with Alan Embry's girlfriend, she and Collier had gone their separate ways. She'd managed all day to keep her mind on the arson murders, but her stomach had been fluttery ever since that moment with him in the parking lot this morning. She'd thought he was going to kiss her.

There *had* been a moment, hadn't there? Yes, she was sure of it. What she wasn't sure of was if McClain really had wanted to kiss her or if he was just playing mind games. He knew he made her jumpy. What really annoyed her was that, at that moment, for one instant, she'd *wanted* him to kiss her.

Even thinking about it now had anticipation jolting through her. But all she had to do to douse that fire in her belly was remember her dad. Roger Russell's numerous affairs hadn't hurt only Kiley's mom. Even at nine and eight years old, Kiley and her sister had known their father was unfaithful. They didn't fully grasp the concept until the day they had heard their parents arguing about it and their mom deciding to get a divorce.

There had been enough hurt and humiliation for everyone. When Kristin was twelve, Roger had put the moves on the mother of one of her friends, and he'd hit on Kiley's tenth-grade English teacher, to name only two instances. Whenever she and her sister were with him, their concerns were put second to his girlfriend du jour or his efforts to nab the next one.

Kiley had once likened him to having the scruples of an alley cat, but on her twenty-first birthday, when she'd been called to bail him out of jail on a solicitation charge, she'd decided that even a tomcat used more discrimination than her father. She knew what it was like to live with someone who went from woman to woman, what it was like to have her heart and her trust broken repeatedly. So what if she wanted Collier McClain? It was only lust and she wasn't going there. Her hormones didn't call the shots; her smarts did.

At the nurses' station on the fourth floor, Kiley was directed to Terra's room. Jack Spencer answered her knock. "Hey, Russell."

His handsome face was lined with exhaustion, but that didn't diminish the megawatt power of his smile. She smiled in return. "Hey, Dad, is this a good time to visit?"

"Sure, come on in." He opened the heavy door wider, and Kiley stepped inside the room that looked more like a cozy parlor than a hospital. Dark wood floors and pale peach walls set off the tapestried drapes and love seat.

Terra sat up in a bed in the middle of the room, holding a little pink bundle. "Hi, Kiley."

The new mother beamed as brightly as her husband. She was fresh-faced, her strawberry-blond hair pulled back in a neat ponytail. "Thanks for the flowers."

Jack moved up the side of the bed toward his wife, pointing to a vase of pink mini-roses set apart from a dozen other bouquets. "They're the ones on the windowsill."

"I'm glad you got them. I brought something for the baby. What's her name?"

"Joey Elise." Terra turned the baby so Kiley could see her little face peeking out from under a soft hat. "We'll call her Elise."

"We chose Joey in memory of Terra's grandfather." Jack put an arm around his wife.

Kiley knew firefighter Joe August had raised Terra after the deaths of her parents. "May I hold her?"

"Sure."

Kiley passed the gift bag to Jack, then reached for the girl. She looked down at the infant's little round face and button nose. Dark hair peeked out from beneath a tiny pink cap. "Looks like she has a lot of hair."

"Yeah," Jack said. "I'm hoping the color will change to be like her mother's."

"She's gorgeous, no matter what." The baby, smelling clean and sweet, slept soundly. From what Kiley could see, the little girl was perfect. And if Jack and Terra were any happier, they'd bust. "She's a doll. When do you go home?"

"In the morning, I hope." The fatigue in the other woman's eyes reminded Kiley not to stay too long.

Jack pulled pastel tissue paper from the gift bag. "The doctor is supposed to come by sometime this evening and let us know."

"If I hadn't had a C-section, I could've gone home late yesterday."

"From what my mom's always told me," Kiley said, "you'd better take rest wherever you can get it from now on."

Jack chuckled, and she glanced at him. He held up her gift, a teddy bear dressed as a cop.

"A police officer bear!" Terra exclaimed. "What about the firefighter?"

Jack grinned. "Obviously Russell has a good head on her shoulders."

"We're always telling kids not to play with fire, Terra," Kiley quipped. "I didn't want to encourage her."

The other woman laughed. "It's very sweet. Thanks."

"I tried to find one dressed as a firefighter," she admitted. "But I didn't have any luck."

"Probably because I got the last one."

Kiley's heartbeat stuttered as she looked over her shoulder. Collier stood in the doorway, his face ruddy from the cold, his green eyes smiling. "The door was open, so I figured it was okay to come in."

"Yeah, do." Jack met the other man at the foot of the bed to shake his hand.

Collier's gaze shifted to Terra as he asked affectionately, "Doing okay?"

"Yes. It's so nice to see you both." Her gaze moved from him to Kiley.

Collier glanced at her. "Hey, Russell."

"Hey," she murmured. An image popped into her head of his calendar picture, that strong naked chest, the scar just below his navel. She sure would like to how he'd gotten that. And just how far down his flat, ridged belly it went. And why she found it so fascinating.

He moved over next to her and peered down at the baby. "She's little."

His breath washed against Kiley's temple, striking a low hum of awareness in her blood, and she fought the urge to ease away.

He reached over her shoulder and skimmed a finger lightly over one pink baby cheek. "Pretty, too."

Kiley was a little surprised. Most men she knew would've given the baby a glance from across the room. He took a step back, reaching inside a blue plastic bag and bringing out a bear dressed as a firefighter.

"Ah, equal representation. I love it!" Terra took the stuffed animal and grinned at its miniature fire helmet and turnout coat. "How are things going with the investigation?"

"So far, so good," Collier answered as Kiley nodded in agreement. "We're following up some leads. I just came from the training center. Everyone sends their best."

Kiley smiled, hoping the others couldn't tell that her nerves were jumping because of the big man standing so close to her.

Terra's speculative gaze slid from her to Presley's newest fire investigator. "Looks like you two are managing pretty well."

"Oh, yes," Kiley said. "Just fine."

"Don't worry about anything while you're off," Collier said. "I might even try to have the office cleaned up by the time you get back."

The other woman laughed. "Don't raise my hopes, McClain."

He grinned and, just like that, Kiley's knees went weak. Her pulse jumped into the red zone. *Aaargh!* She had to get away from him. Problem was, she needed to talk to him.

"Is there anything you want me to do while you're on maternity leave?" he asked Terra. "Now's the time to get it on the list."

"I'm afraid you'll hardly have time to breathe. Just give me an occasional update on our cases and settle in to the office. Make yourself at home. I mean that."

"Knock-knock." A slender dark-haired woman in a white lab coat walked in.

"Hi, Dr. Denton." Terra's voice was grainy with fatigue.

The physician glanced at Kiley. "I see you have the guest of honor."

She grinned. "I guess that's not for long."

The doctor smiled and took the baby, laying her on the bed at Terra's feet and peeling back the pink blanket. She quickly checked the infant, then rebundled her as she looked at Jack. "Here ya go, Daddy."

The big man took the baby, cuddling her close, and Kiley blinked at the tenderness on his face. As a cop, Jack Spencer could be downright intimidating, but he was going to be putty in that little girl's hands. Watching him had her throat tightening. He shared a look with his wife that sent a pang of envy through Kiley.

The doctor lifted a chart from the foot of the bed and studied it for several seconds. "Sorry, folks. I need a few minutes with Terra."

"We'll go." Kiley smiled at the new parents. "She's beautiful. I'm glad everything's all right."

"Thanks for coming," Jack said.

"Yes. Thanks so much." Terra waved as Kiley and Collier moved toward the door. "Come see us at the house if you have time."

"Sure thing." Collier pulled the door shut behind him and started down the hall with Kiley.

"Been here long?" he asked as they reached the elevator.

"Just a few minutes before you."

He reached around her to punch the button. "That was nice of you to come visit."

"You, too." He was too close. His clean masculine scent settled in her lungs, and the moment she'd been trying all day to forget unfolded in her mind. All of it.

The hunger on his face, his featherlight touch on her skin, that dim-the-lights tone in his voice. She had wanted him to kiss her then. She wanted him to kiss her now. She wanted to taste him, to— Work. She yanked her thoughts back to the case. Her focus needed to be on work. "Did you get my messages?"

"I got one on my cell phone. What's going on?"

"I need to catch you up on a couple of things."

"Okay."

The elevator door opened and they stepped inside. Just as the door began to close, a woman and a little red-haired girl hurried on board. A glance at Collier told Kiley he agreed to wait for further conversation about the case until they were alone.

The little girl, who looked to be three or four, was bundled into a pink coat. Red-gold curls hung past her collar. She peeked over her shoulder at Collier.

He grinned.

With a dimpled smile, she turned, training her big blue eyes on him. "We're up here seeing a baby. What are you doing?"

"We're seeing a baby, too."

"It's my aunt's baby."

"Oh, yeah?" He crouched so that he was at her eye level. "What kind of baby?"

"A girl baby."

"My friend had a girl, too."

Her wide-eyed gaze shifted to Kiley. "You have red hair like me."

"Yes." She smiled as the child's attention skipped back to Collier.

"Do you like girls with red hair?"

He likes girls with any color hair, Kiley thought wryly.

"Yeah, I do. Redheads are my favorite."

That flutter in Kiley's belly was due to the elevator's movement, she told herself. *Not* the morning-after rumble of his voice.

The little girl looked at Kiley. "What's your name?"

"Kiley."

"My name's Maddie."

"Hi, Maddie," she said.

"Our baby's name is Petunia."

"No, it isn't." The woman with her hand on the child's

shoulder laughed. "Maddie heard my sister mention that name while trying to decide on one. The baby's name is really Anna."

"Yeah, Anna," Maddie parroted. "What's your baby friend's name?"

"Elise."

The little girl's mother smiled at both of them. "I guess you can probably tell Maddie's never met a stranger."

Kiley grinned and Collier touched the tip of the little girl's nose. She giggled.

The elevator stopped on the first floor and the doors opened. Collier rose as Maddie jumped out with her mother and waved over her shoulder. "Bye!"

"Bye." He chuckled. "Cute."

He and Kiley walked a few feet into the lobby then paused next to the wall. The hospital's glass doors showed it was dark out. A block of cold air hovered in the entrance.

"Let's talk inside. It's brutal out there." Collier's gaze slid over her black wool dress coat. "How's your leather coat?"

"I think it will be all right."

"And your pants?"

"They can be mended."

A corner of his mouth hitched up. "You're not too big for the britches you're wearing right now, are you?"

"I knew you'd have some kind of remark," she muttered, trying not to smile. "What about your coat?"

"Already dropped it at the cleaners."

The one he wore now was long and black wool like hers. Beneath it, she saw the same navy slacks and white shirt of his uniform that he'd had on this morning. Kiley had kept her purple sweater, but changed into gray slacks.

"Did you get any news today?" she asked.

"I heard back from several of the prisons we contacted, but none of them have recently released an arsonist."

"Maybe one of the other prisons will be able to give us

something so we can get a lead on that fake fireman. After we split up this morning, I checked Embry's phone records. He did talk to his ex-wife on the night he said."

"What about his neighbors? Did you have time to go talk to any of them?"

She nodded. "The neighbors to his east are a retired couple. The husband has been in the hospital since the day after Christmas with a broken pelvis and leg from a car accident."

"So they couldn't vouch either way for Embry's being home."

"Right. His neighbors to the west are a family, but they're away on a cruise. No one in the subdivision was sure if Embry was home on Friday night or not."

Collier shoved his fingers through his dark hair, the front spiking a little. "Like we talked this morning, I still don't buy his girlfriend's story about him being with her the night Lazano was shot. Have you changed your mind about that?"

"No. I think you're right. She's hiding something."

He gave her an assessing look. "You were dead-on about her being in her early twenties, blond and built. We'll call Embry's parents in Kansas and check out his and Angie's alibi."

"Sounds good. I also went by Sherry Vail's house on the way here. She still wasn't home."

Because Collier had tipped Terra and Kiley off about Vail filing a complaint against Lazano before she'd been fired five months ago, the two women had tried to talk to the female firefighter the day following Lazano's murder, but had no luck.

The filed complaint had been for harassment, although not sexual, which was what Vail had filed on Rex Huffman, victim number two. The woman had been interviewed after Huffman's murder, not only because of the complaint she'd lodged against him, but also because Huffman had last been seen alive with an unidentified blond woman at a low-rent motel on the outskirts of town.

Sherry Vail was definitely blond. And turning up her connection to Lazano, another arson-murder victim with a link to her, had sent Kiley to the ex-firefighter's house again.

"Her neighbor who lives across the street got a call from Sherry last night, asking him to turn on her water so her pipes wouldn't freeze. He said she told him she'd be flying in tonight, landing around eight o'clock."

"Do you have to be anywhere for the next few hours?"

"No," she said warily. "Why?"

He laughed. "Relax, Russell. I'm not asking you on a date. Let's go get something to eat and stake out Vail's house. She doesn't live far from here. I think we should talk to her tonight."

"So do I." She really did. It was just that seeing him bring that sweet gift for Terra's baby, then watching him with the little girl on the elevator, skewed Kiley's image of him. Which made her jittery.

"We can take my truck," he said. "It's unmarked, so we'll be able to go stealth."

Kiley wasn't wild about sitting in a vehicle with him for any length of time, but she wasn't going to let on. Besides, his truck afforded more room than her sports car. "That's a good idea."

"Need to stop by your car and get anything?" he asked as they started for the front door. "Another pair of pants?"

"Ha ha."

"How about dinner? Are you serving from your car tonight?"

She smiled. "Nope, we'll have to find something."

She was not going to make a big deal out of this. It wasn't like he'd asked her to make out under the bleachers. He was all business; she was all business.

She was still telling herself that an hour later as they sat next to the curb down the street from Vail's duplex. The two-family units took up the first street in this subdivision, and the rest of the neighborhood was composed of single-family housing. Each duplex had its own driveway and a one-car garage. Sitting three house lengths away from the streetlamp's pool of light, Kiley and Collier had an unimpeded view of the woman's small, gray brick home.

His truck was toasty warm, and she felt fatigue creeping over her. Neither of them had said much since eating. Their leftover sandwich and chip bags were stuffed in a sack in the back seat. The air still held a whiff of roast beef and their coffee.

He was on the phone with the fire chief, one shoulder angled into the corner against his door, one hand draped loosely over the steering wheel. Watching him make the occasional gesture had her mind wandering to the way he'd touched her this morning. And last night.

"Everything okay?" she asked as he hung up and returned the phone to its mounted holder.

"Yeah. Chief Wheat just wanted to know how things went at the training center today." He dragged a hand down his face, his gaze settling on her.

In the shadows, his green eyes were dark and sultry. Unnerving. Kiley controlled the urge to squirm, but she was helpless to stop the thrill that shot through her under his regard. Sitting in the darkness, in the quiet of his truck, started a slow throb of anticipation in her blood.

She fought it. She didn't understand how a Romeo like McClain could get to her, but she couldn't deny that whatever it was drew her like Eve to the apple. It really torqued her off.

Searching for something to say, she blurted the first thing that came to mind. "You're pretty good with kids."

"I like 'em."

"You want to have some someday?"

"Yeah." Broad shoulders lifted in a shrug. "I don't know if it will happen."

"Why? Don't think you can settle down with just one woman?"

Heat flared in his eyes; a tension sprang up between them. "I'm not sure there's one out there who'll make me want to."

She never should've started this line of conversation, but she couldn't make herself shut up. "I guess you'd have to date a forever-after kind of woman to start with. Not much chance of that, huh?"

After a slight hesitation, he said, "Never say never."

"Don't have children if fidelity isn't part of your plan. The kids pay for it."

"Are you an expert?"

She shrugged.

His gaze pinned her. "What about you? Do you want kids someday?"

"I haven't decided yet. If I do, I won't have any until I'm ready to settle down."

"You don't strike me as the white-picket-fence type, Russell."

"I could be, with the right man."

"Who's the right man? The guy you're seeing now?"

"I'm not seeing anyone."

Collier was silent for a minute, his attention shifting to Vail's house. "What kind of qualities does the right man have?"

"Why? You gonna set me up?"

"C'mon." His gaze flicked heatedly over her. "Tell me."

"Really?"

"Yeah."

"Well, someone who keeps the promises he makes. Who thinks I'm enough woman for him."

His gaze did a slow slide down her body that jolted every nerve ending. "I'd say you're plenty of woman for any man."

"I meant," she said through gritted teeth, "a man who thinks one woman is enough."

Not like you, she added silently, hating the way her body went to liquid just because he looked at her.

"Somebody's broken a lot of promises to you, Blaze," he said quietly. "Who was it?"

The question alone would've knocked her for a loop, but combined with the nickname, she was stunned. Blaze? No one had ever called her that. And hearing McClain say it so softly sent a pang of longing through her, though she didn't know for what.

Looking into his eyes, she could see he sincerely wanted an answer. What scared the fire out of her was that she wanted to give him one. The same connection she'd felt to him at the dance, the sense that he could see right into her, snapped tight between them. Though delayed, a warning finally blared through her. Things had to stay professional between them, although right now, with her brain in limbo, she couldn't have said why.

A tightness stretched across her chest. She tore her gaze from his and struggled to focus on the front of Vail's house. It took a few seconds for her to register what she saw. A car pulling into the garage. "Oh, look, Vail's home."

Escaping the probing intensity of his gaze, Kiley slid out of his truck and shut her door. Collier followed, his gaze hot on her, but he didn't speak until they reached Vail's driveway.

"I think we should do this together."

She knew he meant the interview, but for a heartbeat she wished it were something else. He had worked in the same station house with Vail, and Kiley had interviewed her before.

"You're right," she said. "We both have information on her. With both of us asking questions we'll be casting a wider net, upping our chances of learning something."

He nodded, reaching the small front porch just before she did. Clear yellow light slid across the high slash of a cheekbone, the bluntly squared jaw. He was a gorgeous, solid stretch of man, and every time she was around him, her hormones screeched, "I want some of that."

She hadn't thought about sex this much in two years, but she couldn't deny she wanted Collier McClain. Thank goodness, some part of her mind still worked. No matter what kind of game they talked, most guys were selfish in bed and out. Probably just one night with Collier would be all it took for her to stop thinking of him as her own personal calendar boy rather than her partner. She might be tempted, but, his reputation aside, she didn't go for casual sex. And he didn't go for any other kind.

He'd been right. Someone had hurt her, and he wanted to know who. Collier couldn't believe he was disappointed that Kiley hadn't confided in him. She'd been right not to tell him. Something like that was too personal. Problem was, he wanted to get very personal with her. In every position he could imagine.

He wanted to get his hands on her soft skin, in her wild hair. He wanted that as much as he wanted to know who'd broken her heart, which threw him. Lust, he could handle. Adding emotion to the mix was something he hadn't done since Gwen. Wasn't going to do ever again.

As they waited at Vail's front door, he slid a look at Kiley. She was back to cool and professional, which only made him more curious. He did not get it. Was this fascination just an offshoot of wanting her? There was something about her, something that reached down deep inside him to a place no other woman ever had. He should've kissed her this morning and gotten her out of his system. All day he'd regretted that he hadn't. But earlier, just like now, his brain was ordering him to keep his distance.

He and Russell were partners. Partners only. Forgetting that would be as stupid as walking into a fire without his gear.

Sherry Vail answered their knock, surprise widening her brown eyes. Collier hadn't been present at her previous interview. He hadn't seen her in the five months since she'd been fired, but the curvy blonde looked much the same. She was a beautiful woman who had modeled for a while before going through the fire academy. Thick golden hair slid around her shoulders. The black skirt that hit her just above the knee revealed a pair of great-looking legs that had remained covered during her days at Station Two.

She was a looker, but only a fair firefighter. Her gaze shifted from him to Kiley. "Detective. McClain, I heard you were promoted. The last time Presley's fire investigator and one of its homicide detectives showed up here, the news was bad."

"Afraid it's bad this time, too, Miss Vail," Kiley said. "I'll need to read you your rights, just as I did last time when I was here with Investigator Spencer."

Sherry looked from Kiley to Collier, then nodded.

Once Kiley finished Mirandizing the other woman, she asked, "Did you know Dan Lazano was killed last Friday night?"

"No."

Collier thought the shock on her face looked genuine. "We need to ask you some questions, Sherry."

"I've been gone since last Wednesday. I don't see how I can help."

"We want to talk to you about the complaint you filed against him."

She hesitated, her mouth drawing tight. Despite the wariness in her eyes, she stepped back and opened the door wider. "Come on in."

"Thanks." Kiley stepped inside the small flagstone foyer just ahead of Collier.

He closed the door, catching a whiff of Russell's subtle, spicy scent. He'd finally decided it was cinnamon. The whole time they'd been sitting in the truck that scent had teased him.

His gaze shifted to Vail. "Where were you last Friday night between the hours of ten and midnight?"

"Is that when Lazano was killed?"

"Yes."

"I was in Denver since last Wednesday, calling on customers."

"Where did you stay?" Kiley slid a small notebook from the side pocket of her coat.

The other woman's jaw firmed, but she answered. "At the Adam's Mark, downtown."

"Are you still working for the Torch Stop?" Collier knew the business that had been established and was run by former firefighters. Over the years he had bought a couple of replacement parts from them for some of his gear.

"Yes. I sell parts and accessories for firefighting equipment."

"Why don't you walk us through what led up to your complaint against Lazano?"

She flicked a glance at Kiley as she moved into a small living area done in green with touches of burgundy and cream. "I'm sure Detective Russell remembers about my sexual harassment complaint against Rex Huffman?"

"Yes." Kiley followed the woman, stopping behind a nubby couch the color of moss. "You first met him at a fire call both your stations responded to. He kept asking you out and you repeatedly refused. After a couple of months he started calling you, saying suggestive things."

"Suggestive, my butt. They were out-and-out sexual. I told him I didn't date firefighters. I never had, never would, but he wouldn't let up. Lazano was one of Huffman's buddies. After I filed on Rex, Lazano started giving me grief. Screwing with my gear at first, then threatening me."

"Physically?" Collier stood at the edge of the room, where the light-toned carpet met the flagstone floor.

Sherry eased down on the arm of a plaid wing chair adjacent to the couch. "No. Threatening to get me fired. About a week later, drugs were found in my locker. They weren't mine. I passed a random drug test, but I couldn't prove they'd been planted. The locks on those lockers are flimsy. Everyone has access to them. Anybody could've set me up."

"No one ever saw you do drugs?" Kiley asked.

"No. And they couldn't prove I ever had, but the amount was such that they said I could've been distributing."

Kiley glanced at her notebook. "You had other violations on file, didn't you?"

Sherry's mouth tightened. "I was written up for being late a couple of times."

And disobeying an order, Collier added silently.

"They fired me for violating city policy."

"So you had more than one reason to dislike Lazano."

He watched her face carefully. Vail looked annoyed, but she didn't appear to be hiding anything.

"Dislike him? I hated him. He got me fired. Am I sorry he's dead? No. But I didn't kill him."

Kiley flipped back a page in her notes. "When we learned about the complaint you filed against Lazano, we went back a little further in your personnel file. You had a problem with Gary Miller, too."

"But I didn't file anything on Gary."

"You talked to your captain about him."

"So?" She shifted uneasily on the arm of the chair.

Collier rubbed at the taut stretch of muscle across his nape. "What was that about?"

"I complained because he was doing the same thing Lazano was," she said impatiently. "He and Dan didn't like that I'd turned Huffman in for being a lech."

"Why didn't you file a complaint against Miller?" Kiley asked.

The other woman's eyes narrowed slightly. She looked as

though she might not answer. "I thought I should tough it out. I got crap like that from other men when I first started as a firefighter. I really thought it would blow over."

Collier remembered the first time Sherry had walked into the station house. He'd noticed her looks, but he hadn't been interested in hitting on her. A few of the other guys had, though. They wanted her to be a pinup, not a firefighter. Most of them hadn't given her a chance to prove herself until after a few months.

"You remember that Miller was our first arson-sniper victim?"

"Yeah." She eyed him cautiously.

Kiley jotted something in her notebook. "Were you friends with Lisa Embry?"

"We knew each other in high school." Sherry shrugged. "We didn't hang out or anything."

Collier picked up the thread. As long as he and Russell were here, they should get as much information as possible. "Where were you between the hours of eight and midnight on the night she was killed? December fifth."

Her eyes widened. "You can't think I had anything to do with that!"

"These are questions we need to ask, Sherry."

She stiffened; her face closed up. She looked from him to Kiley. He could practically see her connect the dots. She had a link to three of their victims, three men who had likely cost her a career in firefighting. Did she also have a reason to hate Lisa Embry?

"I'm tired." She rose from the arm of the chair. "I told you what I know. I didn't do anything to any of those jerks. I'm going to tell my lawyer you showed up here. If you want to talk to me again, go through her. Raye Ballinger."

Collier wasn't surprised. Raye had a reputation for handling harassment cases. "You suing the city, Sherry?"

"I want my job back." She moved around him to the door and opened it.

He shared a look with Kiley as they walked out. "All right, then. If we have further questions, we'll contact Raye."

"Fine." She shut the door.

Kiley jammed her hands into her coat pockets, tucking her head against the cold as they moved across the frozen yard and toward his truck. Neither one of them spoke until they were inside. He started the engine and flipped on the heater.

She glanced at him. "Were you surprised to hear that Ballinger's her attorney?"

"No."

"Neither was I. I'll call the hotel in Denver to check her alibi."

He nodded as he pulled away from the curb, heading back to the hospital for Kiley's car. "We've got a solid tie between her and the three male victims. Do you think she had anything to do with Lisa's murder?"

"I don't know. She was more than willing to talk about the other victims, but she clammed up fast when we asked about Lisa."

"She could've stopped talking because she really was tired, and that just happened to coincide with when we asked about Lisa."

"Yeah, or not. I'm sure you believe in that kind of coincidence about as much as I do. Both women were at your fire house for a while. Did you ever notice anything going on with the two of them?"

"Not really."

"I think we should keep digging. See if Vail had a connection to Lisa that we haven't found."

"I agree. I can pull her personnel file, and we can go over the people who were interviewed by the police and the OSBI about her when she applied to be a firefighter."

The Oklahoma State Bureau of Investigation assisted with background checks if the fire department asked. Collier knew the police department also used the agency at times. "In the morning I'll tell Darla to get the file from personnel."

"Maybe we'll get a lead from that."

"Even if Vail was out of town the night of Lisa's murder, she could've hired someone to kill her."

"Right."

Collier turned onto Tenth Street. "Lisa's the only female victim. She could've been murdered just to throw us off the trail."

"True," Kiley murmured, looking out the window.

About three blocks ahead, he saw the fog-shrouded lights in the hospital parking lot. "I think we should look hard at Sherry. Huffman was last seen with a blond woman who we still haven't been able to identify. The clerk from that seedy motel couldn't be sure the woman with Huff *wasn't* Vail, even though he thought he'd remember a woman that good-looking."

"Could've been a prostitute." Kiley turned toward him, settling one shoulder in the corner. "Or someone wearing a wig."

"I'll go along with the wig theory. I don't know about the prostitute. There were no signs in Huffman's autopsy report of his recently having had sex, which could make Vail a good suspect. If Sherry was the woman with him that night, we know she wouldn't have gone there to sleep with him."

"True." After a minute she said, "Her alibi for that night was that she was in Little Rock, Arkansas, calling on customers. It was solid."

"She still could've hired a sniper." Collier pulled in to the hospital parking lot, going slowly over patches of sleet that had refrozen after sunset. He had just guided his truck into the parking space beside Russell's car when his cell phone rang. He answered, "McClain."

"Collier, it's Raye Ballinger."

That hadn't taken long. His gaze shot to Kiley's. "Hang on a sec, Raye."

Russell exchanged a look with him, indicating she also considered it a red flag that Raye was calling so quickly after they'd seen Sherry Vail. Kiley straightened and leaned in slightly as he returned the phone to its mount and put it on speaker. "I thought I might be hearing from you."

"My client said you paid her a visit." The woman's voice was silky and relaxed. "What was the purpose?"

"Didn't she tell you?"

"She was upset. Why don't you tell me?" Her voice dropped invitingly.

"It was routine." Collier grinned. He doubted the attorney would be so sociable if she knew Kiley Russell was with him. "Sherry filed a complaint against Lazano and we were just following up."

"Maybe we should meet for a drink and talk about this."

"I think I've got what I need for now."

"We could meet, anyway." Her voice stroked over him in a way that didn't turn him on. "You still owe me a rain check for the dance last night."

He could feel Kiley's gaze taking him apart like a bad toy. "I'm up to my kneecaps on this case, Raye."

"One of these times, I'm going to convince you, Collier. It would be so good." She laughed softly as if they were alone in a dark corner. "You know I go after what I want. That doesn't threaten you, does it?"

Kiley rolled her eyes.

"Nope." He wasn't threatened; he just wasn't interested.

"Now remember," she said flirtatiously. "No more talking to Sherry without going through me first."

"Got it. Good night." He jabbed the disconnect button, shaking his head. "Not too subtle, is she?"

"Did I just witness history here, McClain? I didn't know you ever turned anyone down."

He slid her a look. "Well, now you know something about me."

"Oh, I know about you all right. How long has she been chasing you?"

"She's not really chasing. She just likes to play."

Kiley arched an eyebrow. "Don't they all?"

"You don't," he said pointedly, wanting to shake that cool, judgmental look off her face.

She laughed, the smoky sound drawing his body tight. "Does that bug you? That I'm not one of those women who fall at your feet?"

"Hardly," he muttered. An unfamiliar heat charged through his chest. "You've known me what? All of two months, if that, right? Why do you think you know so much about me?"

"This ain't my first rodeo, McClain," she drawled. "I know your type. I *lived* with your type."

"Doesn't mean you know *me*."

"It's a wonder you're not worn-out, getting in a clinch with every woman you meet."

"Haven't with you." He shifted in his seat and leaned toward her, just enough to put a wariness in her eyes. "Are you asking?"

She gave him a flat look. "Yeah, right."

"I don't know who did a number on you, Blaze, but it wasn't me. I'm tired of you painting me with that brush."

"Hey, it's your brush."

He should just ignore her and say he'd see her tomorrow.

She tilted her head, scrutinizing him thoughtfully. "You can probably go from hello to a liplock in under a minute."

"Wanna time me?"

She laughed again, the sound setting off an explosion of anger. And lust.

"Since you've got me pegged, I figure you saw this coming."

"Saw what—"

He clamped a hand on her nape and hauled her to him, slamming his lips against hers.

She gasped, stiffening. His chest caved like he'd taken a fastball to the sternum. His anger lasted two seconds. Until she melted against him, made a soft noise in the back of her throat.

The hot surge of blood in his veins had him wrapping his other arm around her waist and dragging her as close as he could with the stupid console between them. Her arms went around his neck. She sank into him, opening her mouth to his. Beneath her coat, he felt the faint press of her breasts against his chest. Her tongue stroked his, and he felt himself going under. He wanted her in his lap.

Somehow he managed to gentle the kiss, taking it deeper, drinking her in. She smelled like cinnamon, tasted like nine kinds of sin. Right now, he'd give his badge to strip her naked and bury himself in her. She kissed him back with every bit as much enthusiasm as he had pounding below his belt. He only stopped because he couldn't pull in one more breath. Pulse racing out of control, he lifted his head. His hands were on her face, holding her to him. His body was iron hard all over.

She trembled as she slowly drew her arms from around his neck; his hold tightened reflexively.

Her eyes were smoky with desire, but she pulled away, pressed into the door looking shell-shocked. He sure felt that way.

She was breathing hard, her lips wet from his, her hair loose around her face where he'd had his hands. "I can't…believe you did that."

The accusation in her tone ripped off a different kind of heat, infuriated him. "Guess you were right about me after all."

The tip of her tongue touched the center of her top lip.

His body actually hurt from need.

"I'm going now." She tore her gaze from his and fumbled for the door handle. "This never happened."

"You got that right." No way was he apologizing, even though danger signs were slamming him from every direction.

She got out and walked the few feet to her car. It took her two tries to get her door unlocked and get inside. If she was shaking like he was, he understood.

He watched her drive away, staying put as much to make sure her car started without problem as he did because he needed a minute—or more—to restart his brain. He swallowed a curse, his head falling back on the seat.

That kiss had lit him up like a match to lighter fluid; his body was as fully engaged as any blaze he'd ever fought. He'd been trying to prove she was wrong about him. Yeah, grabbing her and kissing her like a sex-starved maniac had been real convincing.

Even as he willed his heart rate to slow down, he wanted more of her lush mouth, her rich sweet flavor. One taste of her was not going to be enough, but it had to be. He was not getting involved with her. It would help if his brain sent that message to his body. Pretty damn quick.

Chapter 6

Sweet Saint Florian! Kiley needed the patron saint of fire-fighters to protect *her*. Two days after her meltdown in Collier's arms, she was still reeling. His kiss had hit her faster, harder than 180-proof liquor.

Just before six o'clock on Friday evening, she pulled up under the old metal sign that hung over the glass front door of the fire investigator's office. She and Collier had some catching up to do on the case. Anticipation buzzed her nerves, just like it had been doing since he'd kissed her. She had managed to keep it in the back of her mind and stay on track by telling herself the reason it—*he*—had affected her so much was because the kiss had been such a surprise.

He'd said she should've seen it coming. *Hmph.* Evidently she didn't have the mother of all radars. Still, when his mouth had covered hers, she should've been the one to pull away. She hadn't done that, either. It had felt good, *too* good. She'd been kissed before by guys who knew what they were doing, but Collier was way out of their league.

Her bones had turned to water, just like her brain. It had been incredible and her body hadn't stopped reminding her ever since. Since she hadn't pushed him away, she would have to be the one to reestablish the boundaries between them.

And she definitely had to tell him to quit with the nickname. His calling her Blaze made her…hot. The way he said it put a flutter in her belly. She hadn't stopped thinking about that, either. Which meant it was a darn good thing she'd been away from him for the last two days.

They had both been dealing with other aspects of their jobs that couldn't be ignored. The time apart had enabled Kiley to put that kiss out of her mind. Mostly. Today.

She'd spent yesterday at the D.A.'s office going over evidence for an upcoming trial. And she'd spent today in another jurisdiction, interviewing a material witness in a homicide. She'd been looking for Erby Fuller for six months, and he had been picked up nearby on a traffic violation. When the Yukon police saw he had a warrant, they called her, and Kiley had spent most of the day in the small town due west of Oklahoma City.

From the two phone calls she'd exchanged with Collier, she knew he'd been tied up yesterday at the training center finishing a class, then today performing some building inspections that couldn't be put off.

She'd told him that kiss never happened. She intended to act as if it hadn't, and she expected McClain to do the same.

She opened the glass front door and walked into the age-washed red brick building that housed his office. Ten or eleven years ago, the fire investigator's division had moved here. Wiring and plumbing had been brought up to code, but there had been no change to the exterior of the place that had been the precursor to Presley's four present station houses.

A hint of smoke underlined by a sharp chemical odor

drifted through the air. Having met Terra here a few times over the past couple of months, Kiley knew the layout of the utilitarian space.

To her left was the secretary's desk belonging to Darla Howell, who had left for the day. The concrete floor led to a metal door at the end of a short hallway. Terra's office was on the left, situated behind where Darla sat and separated by glass walls.

The office was crammed with a squat oak desk. Stacks of files and a computer sat on one edge. Two wooden arm chairs faced one side of the desk and a stuffed leather chair sat on the other. Scratched gray filing cabinets lined the adjacent wall. Photographs of fires and ancient fire engines covered the wall above the files.

The major part of the sturdy building, which had been home to Presley's original fire station, was behind that metal door where Terra tested her theories and some samples. Though the hire of a new fire cop had been approved, the budget didn't include building a full lab. What couldn't be tested here was taken to the lab in Oklahoma City.

Kiley had learned a lot from Terra over the past weeks but not enough that she could work this case by herself. Not that she could've ditched McClain and gone against city policy, anyway.

"Hello!"

"Back here." Collier poked his head out of a doorway across the hall from Terra's office.

As he disappeared back inside, Kiley walked in that direction. Along the wall outside his office stood a dry erase board on wheels. She recognized the precisely arranged photos as being from last week's warehouse fire where Dan Lazano had been killed.

She stopped in the doorway, noting that the files on his desk were stacked as deeply as the ones on hers. She'd known this small office was his, but she'd never been in it before. Her gaze slid over a computer on the far corner of his desk, a pair of firefighter boots against the wall behind. The helmet she'd seen the night of Lazano's murder rested atop a four-shelf bookcase crammed with sample cans and a couple of cameras. His shovel was to her immediate left, and the tackle box containing his hand tools sat in front of it.

"Didn't this used to be a storage closet?"

"Yes." He grinned easily with no hint of the tension that had hummed between them the last time they'd seen each other.

He dominated the room. Not just his sheer physical size, but *him*. The small space seemed even more crowded. Kiley noted no awkwardness in his manner, no hint of the blazing emotion that had been in his green eyes when she'd left him the other night.

Last night he'd called to tell her that he still hadn't been able to reach Alan Embry's parents. Kiley had heard nothing from them in response to her phone messages, either. She was hoping one of the things McClain told her tonight was that he'd finally talked to Embry's lawyer father and homemaker mother.

Scribbling notes in a file, Collier bent over an old oak desk. Seeing the strong angled lines of his face, the mouth that had obliterated every protest in her body had Kiley taking a deep breath to settle her restless nerves. Amid the stacked files on the cluttered desk were maps and newspaper clippings as well as hand-drawn diagrams.

He again wore the white shirt and navy pants of his uniform, but the top two buttons on his shirt were open, and the sleeves were rolled back to reveal corded forearms dusted with dark hair. Her gaze slid to his hands, and she recalled his gentle touch on her face Wednesday night. A knot formed in her throat. She mentally rolled her eyes at herself and pushed away all thoughts of that kiss.

He shoved a piece of paper across the desk toward her. "Look what I got from Michigan City, Indiana."

The Indiana State Penitentiary was one of the places to where they'd expanded their search for anyone recently released who'd served time on arson charges. "A picture of the fake fireman?"

"Yep."

"Great!" Kiley picked up the grainy, faxed mug shot of the man Collier had seen on the video from the last fire murder scene and stared at a guy with a boyishly young face whose features were sharp, his face narrow. Maybe they had finally gotten a break. "I was hoping we'd get lucky today. What's the story on this guy?"

"Meet Monty Franklin, thirty-three years old." Collier picked up another sheet of paper from the stack on his desk and glanced at it. "Served ten years of a twelve-year sentence for second-degree arson. Just paroled for good behavior. He has an aunt who lives outside of Presley. She vouched for him at his hearing and said he could stay with her. Since he had a place to live and a potential job, he was released. But his parole officer hasn't seen or heard from him since his first check-in three weeks ago."

"If he's only been out three weeks, he can't be our guy." She returned the photo, noticing a framed picture on the wall behind him. Collier and three men in full turnout gear stood in front of Station House Two. She recognized the man to his right as his brother, Walker.

Collier followed her gaze, pointing to the two older men. "My daddy and granddaddy. You've met Walker."

"I knew you were third generation." She could see where he got his looks. "I didn't realize Walker was a firefighter, too. Is your sister?"

He shook his head.

"Back to Franklin, what about motive?"

"So far the only connection I've found to Presley is the guy's aunt, but that doesn't mean there isn't another. He can't be our sniper on the other three cases, and maybe he's not our arsonist, either, but we can put him at the Lazano scene."

"If he's done time for arson, he would know that the fire would likely be videotaped. He got a turnout coat so he could be part of the crowd."

"Yeah, and maybe while he was blending in, he saw who started that fire, who shot the rifle."

Kiley nodded. "You haven't had any luck finding him?"

"Not yet, but I've been to see his aunt and his parole officer. The aunt seems like a nice lady. I think Monty's got her snowed. Both she and the P.O. agreed to call me if our boy shows up."

Presley was small enough that all police, including the detectives, worked solo. Kiley had never worked with a partner, but she liked working with McClain. She admired how he was more concerned with solving the case than flexing his macho muscles, but just because she enjoyed working with him didn't mean she should enjoy doing anything else with him. Like kissing.

"I don't want to depend only on the aunt or the parole officer making contact when they see Franklin."

"I don't, either." He grinned. "That's why I called the chiefs at each of our four station houses. We're set up to ride along on as many fire calls as we need to. Monty loves fire—he won't be able to stay away. We may not catch him at the first one, but he'll show up eventually."

"Good idea."

"I'm known to have one every once in a while."

"I'm starting to see that."

He looked surprised at the compliment; she was a little surprised herself.

He dragged a hand across the back of his neck. "We've

gone as far as we can with the samples that started the fires. These are the hardest kind to pin on a torch. Just using a match in the right place in a closed-off area can result in a good fire, which makes it hard to assign blame."

"A *good* fire, McClain?" She shook her head, smiling slightly. "Only you hose draggers think fire is good."

He grinned. "We know these fires weren't accidental, but we have very few clues as to whodunit. I think we both agree that the reason is to get firefighters to the scene and kill them."

"Yes." She wanted to think he was shallow and fast and cared only about one thing, but she was learning differently. He was a good investigator and seemed to have a natural knack for putting people at ease.

And despite the way they'd left things the other night, he acted professional, friendly. Completely unaffected by their kiss. If she were honest, his seeming disinterest needled. Especially when that liplock had darn near burned her common sense to ashes. She should be glad he wasn't acting bothered by it, but what concerned her more was how many women he'd practiced on before her.

She forced her mind back to the case. "If we could figure out the arsonist's motivation, we might be able to stop another murder. Right now we don't even know if he's getting revenge on firefighters who responded to the same call or not. We'll have to work with what we do know, maybe go over the videotapes, witness statements, everything again to see if we're missing anything."

"Speaking of which, I still haven't received a call back from Alan Embry's folks. I guess I'm going to have to go up there."

"*We,* McClain," Kiley said briskly. "*We'll* go. It's my case, too." Whatever this was between them was not going to affect her job. And she certainly didn't want her lieutenant to think she was dodging any of her responsibilities. "Unless something comes up, we can both go."

He nodded, stepping toward her and easing down on the corner of his desk. The tang of his aftershave drifted on the air. "I'd sure like to be able to bust his alibi."

He folded his arms, drawing her attention to the subtle flex of muscle. His slacks pulled taut over lean, powerful thighs.

She dragged her gaze away, wishing she weren't so fascinated with his body. "Yes, we definitely need to get a lead somewhere."

"Embry's so jealous and possessive I have no problem imagining him murdering Lisa or those three guys who warned him to back off when he was hassling her."

Kiley nodded. She felt bad about what she'd said concerning Collier's kissing every woman he met. She had thought back more than once to the way he'd been with Terra's baby and that little girl on the hospital elevator. Seeing such a tender side of the man sure didn't match the playboy image she had of him.

His green gaze rested on her face. "I haven't had any luck getting Vail's personnel file. Darla tracked it down to the city attorney's office, but he took it with him on some out-of-town deposition. He's supposed to be back on Monday."

"Well, since we can't get to the fake fireman yet, maybe we should think about going to St. Louis tomorrow." The way he seemed to see into the deepest part of her was unnerving. Such perception didn't match her image of him, either. "At least we can try to confirm Embry's alibi that he was with his parents the night Lazano was killed."

"That's a good idea. I can make the flight arrangements if you want."

"I can do it." And she would request seats in separate rows. The man was a whole lotta scrumptious. Just being within feet of him was making her palms—and other places—damp. She couldn't sit beside him on a plane.

She'd wondered what his kiss would be like, and now she knew. Man, did she know. It was the best kiss she'd had in...well, ever. La-de-freakin-da. That didn't mean she had to turn into a throbbing mass of hormones. Just because he knew how to kiss didn't mean he was any less selfish than other guys she'd dated. Or any more inclined to be faithful.

She didn't understand. She'd never even been attracted to his type before, but she couldn't deny she was now. At least to him, anyway. But she wouldn't let him get to her. Just like she apparently wasn't getting to him.

She needed him to help solve these cases, but she couldn't let it be more than that. There was enough to juggle with this one investigation to keep her mind occupied, not to mention the other three related cases. She had to focus so they could wrap up their investigation. The quicker they did, the sooner she could get Collier McClain off her radar.

A loud ringing jerked him awake. Collier struggled up out of the thick fog of sleep, his hand closing over the cordless phone. He answered as he tried to drag his eyes open. It was dispatch. Station Three had received a fire call. Witnesses reported seeing an eighteen-wheeler hit a propane truck then crash it into a small storage building. Clearly an accident and not arson, Collier didn't need to investigate, but the resulting fire could be something that would tempt Monty Franklin. A perfect opportunity for Collier and Kiley to try to find the guy.

His head cleared and he rolled out of bed, pulling on his jeans as he glanced at the clock. A little after two. He punched in Kiley's number as he pulled on a T-shirt, then a thick black sweater.

Since his house was closer to the scene, she agreed to drive here. They would ride there together and work out their plan for surveillance on the way. He went out and started his truck. While he waited, he checked the hands-free audio equipment he'd gotten from the police department. Less than ten minutes later she arrived. She hurried to his truck, shrugging into a heavy coat, and he caught a glimpse of a tight white sweater, the full curve of her breasts. Her wild hair was pulled through the back of a dark ball cap.

As she climbed in and closed the door, her sassy scent drifted to him. He laid the microphones on the console and backed out of the garage. "I want to make sure those are working."

"Okay." She picked them up, fitted one behind her ear so that the mouthpiece came to the corner of her mouth. She handed him the other one to put on. "Testing," she said.

"Mine's working."

"Mine, too." She kept hers in place, flipping off the switch. "Do you think we'll spot this guy tonight?"

"Hard to say. If he hears about the fire, I'm hoping he won't be able to resist it."

She nodded, rubbing a hand over her eyes.

"Sorry I had to wake you up."

"No problem. It'll be worth it if we can get Monty Franklin." She glanced over and smiled.

That same friendly, you-don't-make-me-hot smile she'd given him in his office earlier. And just like earlier, it irritated him. "I figure you can mingle with the people who show up, and I'll stay on the perimeter. Whoever spots him first can point the other one in the right direction."

She nodded, her expression polite, distant. It drove him nuts. Despite telling himself not to, his gaze dropped to her mouth, lingered.

"Where's our scene?"

He named a street on the north side of town. "There's a fast-food joint and a mattress store on the same side of the road."

"Oh, I know where you mean. What caused the accident?"

"The driver of the semi fell asleep at the wheel. I've been thinking one of us should get out on the south side and walk up to the scene like an observer."

"I'll do it."

He thought she answered eagerly, as if she wanted to get away from him, but he could read nothing on her vibrant features. "I'll park in the lot of that gas station across the intersection and come in from the west."

"Sounds good."

"Okay." He forced his gaze away from her and to the dark road, finally clear of ice and sleet. The other night in his truck, she'd said she had lived with his type. He took that to mean she didn't live with that person now, and she'd told him she wasn't dating anyone. It must've been an old boyfriend who had broken her heart. He forced his mind to remain on the task at hand. He had a job to do and it wasn't figuring out what made her tick.

As they approached the accident scene from the north, he saw gray-brown smoke spiraling into the air. Red and blue lights flashed from police cruisers parked at either end of the scene. The officers had blocked off the road both east and west as well as the nearby side streets that ran north and south. Yellow crime-scene tape cordoned off the whole block.

If he and Kiley had been working this scene, they would have shown their badges to the officer stationed at the entrance, then spoken with the cop who held the log book to check people in and out of the scene. But not tonight.

He drove through the intersection and stopped about half a block away to let Kiley out, then made a U-turn and drove back toward the light, turning left into the gas station lot before he reached the intersection.

As he walked toward the scene, he could see the propane truck on its side, half in and half out of the building that stored raw materials for making mattresses. The semi sat jackknifed in the middle of the main road.

People always gathered at a fire scene, and chances were good Collier and Kiley might spot their suspect in that group of people.

He showed his badge discreetly to the officer stationed at this end, then started toward the people who were congregating on this side of the yellow tape. The crowd ran the gamut of firefighters, cops, news crews and civilian onlookers. The street was lined with fire engines and police cruisers. Some of the officers who drove those black-and-whites were there specifically to keep an eye out for the sniper. Two news crews from stations in nearby Oklahoma City were already filming.

Stations Two and Three were there with their engines and one ladder truck. Oklahoma City had lent an engine, and Presley's Station Four brought the rescue unit.

Some of the equipment was housed in different locations, but the rescue unit went on major medical calls with other engines to other locations. Both victims of this accident had required immediate attention and were now on their way to the hospital.

As far as Collier and Kiley knew, their arsonist-sniper hadn't yet shown up at the scene of an accident or killed anyone at such a scene. Even though this fire wasn't an arson, the Presley PD and FD were taking no chances.

Engine fumes hung heavy in the air along with the acrid stench of burning rubber and cotton batting. As he neared the scene, Collier felt the heat rolling in waves from the burning truck and building. His gaze swept the crowd. He stopped at the back end of Three's ladder truck and spotted Kiley coming in from the south. She was several yards away, her hair a warm glow of color in the frozen night.

He switched on his combination earpiece and microphone. "You there, Russell?"

"Yeah."

"I can hear you loud and clear."

"Same here. I'll do a sweep of the bystanders."

"Ten-four. I'm next to Station Three's ladder truck."

The streetlights cast a hazy glow over the scene. Collier noticed several people in the crowd were high school kids. He moved to the side of Station Two's fire engine and into the shadows.

Collier saw Kiley then, talking to a young woman in the cluster of those who watched the fire. After a few seconds she drifted among the growing throng of people and spoke to someone else. He stepped up to the nose of Station Two's fire engine, his gaze probing the faces around him.

Sooty water ran into the street, gurgled in the grates. Illumination from the streetlights was overpowered by the orange glow and black-gray smoke. The flames snapped as they shot out of the building's roof and the driver's-side window of the propane truck, the fire swallowing whatever got in its path. Collier knew the fire inside that building roared like a small plane engine.

He studied the crowd, standing so that his hands-free device wasn't immediately visible to anyone who saw him.

"McClain?"

There was nothing suggestive in Russell's tone, but her whisper shot adrenaline through his body. Annoyed, he whispered back, "Yeah?"

"I see him."

Collier straightened, his gaze slicing through the crowd to find her, then looking for the face they'd seen in the mug shot.

"He's at my two o'clock."

His gaze moved to her right shoulder, then out. There was Franklin in a turnout coat on the back edge of the crowd as if he were providing control. The look of dreamy infatuation on his face would've raised Collier's suspicions even if the guy hadn't been Monty Franklin. Oh, yeah, he was a torch all right. And he was the fake fireman on the videotape from the scene of Lazano's fire murder.

Collier eased away from the fire engine, throwing a look at the empty parking lot of the strip mall across the street. The wooded land behind the line of businesses was still undeveloped. "Russell, I'm going in from this side to try and keep him from going across the street. If he gets over there, we could lose him."

"Okay, I'll make my way toward him, too. We'll box him in."

Collier moved slowly, not wanting the guy to take his attention from the flames shooting out of the propane truck. Franklin stepped between two onlookers, getting closer to the fire. Collier adjusted his position and angled toward the guy. Four more steps and he could grab the suspect's arm.

The man glanced around nervously. Collier stayed in place, hoping the guy didn't realize he was a target. Franklin eased his way to the back of the crowd as if he were trying to get a better view between people, then he spun and sprinted for the street.

Hell! Collier took off at a dead run, yelling into his microphone. "Russell, he's heading for that mall!"

"Ten-four!"

He raced across the street and onto the empty parking lot. Floodlights illuminated the fleeing man, and Collier identified himself, "Fire Investigator!"

A cop caught up to him. "Need any help?"

"Yes! Stay back there in case he tries to come this way again."

"Ten-four."

Collier pushed himself harder. Franklin sped toward the open side of the corner building, running parallel to the street. Collier was prepared for the guy to dart into the street, but he turned left and went behind the building.

There was a retaining wall back there, eight feet tall, shoring up the dirt and concrete foundation of the strip mall. If Franklin jumped and ran for the woods, they'd lose him for sure. The possibility sent a surge of adrenaline through Collier, and he rounded the corner, closing the distance between him and the suspect.

The other man dodged a stack of empty pallets, then darted behind a steel dumpster on wheels. Collier sprinted in front of it, thinking he could cut the guy off. Suddenly the dumpster flew at him, ramming a sharp corner into his knee. Cursing, he shoved his way around it, heard it crash against the brick wall. "Franklin, stop! I just want to ask you some questions!"

The man was only feet from the retaining wall. As he glanced back, Collier tackled him, managing to grab the hem of the turnout coat Franklin had probably stolen.

Both men went down hard. Collier lost his grip on the suspect. Grunting as his shoulder slammed into the rough, unforgiving surface, he bounced like a rubber ball. His head slammed into the curb. Ears ringing, pain streaking through his head, he scrambled to his knees and dove for Franklin. His hands closed over the SOB's shoulders.

The suspect jumped, pulling his arms free of the protective gear and leaving the coat dangling in Collier's hold. Breathing hard, sweat running down the side of his face, Collier threw his legs over the wall and dropped. His vision hazed; the dark ground swirled up to meet him. Head spinning, he stumbled back against the edge of the wall.

"Did he jump?" Kiley landed beside him, muttering something. "Are you—"

"I'm fine." He took off, biting back a moan and clenching his teeth against a jarring pain in his knee.

Kiley stayed with him. Collier's body screamed in agony, but he was too mad to stop. The two of them headed across the flat pastureland for the trees where Franklin had disappeared.

He and Kiley stopped at the line of trees, seeing nothing, hearing nothing except their own harsh breathing. There was no way they'd be able to find the loser in the dark. He bit off a curse, thumbing sweat from his temple.

She came around on his left and they started back toward the building. She held her side, breathing hard. "You okay?"

"Just banged up. You?"

"I'm…fine. You got the coat," she said. "That's good."

He looked down, only now realizing he still held the turn-out coat. "It isn't going to tell us anything we don't already know, except maybe confirm that it's stolen."

"I guess so," she panted.

Collier dipped his head toward the end of the retaining wall that ran the length of the building. "There's a flight of stairs."

Kiley changed direction with him, sending a dark glare toward the wall. "I wish I'd seen those steps before I jumped. I *hate* jumping."

He grinned, wincing at the stab of pain in his temple. Now that his heart rate was slowing, he became aware of a throbbing in his shoulder, a bone-squeezing pain in his knee. His head felt as if it had been cracked open. He grabbed the rusted iron stair rail and made his way up the steps with her, going back the way they'd come. "I am too old for this."

The high-wattage floodlamps situated in the parking lot threw enough light over the roof and back of the building for them to see where they were going.

"You sure you're okay, McClain?"

"Yeah." He glanced at her. "That's the second time you've asked me."

She stopped, her face half in shadow. "You're really pale."

He gave a short laugh. "There's not a lot of light out here, Russell. How can you tell?"

She moved to stand in front of him, eyeing him critically. Her gaze skipped over him from head to toe, then jerked back to his face. "McClain!"

"What!" he growled, startled by the alarm in her voice.

"You're bleeding! A lot." She feathered a finger across his temple.

Even in the shadows he could see the concern in her eyes. He reached up to touch his head, his hand brushing hers as she withdrew. His fingers came away sticky with blood. It hadn't been sweat rolling down his face.

"Maybe you should sit down. I'll go get the paramedics."

"I can walk." His whole right side ached. He'd been going full speed when that dumpster hit him, but he'd already determined that his right kneecap wasn't broken.

"Are you hurt anywhere else?"

"Just banged up my shoulder and my knee."

"Your head looks bad."

The worry in her eyes seemed real. As real as the desire he'd seen the other night. "I'll get it checked before we leave."

"Okay."

It took only a few minutes for one of the paramedics to clean and bandage the cut on his head. Since he didn't need stitches, a trip to the hospital was unnecessary. He told them not to bother with the other injuries.

Kiley insisted on driving him home, saying she should be the one behind the wheel so she could get back to her car in one piece.

By the time they reached his house, the pain in his head had subsided somewhat, but his knee ached more sharply than it had before. She parked in his garage and held open the door leading into the house. He limped through the kitchen and into the living room where she helped him off with his coat.

Her warm, spicy scent settled in his lungs. She stepped back into the kitchen, asking if he wanted some water to take his acetaminophen. He directed her to the cabinet where she could find the glasses.

"At least this wasn't an arson, and we had no shots fired tonight." She was once again all business, her earlier concern gone so completely he wondered if he'd imagined it.

"Yeah. I wish we could find the connection between these dead firemen. I can't believe we lost Franklin."

"I know," she said briskly, impersonally. As if they hadn't nearly devoured each other in his truck the other night.

He wanted to touch her, wanted her hands on him. It surprised him how much he wanted that. Maybe it was the whack he'd taken to the head. Maybe it was his ego, but he was suddenly determined to get a response from her. At the very least, an admission that they *had* kissed the other night.

Favoring his right leg, he made his way carefully down the hall to his bedroom, figuring she'd try to find him. He crossed the nubby carpet, went past his dark wood bed and into the master bath. Once there, he tugged his sweater and T-shirt over his head, clenching his teeth against the pain.

"McClain, where are you?"

"Back here." He turned so he could see his shoulder in the mirror that took up most of the wall. His flesh was scraped and bloody, a bruise already forming.

"Ouch, that looks like it hurts."

He looked around to find her in the door, holding a glass of water. He opened the cabinet to his right and pulled out a bottle of acetaminophen, easing down onto the edge of the sink.

He tossed back six of the regular strength painkillers, feeling her gaze on his bare chest as he drank the water. When he lowered the empty glass, she looked away. Which only firmed his resolve.

She backed up a step. "Let me know how you're doing in the morning. I'll call and cancel our reservations to St. Louis."

"Why?"

"You're hurt. We can—"

"We should go on. We're at a dead end with this case. We have to do something, *find* something. Embry's folks might be the ones who give us a lead."

She paused a second. "All right. While we're gone, I'll send an officer over to Franklin's aunt's house as well as his parole officer to see if he's there or if either of them have heard from the scuzzball."

"That's good."

"See you bright and early, then."

Oh, no. She wasn't going anywhere yet. "I hate to ask, Russell, but could you put some medicine on my shoulder? I don't think I can reach it too well."

She hesitated less than a second, agreeing in that same polite, remote tone she'd been using since last evening in his office. It bugged the hell out of him.

He reached into the drawer at his left hip and pulled out a tube of antibiotic cream.

She hesitated then moved up beside him and took the medicine, squeezing a generous amount onto a cotton swab. "Tell me if I hurt you."

He nodded. She leaned over and gently dabbed ointment on the wound.

Her warm breath fluttered across his back. Even beneath the smoke, he could smell her shampoo, some kind of flowery soap on her skin. His body tightened all over. "How does it look?"

"Raw." She carefully touched the scrape, leaning farther into him to reach more of it.

He could feel the warmth of her body. She was too close, too tempting, and he couldn't resist. Very lightly, so he wouldn't spook her into jabbing that swab into his wound, he blew in her ear. She shivered, sending him a sideways look as if trying to decide if he'd done something.

He managed to keep his face blank. He'd never known a woman who could hide her emotions so well, but it didn't occur to him that she wasn't interested. He *knew* she was.

Something had happened between them, something that had knocked him to the moon, and she was going to admit to it. He didn't care if he was being driven by a blow to his pride.

How could she act like he'd never had his mouth on hers? How could she even pretend nothing had happened? She'd practically melted all over him.

She shifted, her silky hair teasing his cheek. She smelled like a dark, sultry night; her skin glowed like pearls. He wanted to put his mouth on her, mark her. He barely moved his head, and his face was in her hair. He nuzzled her behind the ear.

She came up so fast she nearly hit his chin. Her eyes narrowed on him. She tossed the swab into the trash and stepped back, screwing on the cap to the ointment. "There."

"Thanks."

"You're welcome." Her eyes wary, she laid the tube on the countertop beside him and moved toward the door. "I'll see you tomorrow."

He didn't care how he stopped her from leaving, but he *was* stopping her. He was getting ready to bluntly remind her of their kiss, get her good and flustered when her gaze dropped to his leg.

She frowned. "Your knee's bleeding."

He glanced down, saw the dark stain on his jeans.

"You'd better put some antiseptic on it."

"Careful, Blaze. I might start to think you care."

Her eyes flashed. "Can't afford for you to drop off the case, McClain. I don't have time to catch somebody else up on the details."

"Ah, you're making me all misty."

"Yeah, yeah. Listen, I can help you with your knee if you need it. Otherwise…"

"Could you get me a pair of shorts? I'll do the rest."

"Sure."

"Bottom right drawer of my dresser."

She disappeared into his bedroom. She might not be falling all over him, but he'd seen her pulse jump in her neck when he'd nuzzled her, spied a glimpse of the desire he'd seen the other night. Having her so close revved him up. He was sore, but he wasn't numb.

Kiley returned to hand him a pair of gray cotton gym shorts.

"I appreciate it. Wanna help me take off my pants?"

She laughed. "This isn't one of your dreams, McClain."

He grinned.

"Need anything else?"

"You could stay and talk to me."

"You should rest."

"You could stay and rest with me."

She rolled her eyes. "Give it up. You just whacked your head hard enough to split it open."

"What if I pass out or something?"

She pressed her lips together as if trying not to laugh. "Seriously, do you need me?"

"Yes," he murmured, locking his gaze with hers, knowing just what would get her. "I need you to kiss me and make it better."

"I am not going to kiss it—" Her eyes narrowed. "Did you say kiss *me?*"

"Pretty please? I'm askin' real nice."

"McClain," she gritted out. Fire blazed in her eyes.

He could barely keep from laughing. "Double-dog dare ya."

She scooped his sweater off the floor and threw it at him, turning for the door. "I'm outta here."

She wasn't leaving until he got what he wanted. "Blaze?"

"What?" she snapped over her shoulder.

He wanted her to look at him. "That kiss?"

She spun, her eyes wide. "Hey, we agreed that never happ—"

"It happened, and I'm not going to forget it. I'm not going to let you forget it, either."

For a heartbeat, she looked nonplussed, then emotions—panic, exasperation, uncertainty—flashed across her features in rapid succession. She stared hard at him, frowning fiercely. "Well, crap."

She turned on her heel and marched away. Collier burst out laughing, then grabbed his head as a sharp pain drilled through his skull. The door leading out to his garage slammed; he heard her car start.

His ego was satisfied. He was starting to think his body never would be.

Chapter 7

Kiley thought she was prepared to see Collier the next morning, but when she walked up to the waiting area to board their flight and saw him, her stomach dipped. His short hair was mussed as if he'd been running his fingers through it. He looked darkly handsome in a black suit and white shirt; his muted green-and-blue tie made his eyes seem even more green.

The bulky bandage at his temple had been replaced with a small butterfly Band-Aid. His right leg was stretched out, probably because it hurt to bend his injured knee. He glanced up and saw her, folding his newspaper and moving his coat out of the seat next to his.

She really didn't know how to act around him. The way her blood had been rushing since last night, at his house, had her warily eyeing him.

The man had been banged up worse than a bull rider and he'd still been able to get to her. She couldn't believe he'd reminded her of that kiss. She didn't need a reminder. Her brain had locked on to that out-of-body experience tighter than spandex on a hooker.

The best way to deal with him and her hormones was to stick to strictly business. Thank goodness they weren't sitting together during the flight to St. Louis. She could stay focused on the job if she had some space. The more she was around him, the more she liked him. Yes, he was a hound dog, but he was a really nice guy. Of course, most people thought her dad was nice, too, Kiley reminded herself.

She'd snagged two coffees from a nearby kiosk. He saw her and held up two of his own. "Great minds."

She smiled, absurdly touched that he'd brought her some, as well.

Keeping her coat on, she took the seat next to his. He eyed her purse on the floor. "What do you have in there for breakfast today? Biscuits and eggs?"

She laughed. "Nothing. I ate at home."

He grinned, his gaze moving over her dark coat, the black dress boots she'd worn with her slim nutmeg slacks and soft sweater of the same color. "Thanks for helping me last night."

"You're welcome." She'd helped him out just as she would any partner. "How are you feeling this morning?"

"Sore, stiff, but I got here without a cane." He touched the bandage at his temple. "And my headache's gone."

"Good. You weren't so cheery the last time I saw you this early in the morning. Is that a side effect of your injury?"

"I've got some coffee in me. I can function now."

"Maybe you can convince the Embrys to tell us something."

"Maybe." He pushed himself out of his seat. "I'm going to see if our plane is on time. Can I get you anything?"

"No, thanks." She held up both coffees. "I'm good."

He limped away but soon returned, favoring his injured leg as he lowered himself into the chair beside her. He gave her part of the newspaper, and they read in silence. She was in-

Get FREE BOOKS and a FREE GIFT when you play the...

LAS VEGAS
GAME

Just scratch off the gold box with a coin. Then check below to see the gifts you get!

YES! I have scratched off the gold box. Please send me my **2 FREE BOOKS** and **gift for which I qualify.** I understand that I am under no obligation to purchase any books as explained on the back of this card.

340 SDL D7ZT   240 SDL D7ZK

FIRST NAME   LAST NAME

ADDRESS

APT.#   CITY

STATE/PROV.   ZIP/POSTAL CODE

(S-IM-06/05)

7	7	7	Worth TWO FREE BOOKS plus a BONUS Mystery Gift!
🍒	🍒	🍒	Worth TWO FREE BOOKS!
🔔	🔔	♣	TRY AGAIN!

The Silhouette Reader Service™ — Here's how it works:

Accepting your 2 free books and mystery gift places you under no obligation to buy anything. You may keep the books and gift and return the shipping statement marked "cancel." If you do not cancel, about a month later we'll send you 4 additional books and bill you just $4.24 each in the U.S., or $4.99 each in Canada, plus 25¢ shipping & handling per book and applicable taxes if any.* That's the complete price and — compared to cover prices of $4.99 each in the U.S. and $5.99 each in Canada — it's quite a bargain! You may cancel at any time, but if you choose to continue, every month we'll send you 4 more books, which you may either purchase at the discount price or return to us and cancel your subscription.

*Terms and prices subject to change without notice. Sales tax applicable in N.Y. Canadian residents will be charged applicable provincial taxes and GST. Credit or Debit balances in a customer's account(s) may be offset by any other outstanding balance owed by or to the customer.

sanely aware of how good he looked and smelled. Thirty minutes later they boarded.

Kiley breathed a sigh of relief that she wouldn't have to sit next to him on the flight to St. Louis. He moved up the aisle behind her. She spotted her row, and his three rows back.

She found her place and edged in next to the window. She put her purse under the seat in front of her.

Collier sat down beside her.

Her gaze jerked to his. "What are you doing?"

"Taking my seat." He grimaced as he bent his right knee and moved his long leg out of the way of boarding passengers.

She chuckled. He wasn't going to get to her today. She hooked a thumb over her shoulder. "Your seat's back there."

"Not anymore." Smiling, he leveled his gaze into hers. "I switched."

"You switched?" she choked out. "But I made the reservations. They told me—you did it when you went to check on the flight."

He grinned, and her stomach did that funny flip it had done when she'd seen him earlier. She didn't want to sit by him. Last night at his house she'd nearly caved in to his flirting. "What's going on, McClain?"

"We can put our heads together."

"Listen here—"

"On the case. We want to have our ducks in a row when we see Doug Embry."

She couldn't argue with that, but she wanted to. The look in his green eyes dared her to acknowledge that sitting so close to him bothered her. It did a lot more than bother her. It sent reckless, stupid thoughts through her mind, like wishing she had kissed his wounds last night. Along with the rest of him.

No way was she letting on. He felt well enough to bug her so she couldn't even get mad at him for changing his seat. As long as she focused on her job, she could handle him. "All right."

"Should we come up with some kind of excuse to talk to the Embrys? Since they haven't cooperated so far by returning our calls, I don't figure they'll throw the door open and invite us in."

"Good point."

He settled into his seat, his broad shoulder against hers.

As he fastened his seat belt, his arm bumped hers. She could feel the heat and hardness of his lean thigh along hers. She plucked a dog-eared magazine from the pocket in front of her and crossed her legs, eliminating one contact point.

Once the plane reached its cruising altitude, he unbuckled his seat belt and shifted in his chair. His knee bumped hers, but she didn't say anything. It was obvious he was trying to find a comfortable position for his bruised body. She wanted to do something for him to take away the pain.

When she'd seen the blood on his head last night, she'd been truly alarmed. More than she'd ever been for an injured colleague. She couldn't deny any longer that he was getting to her, but that didn't mean she had to do anything about it.

"I hope we get somewhere with Embry's parents."

"Yeah. I'd like to find *something*. If Alan and his girlfriend were in St. Louis the night Lazano was killed, we can mark him off as having been at that murder scene. But not off the list of suspects, since he could have hired the shooter."

"True. It was a good idea to come up here." The tang of his aftershave teased her. "At least we can get in their faces until we get an answer."

"We know Embry told the truth about talking on the phone with Lisa a couple of days after he claims he last saw her."

"And we haven't found anything to prove he's lying about not having a gun or knowing how to use one."

Collier shifted in his chair, adjusting his injured leg.

"So maybe we'll get something out of his parents that will

jump-start the investigation." The plane's engines roared around them, and Kiley leaned in so he could hear her. "We're due a break."

"He's got motive. Being threatened and humiliated by three guys who work with your ex-wife would make anybody furious."

"And rage or jealousy could've caused Alan to kill his ex."

Collier nodded, laying his head back on the seat. "So far, he's the only suspect we have with ties to all four victims."

"Yeah."

He closed his eyes, and she couldn't stop her gaze from tracking the strongly defined angles of his face. He was the type of man she'd avoided her entire life, but she hadn't stopped thinking about that kiss or the way he'd nuzzled her neck last night. She hadn't bought his innocent look for one second. She thought he might've blown in her ear, too.

She wasn't mad, but she was on guard. Just because she had refused to acknowledge it to Collier didn't mean she was unaware. She hadn't been unaware of him since meeting him at that Christmas party.

As she watched, his forehead creased as though he were in pain.

She pitched her voice to be heard over the engine noise. "Does your head hurt? I have some aspirin."

He cracked open one eye. "Thanks. I don't think I need them right now."

She frowned. "Are you sure?"

"Yeah." His gaze dropped to her mouth, and she felt her heart jump.

They were nearly nose to nose. She eased away, schooling her expression into what she hoped was a calm mask.

He closed his eyes again, and she forced her attention back to her magazine.

The way he looked at her made her pulse wheel and her

body go soft in all kinds of secret places. She was starting to think he might not be a selfish lover.

That was surely her hormones talking.

Plus probably the fact that she was forced to spend so much time with him. She had to be careful, remember his reputation as the kind of man she knew all too well. Keep reminding herself that they were *only* partners.

An hour after landing, they arrived at Doug and Jackie Embry's home via rental car. Being a Friday, Kiley and Collier had thought they might find Alan's father at his law office, but they hadn't. The phone book had yielded their home address, and Collier had managed to find his way to their neighborhood.

The middle-class homes had the angled contemporary look that had been popular in the seventies. Kiley double-checked the address of the steep-roofed, white brick home, then got out and walked with Collier up a set of broad steps to the porch. Bright sunshine did nothing to warm the air; frigid January wind swept along the porch, stinging her cheeks.

They rang the doorbell, and a pleasant-looking woman with short graying hair and smiling eyes answered.

"Yes. May I help you?"

Kiley reached for her badge, feeling Collier do the same. They'd made up an excuse on the ride over as a way to get inside the Embrys' home and talk to them, but her instincts told her they didn't need it. "I'm Detective Russell and this is Investigator McClain. We're from Presley, Oklahoma."

"My son lives there." Alarm streaked through her eyes. "Has something happened?"

"Your son's fine, Mrs. Embry," Kiley assured her. "We're conducting an investigation and need to ask you some questions. Just to tie up a few loose ends."

"Is this about my former daughter-in-law's murder, then?"

"Not specifically."

She looked visibly relieved but curious. "Come in and have a seat. May I get you some coffee or something else to drink?"

"No, thank you." Collier slid his badge back into the pocket of his black coat. "We don't plan to stay long."

She led them into a narrow living room with dark walls and light carpet. "If Alan's okay, then what is this about?"

"We need to find out—"

"Don't say anything, Jackie." A deep masculine voice came from behind Kiley. "We don't have to talk to them."

She turned with Collier, who said, "Mr. Embry, we only need a few minutes of your time."

Behind a pair of black frame glasses, the man's eyes narrowed on his wife. "You didn't have to let them in."

"What's the harm, Doug? They're just tying up some loose ends."

"You're the cops who've been calling me."

"Yes, sir." Kiley saw no reason to distinguish between her job and Collier's at this point.

"The reason I didn't call you back is because I have nothing to tell you."

"You said you'd talked to these people." The woman glanced at her husband, her lips thinning. She looked at Kiley. "I'm sorry you had to come all the way up here."

"Don't apologize," Embry snapped. "One of them—him— he's from the fire department. You know what those firefighters did to Alan, threatening to take a tire iron to him."

For good reason, Kiley thought.

The woman's gaze turned troubled, moved from Kiley to Collier then back to her. "What exactly do you want to know?"

Collier kept his voice relaxed. "When was the last time you saw Alan?"

"Last week." Jackie aimed a look at her husband. "Well, Doug didn't see him. He made sure to be gone when Alan brought the kids and left them here for a few days. I took them back to Presley alone."

"Do you remember the dates?"

"Yes. The grandkids come at the same time every year. They arrive on December thirtieth."

"And when did you take them home?"

"Last Tuesday."

January sixth. Adrenaline shot through Kiley. *So Alan had lied about being here the night of Lazano's murder.* "When did you last see your son, Mr. Embry?"

"Jackie, be quiet. I'm an attorney, and I know we don't have to talk to the two of them."

"We know Alan hasn't done anything wrong. It can't hurt to answer their questions."

"They're not here to let us know he received some kind of award," he muttered.

Kiley didn't want to get her hopes up, but there had to be a reason Doug Embry wouldn't cooperate. "Mr. Embry?" she prodded.

"I haven't seen him since Lisa's funeral." He sounded choked.

Kiley could see Collier was calculating the time just as she had. It had been over six weeks since Doug Embry had seen his son. And Mrs. Embry had just told them that Alan hadn't stayed here during the time he said he had.

They'd busted Embry's alibi. Kiley reined in her excitement.

"We'll get out of your way now," Collier said. "Thanks for your help."

"You're welcome." Jackie walked them to the front door. "This settles all your questions about Alan?"

"Yes, ma'am." Collier walked out behind Kiley.

As they started down the porch steps, she heard Mr. Embry say angrily, "What is the matter with you? I told you we didn't have to talk—"

The door closed. Kiley grabbed Collier's forearm. "We got something."

"Yeah, I heard." He grinned. "Yee-haw, Russell, looks like we caught a break."

"It's about time."

As they stepped onto the sidewalk and headed for the rental car, he hooked a thumb back toward the house. "Who do you think's gonna win in there?"

"My money's on her." Kiley withdrew the hand she still had on his arm, reminding herself to keep things strictly professional.

He walked around to the driver's side and opened the door. "Mine, too."

Kiley took a deep breath before climbing inside. She'd been so excited about catching Alan Embry in a lie that she'd wanted to kiss Collier. He really was getting to her, and she didn't know what to do about it.

A few hours later Collier and Kiley were once again in the air. She hadn't said two words since they'd boarded the plane for their return flight. Collier had switched seats for this flight, too, so he once again sat next to her, his injured leg stretched out in the aisle. "You're not mad at me, are you, Blaze?"

She glanced over. "About what?"

"Switching seats?"

"No."

He probably ought to stop before he heard something he didn't want to. "Last night?"

"No. Do you want to go straight from the airport to talk to Embry?"

"Absolutely." Cool, professional, pleasant. Exactly how she'd been all day.

"And then to see Angie the girlfriend? She obviously lied to us about being in St. Louis at Alan's parents, too."

He nodded, his gaze skating over her dewy skin. He knew

how soft it was. He wanted to feel it again, but he knew better. The wary look in her eyes told him that if he tried to touch her in any way, he'd probably draw back a bloody stump.

Her wild hair was down today, tucked behind her ears. Her warm cinnamon scent settled in his lungs. He studied the curve of her cheek, the angle of her jaw until she looked at him.

"Why are you looking at me like that, McClain?"

"How long have you been a cop?"

"Eleven years." She eyed him speculatively. "How long have you been a hose dragger?"

"Thirteen years." He should follow her lead and try to keep their conversation restricted to the case. "Did you go to college?"

She nodded, returning to her magazine. "What's with the twenty questions?"

"Just trying to get to know you a little better."

She frowned at him. "How about if I ask you some questions?"

"Go ahead." He laid his head back on the seat, folded his hands over his belly. "Ask me something."

"Anything?"

He cut her a look. Was she planning to ask him when he'd lost his virginity or what? "Anything."

Her gaze held his for a second then slid down his body. He went tight all over. What was going through her mind?

"How'd you get that scar on your stomach?"

"You hiding one of those firefighter calendars, Blaze?" Fighting to squelch his surprise and the jump in his blood pressure, he kept his voice lazy. "How do you know about that?"

"I saw it that day at your house. When you were walking around half-naked."

Her tone was teasing, but her eyes had gone dark in a way that told Collier she was every bit as aware of him as he was of her.

"Are you going to tell me?"

Talking was not what he wanted to do now. He cleared his throat. "It was my first flashover."

"What's that?"

"The combustion of a room and its contents by simultaneous ignition."

"Ouch."

"It was at an apartment building. I was on the second floor and there was a puppy. I picked him up, tucked him under my turnout coat and started for the exit. The room behind me exploded, and the dog panicked, clawed my shirt to shreds. Coming out of the building, I got hit by a flying piece of burning debris. Burned my wrist." He nudged up the sleeve of his coat and shirt to show her the faint scar on the inside of his wrist. "And my belly."

"Good grief, McClain! It sounds awful." Her eyes were huge, worried. "You were lucky. Was anyone else hurt?"

"No." Her warmth drifted over him. He loved watching her emotions change from disbelief to concern. He couldn't stop a grin.

"What?" Her eyes narrowed. "Are you lying? You're lying!"

"Yes." He chuckled.

She rolled her eyes. "What really happened? Fall off your bicycle?"

"Walker and I were shooting off fire crackers. We were trying to one-up each other, daring each other to hold a bottle rocket."

"Stupid."

"Yeah, we found that out."

"Good grief." She pushed his arm off the rest between them, a wry smile curving her mouth.

He wanted to run his thumb along her bottom lip. "What about you, Blaze?"

"What about me? I don't have any scars, if that's what you want to know."

"Got any family stories?"

"Not like that."

"I know you have a sister. Any other siblings?"

"Just Kristin. I'm a year older than she is."

"Are the two of you close?"

She nodded.

"What about your mom and dad?"

Her face closed up. "My mom lives in Nevada half the year, during the winter."

She didn't mention her dad. Maybe he'd died. "Is your dad still around?"

"Sometimes." Something he couldn't define streaked across her face. "Why are you asking all this, McClain?"

"I'm just—" his gaze dropped to her lips "—interested."

She actually squirmed. "What about your family?"

"You've met Walker. I don't know what to say about him."

Kiley grinned. "He's cute. Is he married?"

"No, and don't get any ideas."

"About what? Setting him up?"

"Going after him yourself."

She laughed. "And you have a sister?"

"Yeah. Walker's two years younger than I am, and Shea is three years younger."

"You said she wasn't a firefighter."

"No, she's a nurse, like our mom."

Kiley eyed him thoughtfully.

"What?"

"I was just wondering about you and Miss Hadley."

He stilled. "What about us?"

"I have a hard time picturing the two of you as a couple."

"My mom said the same thing." Collier shrugged. "Gwen's okay. She's just not the woman for me."

"You don't sound bitter at all. After what she and Lazano did to you, I'd think you would be."

"I was for a long time, but we're better off apart. Some part of me knew we shouldn't have been together even when we were, but I let other things drown it out."

"Like sex?" she asked dryly.

"Sometimes." He stared at her for a long minute. "Sometimes I just didn't want to deal with it or work that hard."

"Wow, that's honest."

"I thought you wanted an answer."

"I did."

He wanted to press his lips to that spot behind her ear, the slope where her neck curved into her shoulder. "After we split up, I found out Lazano wasn't the only guy she'd been with. That's when I realized just how bad her drinking had gotten."

"I'm really sorry. That's awful."

"At least it's over."

"Is that why you don't have a relationship with just one woman? Too much work?"

"Not enough honesty." She was a straight shooter, and Collier liked that about her. "I don't mind working at it as long as I'm not the only one. Why aren't you seeing anyone?"

"Too much work." She grinned, but he saw hurt flare in her eyes for a split second.

He hated her acting like there was nothing between them. He'd had enough of women who pretended.

Of course *he* was pretending right now. Pretending that sitting beside her wasn't winding him up inside. He wasn't sure how much longer he could fight what was between them. He didn't know if he wanted to anymore.

Three hours after leaving St. Louis, Kiley stood with Collier in Angie Bearden's living room. Small and neat with a wood floor and a colorful throw rug in front of a brick fireplace, the room was cozy.

Driving separate cars from the airport, Kiley and Collier had gone first to see if Alan Embry was home from work. When they found no one there, they decided to see if they could catch his girlfriend at home. They'd found both Angie and Alan.

Kiley had just finished reading them their rights.

With a tool belt hanging low on his tight jeans, Embry looked like the electrician he was. He glared at her. "I've already answered all your questions."

"We've been up to see your folks," Collier said quietly.

"So?"

His tone was belligerent, but Kiley caught a flash of panic in his eyes. "You lied about being there with your kids during the dates we discussed."

Embry cursed. "I should've known my dad would hang me out to dry."

"Actually it was your mother." Kiley moved toward the fireplace, deliberately studying the room as if searching for something. Maybe that would rattle some information out of them. "She's so sure you couldn't have done anything wrong that she didn't have a problem telling us what we wanted to know. Why lie? Why not just tell us you took your kids to St. Louis, dropped them off, then came back to Presley?"

"I'm not telling *you* anything." Embry edged around Angie and stopped a couple of feet from Kiley.

She could've let Collier step in, but she was sick of this jerk's attitude. "You can talk to me here or at the station."

Collier moved to her side, his shadow falling over the other man. "Why do you want to make things harder on yourself, Alan? You could clear this up in a few seconds."

"He was with me!" Angie cried out, curling her arm through her boyfriend's. "We were together, just not in St. Louis."

"Where, then?"

"We were here, at my house. You know, in there." She tipped her head toward what Kiley assumed was the bedroom.

Ugh. "The entire seven days?"

"Yes. Alan was with me," she repeated.

"Can anybody verify that?" Collier asked.

"I doubt it since we stayed in bed the whole time," Alan said with a smirk.

"That doesn't explain why you lied about where you were." Kiley's gaze homed in on Angie. "Why would anyone care if the two of you were holed up here doing the wild monkey dance for nearly a week?"

"Maybe y'all really weren't together for all of that time," Collier suggested.

The girl met his gaze stubbornly. "We were."

"Surely someone saw y'all. Maybe when you got your mail or the paper?"

Angie shook her head.

"Did you go out to eat? Go to put gas in your car?"

"She already told you we didn't go anywhere." Embry's face and neck were flushed with anger. "I lied about it because I told my supervisor I had to be out of town for a family thing. I was on call for both New Year's Eve and day, and I didn't want to work it, for once."

Kiley folded her arms and stepped back onto the throw rug. "So you told one lie to cover for another one?"

"Yeah."

"Makes me wonder if you're doing that right now."

She actually saw a vein bulge in his neck. "I'm telling the truth!" he roared.

"Call your attorney," she said in clipped tones. "Have him or her meet you at the station."

"No way."

"You're busted, Alan." Collier gave him a hard look. "You

have motive to kill all four victims, and now we'll recheck your alibis for the dates of the other murders."

"I didn't kill Lisa or Lazano or anybody else," the man said hotly.

Kiley stared at Angie for a long time then shifted her gaze to Alan. "Maybe the reason you lied is because you didn't want Angie to know where you really were."

"He was with me!" the other woman cried.

"And you can't prove I *wasn't*." Alan got right in Kiley's face. She slapped a restraining hand on his chest. "Back up."

He wrenched her arm away from her, shoving as he did so. The throw rug beneath her feet slipped on the slick wood floor and she stumbled against the raised hearth. She tried to right herself, lost her balance and pitched headfirst toward the brick facade. Angie cried out; Kiley thought she heard a masculine grunt, then a curse. She hit her right cheek but managed to catch herself before her face plowed into the rough surface.

She quickly regained her footing, spinning around in time to see Collier ducking a punch from Embry. Collier rammed a shoulder into the other man's stomach and pushed him to the wall. The legs of an end table screeched across the wood floor as the two men plowed it out of their way.

"I want him, McClain!" Kiley rushed over to the two men, whipping out her handcuffs.

Collier either didn't hear or ignored her. He had Embry's hands behind him and the jerk kissing the wall by the time she elbowed her way between them.

"He's mine, McClain."

He shot her a look, laying an arm flat across Embry's shoulders to immobilize him while Kiley snapped on the cuffs. She pulled the loser around to face her. "You're under arrest for assaulting an officer."

Fury boiled inside her—at the jackass she'd just cuffed, at

herself, at Collier for jumping in the way he had. Yanking her cell phone from her coat pocket, she hit speed dial and requested a black-and-white to come to the scene and transport Embry.

Angie was crying. Alan turned his head and snarled, "Call a lawyer, Angie!"

Kiley prodded her collar toward the door. "Move."

"It was an accident."

"You went for her." Collier's eyes glittered savagely. "Not smart."

Kiley threw him a heated look as she pushed Embry forward. The creep stopped cold in his tracks. He outweighed her by at least eighty pounds. She certainly couldn't pick him up and carry him. She reached down, crushed his knuckles together and squeezed the way she'd been taught in recruit school. That got him moving.

Collier followed her outside. "How long before a patrol cop gets here?"

"Any second." A siren sounded and a black-and-white rounded the corner at the end of the block, headlights sweeping the street.

Kiley seethed. As soon as the car stopped, she yanked open the door and stuffed Embry into the back seat. "I'll follow you to the station," she told the patrolman.

As soon as the cruiser started away, Kiley turned on Collier. "I had it covered. Why did you jump him?"

His jaw dropped. "You've got to be kidding! He put his hands on you. Do you think I'm going to sit still for that? Do you think anybody would?"

"I was handling it. I wasn't at risk."

"From where I was standing, you were," he said in a dangerously quiet tone she hadn't heard before.

"I can take care of myself, McClain. I don't want you pulling that Sir Galahad stuff again."

"Get over yourself, Russell." He looked as though he

wanted to throttle her. "I would've done it for a man or a woman."

She fought back her anger. "I'm going to the station. Are you coming?"

"Depends. Do you plan on interviewing Embry when you get him booked?"

"No. I'm going to let him sit in a cell for that push he gave me. That might convince him to talk."

"Then, you can book him on your own."

"Fine." She marched to her car, got in and drove away.

By the time she'd booked Embry and left him to cool his heels in jail, Kiley had calmed down. She was embarrassed for jumping down McClain's throat the way she had. And she was mad at herself for letting Embry get past her defenses. She really wanted to go home for a long soak in the tub, then to bed, but she couldn't leave things like this between her and Collier.

The idea of finding him and apologizing held about as much appeal as getting a root canal without anesthetic, but she backed out of the PD's lot and headed for the fire investigator's office. If she didn't find him there, she'd try his house.

Less than fifteen minutes later she pulled up next to his truck in front of the old brick building. A light burned in the front section of the office. Kiley walked inside and went toward his office, which was also lit. She stopped in the doorway.

He stood across the small room in front of his bookcase, writing on a label affixed to a pint-size aluminum paint can that she knew he used to store samples. His coat and suit jacket were draped across the back of the chair behind his desk. The top button of his white dress shirt was undone, his tie loosened. With his sleeves rolled back, he looked relaxed, but Kiley noted the rigid set of his body.

He had to know she was there, but he continued writing. Finally he glanced at her, his green eyes hard.

"I need to talk to you."

"Not a good time," he said brusquely.

"About what happened with Embry—"

"I'm not apologizing for what I did, Blaze. You're wasting your time if you think I'll ever apologize for backing up a partner."

"I don't." She took a chance and walked over to him. "You went off on him, Collier. What if you get written up? What if you hurt yourself again?"

He set the can on the top shelf and stepped around her to go behind his desk. "Afraid I'll put a kink in your investigation?"

"No," she said firmly. She turned, moved close enough to put a hand on his arm. "I was mad at myself for letting Embry get the drop on me, and I took it out on you."

He looked down at her hand then back at her. "Forget it."

He shook her off and moved to the end of his desk closest to the door. Putting as much space between them as he could without leaving his office.

She had really screwed up, letting her temper get the better of her. "C'mon, Collier. I'm truly sorry. What I did was way out of line. Will you accept my apology?"

His eyes were unreadable, his expression closed.

"It's the red hair." She tugged at a strand, giving him a hopeful smile. "It makes me get mad faster than other mere mortals."

He still said nothing.

Frustrated, she walked past him and stopped in the doorway. "I don't want things to be this way between us."

Just when she thought he wouldn't respond, he said, "I don't, either."

"So you'll accept my apology?"

He nodded.

Relief rolled through her. "Good. Thank you."

"You drive me crazy. You're my partner out there, Blaze. That means I have your back." He eased down onto the edge of his desk. "You better have mine, too."

"I will. I do." Relieved that Collier wasn't holding a grudge, she laughed softly. "I thought you were going to beat up Embry."

"I thought you were going to beat *me* up."

His grin had her finally relaxing. "You were really mad at me."

"No madder than you were at me."

"Ouch."

"Are you okay?" He gestured to her right cheek.

She nodded. "It's just a scratch."

"Let me look at it."

She hesitated.

"Hey, you doctored me last night. Just returning the favor."

"You're not using this as an excuse to lay some hurt on me?"

He chuckled. "Come here. I've got some antiseptic."

She stepped over to him as he reached around to the back of his desk and opened a drawer. He pulled out a small white bottle and a clear plastic bag containing swabs. He wet the cotton tip with the medicine and looked up at her, crooking his finger. "You're gonna have to get closer."

She moved just inside his knees, her stomach clenching at the flesh-warmed scent of clean, musky male. The barely there brush of his hard thighs against hers.

"It'll probably sting," he murmured. He moved the swab carefully over the scrape on her right cheek.

She yelped, flinching.

"Don't be a baby," he teased. He doctored the spot again, then blew on it.

She started, making a sound of surprise. "No one's done that since I was little."

He laid down the swab. "Still burning?"

"A little."

He blew on it again. She laughed. "That tickles."

His gaze flared hotly, putting a flutter in her belly. Before she could move away, before she knew what he was doing, he leaned over and brushed his lips across the spot. "How about now?"

Now? Now what? Sensation jolted her nerves like she'd stuck her finger in a light socket. He had to be able to hear her heart pounding like a jackhammer.

"Does it still burn?"

His big hands were beneath her coat, bracketing her hips. She didn't remember him putting them there. He pulled her between his legs, right up against him. He was hard and before she could stop herself, her surprised gaze flew to his. "Collier."

"I need another taste, Blaze," he murmured.

A shiver rippled through her. His eyes were dark with desire and intent. Her brain short-circuited. Surrounded by his heat, his body, she couldn't manage a single thought.

He lifted a hand, ran his thumb back and forth across her bottom lip. Anticipation coiled inside her. If he didn't kiss her, she was going to scream.

He leaned toward her, tugging her chin down with his thumb, opening her mouth. "Let me in."

She did, her senses on overload. He didn't kiss her hard and fast and wild like last time, although she probably wouldn't have had any defense against that, either. This kiss was slow and thorough, as if he intended to learn every inch of her and planned to take his own sweet time doing it.

She was vaguely aware of the needy sound that came from her throat. Her knees went weak and she gripped his arms, feeling the steel bands of muscle beneath his white dress shirt.

His hands glided to her lower back, curved over her bottom. She pressed into him, skimming her hands up his hard arms to his shoulders, slipping her fingers into his hair. It was warm and silky against her flesh.

He left her lips; trailed kisses to her ear, down the side of her neck. Burning up, she brought his mouth back to hers.

He stroked one hand up her back, around to rest just below her breasts and thumbed her nipple through the wool of her sweater. It tightened in a glorious rush of sensation.

She had to stop before she completely lost control of herself. She pulled away, her senses whirling.

Breathing as hard as she was, he rested his forehead on hers. She struggled to calm the churning, restless thoughts that rushed in on her. "Collier—"

"If you say you didn't want that, you're a liar."

"I wanted it." She dragged in a lungful of air. "But I can't get involved with you."

"Why?" He lifted his head, his gaze burning into hers. "Because we work together?"

"Oh. Didn't think about that one. But no. I like you. A lot." Her gaze involuntarily dropped to his mouth and she said regretfully, "And you are one good kisser."

"But?"

It was hard to concentrate with his hand resting so close to her breast. Her body hummed on high speed.

"If you're going to turn me down, at least tell me why."

"I…you're…" She looked him straight in the eye and said around the lump in her throat, "Guys like you scare me."

He frowned, watching her intently. Listening.

"Flings work for you. They don't work for me. I'm not wired that way. I can't do it." She looked at his mouth again. "Believe me, right now I wish I could."

"It would be good."

"For a while."

"Why don't you give me a chance to change your mind?"

"I can't."

"You want me. Admit it."

"Obviously, I do," she said dryly. "You're hot, McClain. How's that for you?"

One corner of his mouth hitched up. "Then what's the problem?"

She liked that he didn't try to pull her back into him. Or kiss her again. He just waited. She rarely talked about this, but she needed for Collier to know. To understand. "My dad was a compulsive womanizer."

"How compulsive?"

"While married to my mom, he had affairs. Plural. I don't know how many, and I don't want to know."

"I'm not trying to be a jerk, Blaze, but wouldn't that affect your mom more than you?"

"You'd think, but I saw him repeatedly lie to her, to us. As Kristin and I got older, he tried to get us to lie for him, too. When they finally divorced, I was twelve."

"Did you see him after that?"

"Yes. Whenever we were with him, he had a different woman. My sister and I always came second to whoever that was. Occasionally they would be the mothers of my friends or one of our teachers."

He made a rough sound.

"When I was in college, I came back to my dorm one evening after studying and found him with my roommate. Another time I had to bail him out of jail for soliciting."

Collier's thumb moved soothingly back and forth in a spot just below her breasts. Kiley wondered if he was even aware of doing it.

His gaze searched her face. "I'm sorry. I didn't know."

"That's why I told you." She gave him a small smile.

"And you're afraid I'd do something like that?"

She hesitated, then nodded.

He flinched, shoving a hand through his hair. "I can't say I don't always know where I stand with you, Blaze."

"We're just too different, Collier. I'm not saying it wouldn't be good while it lasted, but I've never gotten the hang of casual relationships. I don't want to. I don't like them."

"And casual's my reputation, right?" he asked evenly.

She thought she heard a thread of hurt beneath his words. She didn't want to hurt him, but she wouldn't lie. "You know what works for you and I know what works for me," she said brightly.

He studied her. "You can't blame a guy for trying."

"No." She tried to dismiss the stab of disappointment. He was only doing what she'd asked. She swallowed hard, looked down for a minute. "Are we going to be okay? As partners, I mean."

He drew away, folding his arms. Closing himself off from her. "Do we have a choice?"

"No." She backed toward the wall. "But I want to know you're okay about working with me."

"I'm fine."

She searched his eyes, saw he was telling the truth. "Call me when you get Vail's file from the city attorney, okay? Or if you have any news about the fake firefighter, Franklin."

"You know I will."

Somehow she made it to her car on legs that were as limp as wet string. She had to sit there for a few minutes before she felt steady enough to drive. She liked Collier, really liked him. Not just the way he kissed and touched her, but him.

If he tried pursuing this thing between them, her defenses wouldn't last long. She didn't know how to protect herself except to stay away from him, and that was impossible. They were partners until this investigation was closed. She needed his expertise, his cool head.

She had to figure out a way to work around this sizzling attraction before she gave in to it.

Chapter 8

Two days after that kiss, Collier's body still hummed. Once he had put his mouth on Kiley's, she hadn't even hesitated. She wanted him as much as he wanted her, and he knew he could wear her down by using that to his advantage. In fact, he figured another kiss or two would get her right where he wanted her.

Still, he couldn't ignore what she'd told him about her father. Collier now understood her skittishness about him, and it did have him tapping his mental brakes. He wanted her, but he didn't know what he was going to do about it.

A little before six-thirty that Monday evening, he drove east on I-40 toward Oklahoma City then hit I-35 and headed north for Presley. The interview he'd just finished with a long-ago neighbor of Sherry Vail's had yielded some prime information.

Kiley had been in court all day. Before he'd left his office this morning, Collier had called to catch her up on what he'd found in their suspect's personnel file. When Sherry had applied to be a firefighter, the police and agents from the Oklahoma State Bureau of Investigation had conducted interviews with people she'd given as references and, as was the norm, also with some she hadn't. A note written beside the name of Sherry's former neighbor had put Collier on the woman's trail.

He'd finally tracked down Marti Linn, who now lived in Minco, a small town southwest of Oklahoma City. Kiley was going to be sorry she had to hear this secondhand.

The trip took him a little over an hour. After exiting the highway and reaching Presley city limits, he punched in her cell number on his mounted car phone. Getting no answer, he tried her at home.

"Hello!" She sounded winded.

"Russell?"

"Oh, McClain! Let me call you back. I've got Niagara Falls flooding my house and I'm waiting to hear from a plumber."

"What's overflowing?"

"My washing machine."

"From the top? Bottom? Behind?"

"I don't know! It looks like it's coming out from under the machine."

"Sounds like the fill hose. I can probably fix it."

"I need help *now,* McClain."

"I'm on my way into town as we speak."

"How can there be so much water in that thing!"

"Can you see behind the machine? To where it's hooked up?"

"Wait." He heard sloshing, then a hollow bang. "Okay, I'm on top of the washer—oh, I see what looks like a hookup. What do I do?"

He grinned, picturing her climbing on top of the appliance. "Do you see a faucet knob in the wall?"

"Yes."

"Turn it off. That will stop the water until I get there."

"Okay—oh, there I got it. You're hired."

"Give me your address." After she did, he said, "I can make it in about ten minutes."

"My laundry area leads into the garage so come in the front door. That should keep you dry, more or less."

"See ya in a few."

Several minutes later he parked in the driveway of an older, Colonial-style home, red brick with black shutters and white trim. After getting his toolbox from behind his pickup seat, he walked up a couple of steps to the porch and opened the front door. Teased by a fruity-spicy scent, he stepped into a wide foyer that looked into the living room. "Russell?"

"I'm back here! Come down the hallway with the wood floor then through the kitchen."

He did, noticing the dark planks were real wood, and hand cut and fitted. Walking past a small dining room, he heard Kiley muttering, then the soggy slap of a wet towel. The kitchen was small but open, and done in cheery red and white. He crossed the corner of the bright, airy room in three steps and rounded a wall.

Have mercy.

The first thing he saw was her gorgeous backside covered in soft pale pink. She was on her hands and knees sopping up water. Her hair swung around her face and shoulders, but what had his mouth going dry was the sight of her slender curves gloved in form-fitting workout clothes. If those were sweats, they weren't like any he'd ever seen.

Except for her bare feet, she was completely covered, but that didn't stop Collier's entire body from going tight. The zip-front jacket rode up the smooth slope of her back, revealing creamy skin between the jacket's hem and the top of hip-hugging pants that sleeked down her long legs. Freckles dusted the dip of her spine, and that stretchy material molded to the high firm butt he'd had his hands on two days ago.

Tossing a soaked towel to the side, she reached left and yanked a fresh one from where it hung over the open dryer door. She glanced over her shoulder and saw him, relief streaking across her face.

Sitting back on her feet, she shifted toward him. "Am I glad to see you! There must be a million gallons of water in that thing. Who knew it took so much to do a load of laundry?"

She was as cheery as usual, but there was a tension beneath her words that hadn't been there two days ago. The floor looked slippery in places, but the calf-high stack of wet towels against the wall testified to how much water she had already mopped up. "Looks like you're making progress."

She shoved her hair out of her face, the motion causing her jacket to hitch up and tease him with a peek of her flat belly. "I think I've got most of the water cleaned up. At least you can walk across the room without ruining your shoes."

He said something that must've made sense because she surveyed the small space and nodded. At the moment he was aware only of the hard thrum of need in his blood. She looked delicious. All pink and fluffy and soft. He wanted to drink her up.

His hand clenched so tight on the handle of his toolbox that he felt the metal clear to his knuckles. He knew he'd left her with the impression on Friday that he was going to back off, but right now the chances of that happening were about as likely as hell churning out ice. He wanted to pull down that jacket zipper and see what she wore underneath. How was he going to keep his hands off her?

For starters, McClain, get busy on the washer, his inner voice instructed.

He set down his tools and slid off his lined uniform jacket, walking into the kitchen to drape it over the back of a dining room chair. He let out a ragged breath, trying to stem the raging current of lust in his blood. Unbuttoning his cuffs, he rolled back the sleeves of his white dress shirt as he returned to Kiley.

She stood, her gaze flicking over him. "I don't want you to mess up your clothes."

"They'll be fine." Noticing a mop against the opposite wall, he moved across the damp tiles and checked behind the machine. Leaning over, he lifted the short hose that connected the water supply to the washer and examined it. "Yeah, there's a hole here."

"Is it the fill hose? Like you suspected?" she asked from beside him.

Surprised at how close she was, he stepped to the side. "Yeah. It puts water into your washer."

"But because of the hole, it wasn't reaching the machine?"

"Right. Just the floor."

"You figured that out really fast." Admiration gleamed in her eyes.

"It's happened to my mom a couple of times."

Kiley nodded, her gaze tracking over him. There was no heat in her eyes, just thoughtful study, but Collier's entire body locked up. What was going on with her?

"So now what?" she asked.

"I don't recommend patching it because of the pressure buildup when the water runs through. I can get you a hose, tonight if you need it."

"No, there's nothing I absolutely have to wash tonight."

"Okay. I'll pick one up in the morning and stop on the way to work to put it on."

"Are you sure you don't mind?"

"I'm sure." She was still studying him, and he ran a hand across the taut muscles in his nape.

"It's lucky for me you know this stuff, McClain." She eyed him curiously, as if she were dissecting him. "I was a little rattled."

"I noticed." He grinned.

"Have you eaten yet?"

"No."

"I've got grilled cheese sandwiches and tomato soup. Do you like that?"

"You don't have to feed me."

"Sure I do. I might need you again sometime."

He wished he could decipher that tone in her voice. It wasn't flirty exactly.

"Besides, you still have to tell me about Vail, and there's no reason you can't do that while we eat. If you hate grilled cheese, I can call out for pizza or Chinese food or whatever you want."

"The sandwich is fine."

"Good. Let me start the soup."

It took her only a moment to open three cans and pour the contents into a pot on the stove. She walked around him and into the hall. "I'm going to change clothes. I'll be right back."

"Do you want me to do anything in the kitchen?"

"No. Just make yourself at home."

Habit had him checking to make sure all the stove's burners were off except the one being used, then he walked through a doorway that led into the living room he'd seen upon entering the house.

Her chestnut leather sofa and two oversize chairs looked comfortable. Framed pictures sat atop a sofa table along one wall and the mantel. He recognized her sister in several. His gaze lingered on a black-and-white one of her and Kiley together. The photo next to it was of them on either side of an older woman. Their mom?

"Want something to drink?"

He looked over his shoulder, saw her in the doorway he'd just walked through. She had put on socks and changed into baggy gray flannel pants and a tight red tank under an unzipped gray sweatshirt cardigan. "Iced tea, if you have it."

She nodded, her gaze speculative.

"Nice pictures."

"Thanks. That's my mom with Kristin and me."

"Pretty lady." He glanced back at the photo. "You both favor her."

"Thanks." Faint color crested her cheeks. "I'll start on the sandwiches."

While she did that, he returned to the washing machine and unhooked the fill hose. He could hear her moving around on the other side of the wall, smell the buttery scent of toasting bread. Carrying the hose to his tackle box, he knelt to put it inside, wincing when his scraped knee banged the floor. He glanced at Kiley over by the stove. "I'll take this to the hardware store when I go. Just to make sure I get the right fittings."

"I really appreciate your help, Collier."

"You're welcome."

"I guess I shouldn't be surprised you're such a handyman, since you're doing all the work on your house." She carried two bowls of steaming soup to the small dining room table. "Dinner's ready."

He walked into the kitchen and past the table to the sink to wash his hands. A couple of sandwiches were stacked on the plate in front of the chair where she indicated he should sit.

"Smells good," he said as he slid into his seat.

"I didn't burn anything, so I'm optimistic. This is about the extent of my culinary talent."

"All I can do are eggs and pancakes."

She grinned, starting on her soup. They ate in silence for a few minutes. A couple of times he caught her looking at him with hot, curious eyes. Not just his face, but his mouth. Whatever was going on with her was driving him crazy. He tried his darnedest to keep his mind on the case, on his food, on the washing machine. Anything but her lips. Or the sweet flesh hidden beneath those sweats.

"Did you find the woman you were looking for today? Sherry Vail's neighbor?"

"Yeah. We may have caught a break."

"Really?" She rose, silently offering him more soup, and he nodded. "What exactly made you zero in on her?"

"A notation made in Vail's file by an OSBI agent. After she applied to firefighter school, they interviewed her references and acquaintances. Written next to the neighbor's name in quotes was the sentence, 'I'm impressed with the way Sherry turned out after what happened to her mother.' I figured we'd better find out what that meant."

As Kiley dished more soup into his bowl, Collier found his gaze wandering over her, lingering on her butt. He forced his attention to the information he'd gotten. "The woman I spoke to used to live in Oklahoma City, but now she's in Minco. She's been married and divorced three times since she was the Vails' next-door neighbor, so it took me nearly all day to track her down. Sherry's dad died when she was ten, and after about five years, her mom started dating someone. Lisa Embry's dad."

Kiley's mouth fell open as she slid into her seat. "You are kidding! How'd they meet?"

"Remember that Sherry said she and Lisa went to the same high school?" At her nod, he continued, "The neighbor wasn't sure how their parents hooked up, but she thought it was at a football game."

"Vail mentioned going to high school with Lisa as if she barely knew her."

"We were right about her holding something back."

"Something big."

He grinned at the excitement in her eyes. He'd felt the same rush upon discovering Vail's very personal connection to their third victim. "There's more."

Kiley pushed her bowl out of the way and leaned toward him, drawing one leg up under her. "Tell me."

"Sherry's and Lisa's parents became engaged, but to hear this woman tell it, Lisa hated Sherry's mom." Collier found his gaze locked on Kiley's mouth and looked away. "Lisa threw fits about the relationship on a regular basis and finally ran away. Her dad broke up with Vail's mother, and when he did, she committed suicide."

Kiley's eyes widened. "So Sherry Vail might blame Lisa for her mother's death."

"Wouldn't be a stretch to think so."

Looking thoughtful, Kiley tapped a finger on the table. "And maybe Sherry finally starts to recover from that, joins the fire department and here comes Lisa, transferring into the same station house. Now she's right in Sherry's face, bringing it all back."

Collier pushed his empty plate and bowl aside, stretching out in his chair and linking his hands behind his head. "And if Vail did murder the three male firefighters, maybe she thought she should take care of Lisa at the same time."

"She didn't set a fire with Lisa, just shot her in her own garage," Kiley mused. "So she could watch Lisa die?"

"Maybe. I'd think someone with a grudge like that would want to see their victim suffer."

"So now we know Vail has motive to kill all four victims."

"Just like Alan Embry." Collier's mind went back to his and Kiley's last visit with Alan Embry.

When that scumbag had put his hands on Kiley, Collier had lost it. Some protective instinct had unexpectedly exploded inside him. He wanted to chalk it up to her being his partner, but that wasn't the whole reason. He'd reacted as if she belonged to him, and she didn't. Besides, the woman carried a gun, for crying out loud. She knew how to protect herself. Especially from guys like him.

Kiley pushed her hair over her shoulders. "Alan had clear motive to kill Lisa and Lazano, but what about Miller and Huffman?"

"Maybe he killed the other two victims so it would look like there's a connection when there really isn't."

"I think we need to go see Vail and find out why she kept silent about having more of a connection to Lisa than she led us to believe."

"We've definitely got a reason to look even harder at her now."

"Do you think it's too late to go tonight?"

"Let's give it a shot."

"I'll change clothes." She rose and started past him. "Thanks again, Collier. I really appreciate you looking at my washing machine. Call me if you ever need help with…I don't know. Something besides a washer."

Two days ago he would've told her to help him by sitting in his lap and letting him get her naked. But not now. Not after hearing about her father, not after seeing that raw vulnerability on her face. He'd realized that as he sat here with her.

She'd said he was wrong for her and she was right. He was exactly the no-strings, hit-and-run kind of guy that she avoided.

The deep hurt in her eyes when she'd told him about her father had hollowed out Collier's gut. He never wanted to be responsible for putting such a look on her face. Even if it killed him, he would try to respect the line she'd drawn between them.

Kiley had meant every word she'd said to Collier about not getting involved, so why couldn't she stop thinking about it? His mouth on her skin, his hands on her skin. *Him* on her skin. Whatever smarts she'd prided herself on, where Collier McClain was concerned, had been drowned by hormones and lust. She was much too aware of his lean, rangy body, the faint flesh-warmed scent of his aftershave.

Forty-five minutes after leaving her house, she and Collier

were in a small boxy room at the police station. Kiley dragged her thoughts from Mr. July and focused on the suspect she was about to interview. Sherry Vail had refused to speak with them at her house, so Kiley had instructed the ex-firefighter to call her lawyer and meet them at the police department.

Collier had switched on the tape recorder and taken a place in the chair at the end of the short, rectangular table. Sherry and her attorney, Raye Ballinger, sat to his right along one side. Standing a couple of feet to Collier's left, Kiley had just finished reading the suspect her rights. She and Collier had agreed on the way over that she would start the interview, then they would play off each other.

"Let's go over what we've discussed before, Sherry, so we can get it on record."

Vail shot a sharp-eyed look at her attorney, who nodded. Sherry's face was stoic, but the death grip she had on the table's edge told Kiley that the woman was jittery. She flipped open her notebook. "When Gary Miller was murdered on October first, you were where?"

Vail opened the day planner her attorney had advised her to bring and turned a few pages. "Calling on customers in Arkansas."

"Did you spend the night there?"

"Yes. I was in Little Rock that night and the next. I spent the two previous nights in Fayetteville."

Collier kept his manner relaxed. "What about the night of Rex Huffman's murder, November fourth?"

Sherry consulted her calendar again. "At a trade conference in Houston."

Kiley placed her hands on the table and leaned down, watching the woman carefully. "We have a witness who saw you at the motel where Huffman was murdered."

"Then your witness is lying! I wasn't even in town, and I have the stub from my plane ticket to prove it."

Kiley gave her a steely-eyed look. She and Collier really didn't have a witness, and from the way Vail had responded, Kiley thought the woman was telling the truth. "What about the night of Lisa Embry's murder? December fifth?"

"I was in town. At home."

Collier drummed his fingers on the table. "Can anybody verify that?"

"I wasn't with anyone—wait. I may have a receipt." She pulled a manila file folder from her purse and began to flip through it. "I keep copies of the receipts I turn in with my expense report."

In their last interview with her, they'd questioned Sherry's whereabouts on the night of Lisa's murder without getting an answer. Raye must've told her client to bring any evidence she could find if it would help prove where she'd been.

"Here it is. A receipt for gas dated December fifth. At 9:42 p.m."

So what if Sherry's alibis were solid? They only meant she hadn't been at the scene, not that she hadn't murdered Lisa or the others. She could've hired someone to pull the trigger. Still, Kiley wanted things done by the book, and that meant getting Vail's alibis out of her own mouth, for the record. "What about January second? Ten days ago. The night of Lazano's murder?"

"She was in Denver, calling on customers," Raye said coolly. "The Adam's Mark has a record of her stay."

Collier drummed his fingers on the table. "Sherry, have you ever been to the Clear Lake Motel on the outskirts of Presley?"

"No."

"Huffman was spotted with a blond woman before he was found murdered there."

Sherry looked full at him. "It wasn't me."

Kiley drew the woman's attention back to her. "Did you ever meet Rex anywhere outside of work? Maybe to tell him to back off?"

"No. The jerk would've thought I had changed my mind about dating him."

"Do you own a gun?"

"No."

"Know anything about them?"

"I know what they look like. That's it."

"You have motive, Sherry." Collier's voice hardened. "To kill all three male victims."

She stared at him in stony silence.

For someone who didn't interrogate that much, Kiley thought Collier was good at it. She leaned against the wall, eyeing Vail, deliberately making her tone skeptical. "You claimed one of those men sexually harassed you."

"He did!"

"And you said the other two men threatened you because of the complaint you filed against their friend. You lost a job you love because of them."

"You filed a complaint against Huffman, but that didn't stop him." Collier leveled his gaze on the blonde. "You're not the type to sit back and put up with something like that. You would take matters into your own hands."

"Y'all are so far off." Raye shook her head, light bouncing off her gold earrings. With her tawny hair in an elegant twist and her tailored black suit, she looked like a young Grace Kelly. "Yes, she took action, but it was appropriate. She went through the channels. That's on record. You two are just fishing. You have another homicide, the Embry woman, and my client had no reason to hurt her."

"Actually, she did." Kiley loved springing stuff like this on suspects, but Collier had been the one to learn the information. He should be the one to drop the bombshell. She urged him on with a look.

"We know about your mother's suicide," he said baldly.

Sherry blanched. Kiley studied her as Collier continued.

"We know your connection to Lisa Embry is much more personal than you led us to believe."

The woman's skin took on a waxy sheen.

"Your mother was dating Lisa's father and he broke things off with her because Lisa didn't like her. That's when she killed herself."

"Shut up!" A dull flush spread across Sherry's face.

Kiley kept up the pressure. "You and Lisa were nearly stepsisters."

"Even if our parents had gotten married, I wouldn't have claimed Lisa Embry as my stepsister. As my anything," the woman spat out. "I hated her!"

"And you blame her for your mom's suicide, don't you?"

"She was responsible for it!"

Raye put a calming hand on her client's arm, but Sherry shook it off.

"I actually thought I'd made progress, learning to live with what my mom did without feeling guilty that I hadn't seen what she planned to do, that I couldn't stop her." Her voice rose. "Then here comes Lisa, right into my station house. I tried to keep out of her way, but she was always around, always in my face. One time she tried to apologize, as if she meant it!"

"Maybe she did," Collier said.

"No, she didn't!" Sherry screamed. "She only did that to bring up the pain of my mom's death."

"And you wanted to hurt her back." He rose, towering over her. "So you killed her."

She drew up short. "No," she said shakily. "No, I didn't."

Kiley leaned down to Sherry's eye level. "We have a woman willing to testify about how upset you were with Lisa."

"It doesn't prove I killed her. Or anyone else," she added quickly.

"You talked about getting back at her."

"I was seventeen!"

"Maybe you tried to get past it and couldn't," Kiley mused. "Maybe you finally saw a chance to make her pay."

"And it's not only Lisa's murder you should be concerned about," Collier put in tersely. "Now we know you have motive for all four murders, Sherry. Four. That looks bad."

"Don't say anything else." Raye touched Sherry's arm, her eyes hard as diamonds as she looked at Collier and Kiley. "Is she under arrest?"

"Not at this time," Kiley said through gritted teeth.

"This interview is finished. We're leaving."

She rose as did her client, and the two women walked out, heels clicking loudly against the tile. Vail had ample motive, but Kiley and Collier couldn't prove anything. Kiley tossed her notebook on the table in disgust. She wanted to hit something. The stormy emotion in Collier's eyes told her he felt the same frustration.

"We're not getting anywhere. With anybody." He shoved a hand through his hair. "In all the excitement with your washer, I forgot to tell you that earlier today I stopped by to talk to Monty Franklin's aunt and his parole officer again. Both say they haven't seen or heard from our fake firefighter. His aunt probably told him we were looking for him, and the loser's in Timbuktu by now. I don't think he's our murderer, but I thought he might have some useful information."

"It's frustrating," she admitted, her gaze going to the bandage on his temple. "But we'll get a break. We have to."

"When, dammit?" He grabbed his coat from the back of his chair and walked out. "Let's go."

Kiley slipped into her own coat and followed him. Once in his truck, they headed for her house. It hit her then that she hadn't even thought about driving her car to Sherry Vail's house. She and Collier had automatically climbed into his truck and taken off.

Long minutes passed without either of them speaking. Kiley's irritation faded as she tried to find a new angle from which to approach the case. A quick glance at Collier showed that his jaw was no longer hard, but tension pulsed from him and a heaviness she hadn't sensed before. "What is it? What's wrong? Is it Sherry?"

"Why can't we get anywhere?" He hit the blinker forcefully, then turned onto Kiley's street. "I can't tell those guys again that we're still nowhere with this arsonist-sniper."

"The other firefighters?" she asked quietly, struck by the self-recrimination she heard in his voice.

"They're out there with a target on their back every time they respond to a call. They need these murders solved. So do I."

"I know." She knew his sense of responsibility didn't stem from being close friends with the murder victims. It was because he'd walked through fire with them, faced death with them. Watched their backs just as they'd watched his.

He pulled into her driveway and parked. "I really thought we might spook something out of Vail. Every time we get a lead, it's a dead end. Why can't I find anything?"

Kiley noticed that he hadn't included her in the investigation, and she understood then that the pressure he felt was about more than his getting justice for fallen comrades. This was his first solo case. His boss was watching, and so was hers. "Terra would be exactly where you are, Collier," she offered.

With a look of surprise, his gaze shot to her.

"She would. We're doing everything right, everything we can. Terra would never even consider that you weren't suited for this job. She didn't make a mistake by hiring you."

Kiley realized that at some point she'd reached out and put her hand on his arm. She withdrew it.

"Thanks." His gaze measured her, as if he were trying to see inside her head. Then he angled his shoulder into the corner, laying one arm along the back of the seat. "We're missing something. I'm going back to the office to go over everything we have."

"You've got to be exhausted. I am, and I wasn't the one who chased down leads all day, then played repairman for my partner."

One corner of his mouth hitched up. "We need a lead, Blaze."

"I know, but you don't have to try and find it all on your own. Come inside. I'll make some coffee and we can go over everything together."

"You don't have to go backward on this case just because I am."

"We're not going backward," she said firmly. "We found out what Sherry was hiding about Lisa. We'll keep digging until we find out what else she's not telling us."

He pinched the bridge of his nose, closing his eyes briefly.

"It's frustrating, but something will give. It will, and then all the pieces will fall into place."

"You sound so sure."

"Just one of my many talents." She smiled. "Come on. Come inside."

After a brief hesitation, he nodded. "Okay."

She led him through the garage and into the laundry area. Leaving him in the kitchen, she took his coat and draped it with hers over the back of the sofa in the living room. When she returned, she found Collier sitting at the table in the same place he'd sat for dinner. She filled the glass pot with water, scooped some grounds into the filter and started the coffee.

"How's your head?" She slid into the chair next to his, gently touching the small bandage. "And the rest of you?"

"I'm all right," he said evenly, eyeing her curiously. "Do we have anything on Vail besides motive?"

"Not yet, but motive to kill all four victims is a big deal."

"We need more. I really thought we'd get somewhere with that information about Vail's mother's suicide."

"I did, too." She bent and tugged up the hem of her jeans, unbuckling and removing her ankle holster and Walther PPK. Double-checking the safety, she placed the weapon on the table beside her.

She looked up to find Collier's gaze moving hotly over her, and she couldn't halt a little shiver as she struggled to call to mind details of the case. They laid out what they had on Alan Embry, went back through the names of those who had been interviewed after each murder. Kiley got up to pour them both a cup of coffee and brought the mugs back to the table, the rich aroma drifting around them.

They reviewed the fire and rescue calls responded to by all the victims. Besides the four dead firefighters, there were twenty-four others who'd answered those same calls due to the need for manpower, yet none of them were dead. What was the common denominator?

Kiley participated in the conversation, but her train of thought wandered frequently. Collier was a good investigator, conscientious and fair-minded. She liked what she'd come to know about the investigator *and* the man. Especially the man. More than once she'd thought about how kind he had been to his ex at Lazano's wake, how sweet he'd been with that little girl at the hospital.

She caught herself twice replaying that bone-melting kiss between them the other night. As she inhaled his musky, male scent, she remembered the way he had looked at her, as if she were too good to be true. No man had ever looked at her the way he did, but since showing up to repair her washer tonight, he hadn't looked at her once that way. Hadn't flirted or teased her. Had treated her like a partner. Only a partner. Just as she'd requested.

She hated it.

She wanted him to kiss her again. She wanted more than that. The pull between them was strong, sweeping her under further every time she was near him. She was tired of resisting, but what if he had decided he didn't want to pursue this thing between them?

Glancing over, she took in his strong features, the lips that had kissed every protest out of her head. Right now he didn't seem interested in anything other than her coffee and the case.

With one hand he massaged his neck. "Everything still leads us to Alan Embry and Sherry Vail. Don't you think?"

"Yes." She rose and walked to the coffeemaker, trying to decide if she should broach the subject or just forget it.

He stood and moved next to her, turning to brace his hands on the edge of the counter and lean his backside against it. He watched her refill the pot with water. "And we can't prove *anything* about either of them."

"We just have to keep chipping away, Collier."

"Yeah." He dragged a hand down his face. "Thanks for the coffee, and for going over everything again."

She loved his slow drawl. "You're welcome."

He smiled. "You're not so bad, Russell."

"Neither are you," she murmured, her stomach fluttering. In that second she decided. She set down the coffeepot and squared her shoulders. "I've changed my mind."

He started to nod, then frowned. "About what?"

"About me." She swallowed hard. "And you."

He stilled, his green eyes going smoky. "Changed your mind about you and me and what?"

She cleared her throat, looked him right in the eye. "Sex."

At least five seconds dragged by.

"Sex," he finally repeated in a strangled voice. "Sex?"

The absolute shock on his face would've been comical any other time. Right now it just made her nervous. She shifted from one foot to the other. "Does that mean yes, sex? Or no sex?"

Chapter 9

Why had Collier ever thought he understood women? He didn't have a clue. At least not with Kiley. "You want to have sex with *me?*"

"Uh, yes. That's why I'm talking to *you* about it."

He stood completely still against the counter, his hands now gripping the edge. "I've been trying to respect what you told me the other night."

"I know, and I appreciate it."

"And give you some room. You said you wanted room."

"Yes, I did."

"I've been leaving you alone. You know that, right?"

"Yes, Collier." She moved in front of him and laid a hand on his chest, flexing her palm against him. "I'm taking full responsibility."

He searched her face. "You're just yanking my chain, right?"

"No." Her heated gaze traveled meaningfully over him. "Not yet, anyway."

Hell. He grasped her upper arms, but he wasn't sure if it was to pull her closer or keep her away. "I need to catch up here. We should think about this."

"I have thought about it. I've done nothing *but* think about it. The only way I'll stop thinking about it is if we do it."

"What changed your mind?"

"The way you've been treating me all day."

He frowned. "I haven't done anything."

"That's my point." Her index finger stroked the hollow of his throat, bared by his unbuttoned collar. She toyed with his shirt, slipped a button free. "You haven't flirted with me, teased me, tried to get me to do something I don't want."

"You told me—"

"I know, and I meant it. But now I've changed my mind." She shrugged, looking a little self-conscious. "I like you, Mc-Clain. In fact, I like you so much it's starting to distract me, so I think we should just have at it and get this out of our systems."

"*Have at it?*" he choked out.

"You know what I mean."

How could she be so calm? She sounded as if she were doing nothing more than offering him another cup of coffee. His mind might be trying to process, but his body already had. His pulse raced. His skin felt taut, hot. And he was hard enough to "have at it" all night. "We should talk about this."

"We are."

"I mean, later." Her breasts brushed his chest. He could smell the subtle scent of skin and soap, of her shampoo. "Give ourselves a little time."

"You really want to wait?" The disbelief in her eyes mirrored what he had felt since she'd turned his world upside down a minute ago. She dropped her hand from his chest and backed up a step, color flushing her cheeks. "If you aren't interested anymore, you can tell me. I won't fall apart."

"That's not what I said. I didn't say anything like that."

"I didn't think I would have to convince you." She turned away.

Was she walking out? He hooked an arm around her waist and pulled her back into his chest. Lowering his head, he nuzzled his stubbled jaw against her cheek. "I want you, Blaze, but I want you to be as sure as I am. I don't want you to regret being with me. Ever."

She turned her head so she could look up into his face. Uncertainty, surprise, wariness flashed through her eyes, then was gone. "I am. Sure, I mean."

His gaze searched hers until he was convinced. "I can't believe you really thought I wanted to wait."

"You don't?"

He pressed her tight into him. "Does that feel like a man who wants to wait?"

"You were teasing me?"

"Yeah, and I plan on doing more of it before this night is over." She stiffened.

He laughed. "I didn't say I was going to bite you, although I do take requests. Relax."

"I'm trying."

"It doesn't feel like it."

"I want to touch you."

"I want to touch you *first*."

"I want you to kiss me."

"Oh, I'm going to do a lot of that," he said in her ear, lightly nipping her lobe.

Resting against his shoulder, she curled a hand around his neck and brought his head down to hers. "Then stop talking."

Her lips parted beneath his, drawing him into her sweet warmth. The kiss grew more heated, deeper, desperate, and she tried to turn. He pulled back a fraction, held her in place.

"No," she said raggedly when he lifted his head. "Come back here."

Every muscle in his body clenched.

"Collier."

The way she breathed his name had hard, hot need slamming into him. She tried to turn around again. He stilled her movement, keeping her back molded to his chest, her rear to his hips.

"This isn't gonna be fast, Blaze," he said softly. "I've waited too long to get my hands on you."

He gently sank his teeth into the spot where her neck met her shoulder.

"Oh." Her knees gave out and she sagged weakly against him.

"Now," he murmured against her warm flesh. Finally getting her where he wanted her, he smoothed his hands down her arms, bracketed her hips.

Pressing hot, open-mouthed kisses down her neck, he moved her hair aside for more, burying his face in the fragrant thickness. He squeezed her waist, then dragged his hands up, closing them over her breasts, kneading her flesh through the soft angora of her gray sweater.

Her breathing broke and she pushed into him. He could feel her tight nipples through the downy fabric and his pulse revved up. "I want to see you," he said hoarsely.

He tugged her sweater up and over her head, dropping it to the floor then pressed his cheek to hers, nuzzling her hair out of the way. Full creamy breasts, rosy nipples strained against her sheer black bra. Bracing himself against the savage rush of blood through his body, his hands covered her. He cupped and stroked, his fingers reaching past the edges of her bra to the swells of her breasts. "You feel so good."

Making a tiny sound, she turned her head and found his lips, kissing him hungrily.

Caressing first one breast and then the other, he slid his free hand down over her stomach, opened the button of her jeans and slipped his fingers inside. The zipper parted as he went lower.

She trembled. "You are killing me."

"You can thank me later." He pressed kisses to her jaw, the side of her neck, her ear.

His palm, hot and a little rough against the warm satin of her skin eased beneath the elastic of her panties, delved between her legs. Very lightly he touched the knot of nerves there.

"Ohmygosh." She melted all over him.

Her head fell back on his shoulder and he felt the small convulsions of her body. His own body stretched painfully taut as raw, searing need coursed through him. After a minute he shifted, swung her up into his arms and started down the hall.

She looped an arm around his neck, nibbled at his jaw. "Where are we going?"

"Your bed. I need some room, Blaze."

She bit him lightly on the neck, then his earlobe. Lust knotted his belly.

The large room was warm and cozy, smelling of soft cinnamon and a light airy fragrance. He stepped inside, saw the bed situated between two windows. A light shown from the half-open door of her bathroom opposite him, shadowing the large bureau against one wall, a long dresser with a mirror against the adjacent one. Moonlight glowed from around her drawn blinds.

The bed was big with an acre of pillows. He laid her on the thick, light-pink downy spread, palming off her shoes and socks. While he leaned over her to tug her jeans down her hips, she stretched her arms over her head and knocked pillows out of the way. Collier's pulse thudded hard when he dropped her pants and got a look at the tiny scrap of transparent black that passed for her panties.

She gripped his shoulders, then started working on the buttons of his white dress shirt, saying urgently, "I don't see how you can go so slow."

"I'm not an in-and-out kind of guy, Blaze." As he looked down at her, he peeled off his shirt, then his T-shirt. Her hair tumbled like fiery silk against the paleness of her bed covers. She trembled beneath his gaze. "I like the trip as much as I like getting there."

She groaned. "If you don't stop saying things like that, the trip will be over for me before we get started."

Grinning, he bent toward her to outline her body with a slow drag of his hands. He wanted to look at her with the soft light falling over his shoulder, gilding her skin with gold.

He trailed his fingers between her breasts to her navel and she shivered. Bracing his hands on either side of her, he came down on top of her for a deep, languid kiss. Her arms went around him, and she shifted, making a place for him between her legs.

He could feel her silky heat through his slacks. After long seconds he dragged his mouth from hers, nipped and laved his way over the swells of her breasts, down her torso, over her stomach. His pulse hammered; his groin ached. He skimmed a hand over her breasts.

"Collier." She shifted restlessly.

She smelled sweet, tasted smooth and rich. He knelt, ignoring the pain in his injured knee, his shoulders pushing her thighs apart as he slid his hands beneath her hips and pulled her to him.

She inhaled sharply, quivering when he put his mouth on her through the silk of her panties. Panting his name, she arched into him, her fingers curling against his scalp.

After long seconds, or maybe minutes, he looked up. Her half-lidded gaze met his. She looked dazed. Hungry. He moved to lie down beside her, propping himself on one elbow while his other hand slid between her legs. "I want to be up here so I can see you," he murmured.

Her eyes were hot, needy; her creamy skin flushed. She

reached up and lightly grazed the bandage at his temple then his injured shoulder. "Are you too sore to do this?"

He laughed. "Blaze, all I feel is you. And you feel too good to quit."

He kissed her, slow and long as he stroked a hand up her smooth inner thigh, one finger stealing beneath the elastic leg band and into her silky heat.

Making a small sound, she pushed into his touch, baring her throat, her body.

He pulled back, watched her face as he slid in another finger. "You're gonna kill me."

"I'm...pretty sure...you'll kill me first." She was breathing hard, her breasts straining at her bra.

Still massaging her intimately, he dipped his head and curled his tongue around one budded nipple, drawing her into his mouth and tasting her through the flimsy fabric. He did the same to the other breast, pushing off her panties.

Her fingers delved into his hair, and she tugged him up. "Kiss me."

He took her mouth, moved his hand to flick open the front catch of her bra. She spilled into his palm, white and soft and perfect. His thumb rasped across one rosy nipple.

She shifted restlessly, unzipping his pants. Her voice was honey and smoke when she said, "I want to touch you, Collier."

Heat shot through him like a rocket. He wouldn't last five minutes if she started in on him.

She rolled into him, nudged him onto his back. He ran his hands up the backs of her firm silky thighs, cupped her bottom.

"Don't distract me. I really want to see that scar. And the rest of you."

He toed off his shoes as she worked his slacks off along with his boxers. She followed the clothes down his body, kissing his chest, his stomach, his scar, lower. Need boiled inside him. She laved his injured knee, then flicked her hot tongue against his straining flesh before coming back to his belly. She scraped her teeth lightly over the old burn, and he nearly jumped out of his skin.

"Come here, Blaze." He dragged her up his body. "Give me your mouth."

She met his kiss fiercely. Wrapping his arms around her, he sat up on the edge of the bed. She locked her legs around his hips and sank down, gloving him in tight, velvet heat. Pure, sharp pleasure pierced him, and for an instant Collier thought his heart stopped.

He looked into her gorgeous blue-green eyes, felt his chest tighten as a savage urge to take, to *claim* swept through him.

She clasped his face in her hands and kissed him as he trailed his fingers down her silky back and curved his hands over her bottom. She moved on him, her soft breasts teasing the hair on his chest. His heartbeat roared in his ears. Wanting to see her, he broke the kiss.

Her eyes were closed, her face flushed and glowing. Radiant.

"Kiley, look at me. Open your eyes."

She did, and the near surrender, the dark desire there sent him hurtling toward the edge. He held off until he felt her reach her peak. Then he nudged her over and shot with her into oblivion.

She moaned his name and he collapsed back onto the bed, bringing her with him. Still joined, they lay there in languorous silence as their pulses slowed. Her cinnamon scent and the tantalizing smell of warm woman mixed with his aftershave. He stroked one hand up and down the velvet column of her back, kept the other one on her neck, holding her to him.

"That…was incredible," she said lazily into his chest.

And then some. He grunted in agreement, feeling as if his

spine were jelly. Her skin was lotion soft, creamy and pink with an occasional smattering of freckles in unexpected places like a little secret hidden just for him. On her left shoulder. The small of her back, behind her right knee. One lone freckle on the swell of her breast. He wanted to kiss them all. "Man, you are gorgeous."

She looked up, pleasure flaring in her eyes. "You surprise me, McClain. You're not like what I thought you'd be."

"In a good way or a bad way?"

"Good." She lifted herself enough to kiss him, long and soft, sighing when she drew away. "Definitely good."

The taste of her, the feel of her bare skin against his pumped through his system like a drug. "You ever been engaged? Or married?"

"No," she said, shifting a little to the side, scraping her fingernail lightly over the scar on his belly.

Her teasing touch had his muscles clenching. "I was just thinking that you know about my past, but I don't know much about yours."

"Judging from what just happened," she murmured, "I'd say you know the important stuff, McClain."

He grinned. "Glad you enjoyed it, but I'm talking about long-term relationships. Ever had any of those?"

She stilled, unease suddenly pulsing from her.

"Why hasn't some guy snatched you up by now?"

After a slight hesitation, she answered breezily, "They're all afraid of my gun."

He hugged her to him. "C'mon, tell me. Are you the girl who can't be caught? Because of how your dad treated your mom?"

Another pause, then she shrugged. "He sure didn't make me want to get married."

"Not ever?"

"No. What about you?" she asked quietly, brushing her

thumb back and forth across his nipple. "Think you'll ever get engaged again? Married?"

For once his usual vehement denial didn't surface. "I don't know."

"If you do, I hope it won't be for a long time." Just like that, she rolled away from him and rose, snatching a long, terry cloth robe from atop a hope chest at the foot of her bed.

He sat up and snagged her wrist, the bedding a rumpled tangle beneath him. "You all right?"

"Sure. I'm just going to take a shower." She pushed her thick mane of tousled hair over her shoulders, glancing around the room. "Um, I think your pants are under the bed. If you're gone by the time I finish, I'll see you in the morning at the police department to interview Alan Embry."

He recalled her words about getting each other out of their system. His thumb brushed across the pulse in her wrist. "Are you kicking me out, Blaze?"

She blinked. "No. Not at all, but I don't want you to feel you *have* to stay. I don't expect you to."

"You didn't really think I was finished, did you?"

Her eyes widened, her gaze sliding down his body. "Well, yeah."

He tugged her onto his lap and smiled when her gaze shot to his as she felt his growing arousal against her hip.

She licked her lips. "Guess I was wrong."

Grinning, he tumbled her back onto the bed and rose over her. "I don't have you out of my system yet."

He settled his mouth on hers, hooking a hand into the vee of her terry cloth robe and tugging it open. Cupping her breast, he lifted his head and stared into her eyes, gone dark and dreamy with need.

"Mmm," she breathed, her hands stroking his back. "I think I like being in your system. How long do you think this might take?"

"Probably all night."

She laughed low and smoky, slamming heat into him. "Prove it."

"I plan to." He kissed her again. He definitely wasn't done with her. Not by a long shot.

Collier woke the next morning alone in Kiley's bed. The red digital numbers on her clock read 6:30. It was Tuesday. The water running in the master bath told him where she was. He sat up and swung his feet to the floor, looking around for his boxers. They were at the foot of the bed where she'd dropped them along with his pants, dress shirt and T-shirt.

He wondered how she was this morning. There had been that one instant last night, after their first time, when he'd thought she meant to kick him out.

He hadn't spent the night with a woman since Gwen. And it suddenly hit him that he hadn't once thought about leaving Kiley. He pulled on his boxers and slacks then pushed open the bathroom door which was already slightly ajar. Soap-scented steam wafted around him, fogged the mirror. Through the frosted glass of the shower door he could see the outline of her body, the bare curve of her breast. He was thinking about joining her when she shut off the water.

"Collier?"

"You better not be expecting anyone else."

Opening the door, she peeked out, wrinkling her nose at him. "Good morning."

"Morning." She was wet and sleek and slippery. He wanted to kiss her, but since he knew he wouldn't stop there, he settled for plucking a dry towel from the chrome bar on the wall and handing it to her.

"Thanks." She wrung out her hair, the strands crimped even though wet. "There's an extra toothbrush by the sink if you want. And a disposable razor."

"I'll skip the razor." He turned, saw the items on the ivory-marbled vanity top.

Rubbing a hand across his bristly jaw, he walked over and opened the box holding the toothbrush. A tube of toothpaste rested on the opposite side of the sink. As he threw the box into the trash can, he wondered if she typically kept tooth-brushes in supply.

He hadn't planned to spend the night, and he didn't think she had planned for him to, so she wouldn't have known to have a toothbrush for him. Just how many of these did she have? The thought had his shoulders knotting up. And did she use that razor? Or keep it for someone else to use?

As he brushed his teeth, Kiley moved up beside him. She'd wrapped the towel around her, sarong-style, her breasts swelling over the top. Using another towel, she squeezed more water out of her hair.

Two days ago anything this domestic would've had Collier breaking out in a cold sweat, but the only thing stirring him up right now was the toothbrush question. He rinsed his mouth, wondering if he should take the toothbrush or leave it. Hell.

"Feel better about the case today?" She spritzed something on her hair and finger-fluffed the wet, heavy mass.

He eased down on the counter's edge, his gaze tracing the damp curve of her neck, the slope of her shoulder. "Even though we still don't have any proof showing Embry's or Vail's guilt, I'm glad we went over it all again."

"Maybe we'll get something from Alan this morning." Her gaze flicked to him, then shifted nervously to a point in the mirror. "You want to shower here?"

"I'll do it at home. I want to change clothes, too. And use a razor that won't take off half my skin."

"Okay."

She didn't avoid his gaze, gave nothing away with her

tone, but Collier felt...something. A subtle tension. He reached over and took her hand. "You sorry about last night?"

"No." She met his gaze instantly, unflinchingly. Then she frowned. "Are you?"

"Not a chance." He tugged her between his legs, running a knuckle along the swell of her breasts. "Is something wrong?"

"Am I acting weird? I don't mean to." She gave a short laugh. "It might take me a little while to get the hang of this."

"You're fine." Her words struck an uneasy chord inside him. By *this* he knew she meant their fling. Casual sex. But nothing about what they'd done last night felt casual to him. "I just wanted to be sure."

"And you're okay, too?"

"Yep." He wondered why she was putting this distance between them. And why the hell he wasn't.

Her light fresh scent drifted around him. He curled a thick strand of her wet hair around his finger. Why couldn't he stop thinking about her supply of toothbrushes? The thought that some other guy might spend the night with her—*put his hands on her*—had Collier's jaw clenching tight enough to snap.

She kissed him, then swatted him on the butt. "Get out of here so I can focus on getting ready."

"You could focus on getting me ready."

She glanced down at his arousal and said wryly, "I think I can check that off my to-do list."

He grinned, hooking a finger in the towel between her breasts and pulling her into him as he lowered his head. He gave her a real kiss, not one of those quickie jobs.

Her arms went around his neck and she pressed into him, her skin soft and damp and warm. She let him in, tasting of the same mint toothpaste he'd used. He wanted her again. He stroked his hands up her thighs, ran them under the towel to her hips.

After a long minute she pulled back, breathing hard. She pushed lightly at his chest. "Go away. I'll never get dressed at this rate."

He stood. "I'm going. I'll see you tonight, Blaze."

She tilted her head. "Did you forget we're meeting later at the police station to interview Embry?"

"I didn't forget." He closed his fist on the top of the towel and drew her close. "You're talking work. I'm talking…after work."

Her eyes widened.

He gave her a quick kiss, then stepped toward the door, yanking the towel away from her as he went.

"McClain!" She caught the wrap before it hit the floor and held it to her breasts.

He chuckled and walked out. She threw the wet towel at his head.

Chapter 10

As Kiley drove to the police department about an hour later, she could not stop thinking about Collier. How he'd touched her, what they'd shared. She'd been so sure last night about what she was doing, but now.... No other man had ever been so in tune with her, physically or otherwise. Had it been only three nights ago that she'd said she couldn't get involved with him?

Tonight, after work. Collier's words had set off a low drum of anticipation that still teased her as she walked into the squad room. He had made it plain that he intended to do more of what they'd done last night. Her erogenous zones were ready. Her brain wasn't.

He had wanted to know about her past involvements, but confiding in him about David Barnsdale was too...personal. She didn't know another word for it. The less sharing of that nature, the better.

His question might've gone unanswered last night, but it hadn't gone unnoticed. It had dredged up annoying memories of her first and only serious relationship. She had dated David from their junior year in high school until their junior year in college. He'd had a bad-boy reputation until they'd gotten together, then he'd settled down. Kiley's naive sixteen-year-old self had believed he had changed his life. Apparently, his bad-boy genes had only been in remission. After almost five years together, Kiley thought she had known the man she loved. And then she'd caught him with another woman.

She would never have imagined David could do such a thing. The emotional blow had devastated her. She'd prided herself on falling for a man completely unlike her father. What a joke. She'd learned the hard way that even reformed bad boys like David, who seemed trustworthy, couldn't be trusted, and she hadn't let herself forget.

Since then she'd dated nice, steady guys who would never cheat on her, and none of them had. But she'd broken up with the last one after three months of boredom. She might like Mr. Nice Steady Guy, but if boring was his middle name, she couldn't live with him for the rest of her life. Collier, on the other hand, never bored her, probably for the very reasons she fought getting involved with him other than physically. She hadn't been kidding when she'd told him she was terrible at flings. He, on the other hand, had seemed completely at ease this morning in an unfamiliar bathroom, using a toothbrush other than his own. He definitely had the hot sex, no-strings thing down.

She'd really thought that giving in to the desire she felt for him would scratch her itch. Either that itch had moved or she had a whole new one because she couldn't stop thinking about him, about *them*. Wanting…more. Last night she had felt an unexpected, deep connection. More than physical.

Panic flared, but she reminded herself that what was between them was temporary. The connection they had was sex. Period. Okay, great sex, but still just sex.

She'd known his kisses were mind-blowing, but the rest of what he'd done? Whoa. Heat raced under her skin as she recalled what had happened after he'd pulled her back down on the bed, the way he'd driven her to climax three times before he had done anything for himself. Or let her do anything for him. She'd been wrong about him being a selfish lover. There wasn't a selfish bone in his body and she'd swear to it in court.

She arrived at the PD trying to curb the giddiness riding low in her belly. Their affair couldn't leak over to the investigation. She had to be careful not to let on that things had changed between them. She hoped Collier would, too.

Turning her full attention to the case, she walked into the large, dingy room with gray-veined flooring and rows of putty-colored, age-warped metal desks. She spoke to several detectives who were already there, some clustered in a group talking and others at a table against the far wall pouring a cup of the squad's horrible coffee. Sipping the cup of coffee she'd bought at the store on the corner, she checked the clock hanging on the opposite wall. A little before eight. Collier would probably be here soon and they could get started with Alan Embry, who had spent the night in jail.

She eased down into the chair behind her battle-scarred desk and opened the Lazano file, flipping to her notes on Embry.

"Detective Russell? You've got a visitor."

She glanced up and saw Officer Lowe in the doorway with Angie Bearden. The woman's pretty face was stoic, her eyes hard. She was without an attorney. If Angie were here about Alan spending time in jail, she would've brought a lawyer. So what did she want?

Kiley rose and walked the few steps to the door. "Hi, Angie." She smiled at the baby-faced cop. "Thanks, Bobby."

He lifted a hand and walked back down the hall.

"Come in and have a seat." She led Alan's girlfriend to the chair scooted against the side of her desk. "May I take your coat?"

"No, thanks." Angie pulled off her black gloves and slid them into the pocket of her dark wool coat.

Just as she sat down, Collier entered, shrugging off his tan cashmere overcoat. His face was ruddy from the frigid air outside. Surprise flared in his green eyes when he saw their visitor. His gaze met Kiley's. "Y'all in the middle of something? I can step out for a minute."

Before Kiley could ask if that was what Angie wanted, the woman said, "No. I want to talk to both of you."

He nodded and walked around the desk to stand beside Kiley. From his slightly ruffled dark hair to the black sweater and slacks that emphasized his lean build and broad shoulders, he was six-plus-feet of yum. She'd seen him less than two hours ago, but her pulse skipped, anyway.

His jaw was freshly shaven, and he smelled of soap and man and fabric softener. She kept her gaze from sliding over him, but that didn't dim the memory of his warm, muscled flesh against hers. His body inside hers. A shiver worked up her spine. She was afraid he could see the want in her face and she struggled to hide it.

His green gaze met hers and set her nerve endings tingling, even though nothing in his eyes hinted at last night. There was only professional interest and mild curiosity about the woman in front of them.

If Angie had come to see Alan, Kiley figured she probably would've already broached the subject. "Can I get you some coffee, Angie? Or something else to drink?"

"No," she said tersely. "This won't take long."

"All right." Kiley sat down, edging her chair closer to the woman, putting a little space between her and the man who affected her way too much.

"Alan wasn't with me the night Dan Lazano was murdered."

The bald statement put Kiley's senses on alert. Beside her, Collier snapped to attention, too. "But you said he was," she reminded quietly.

"I lied." Angie curled a fist against her soft-sided leather purse.

Collier eased down onto the far corner of the desk, his voice easy, nonthreatening. "Why tell us now?"

"Because he lied to *me*." Fury sparked in the woman's brown eyes. "He told me he was at work that night. After the two of you left on Saturday, I asked him about it. He gave me some answer that didn't even make sense."

"Do you know where he really was?" Collier asked.

"He was with his old girlfriend, Neva Sasser." Angie cursed. "I *thought* she was his old girlfriend. Evidently he's been seeing her while he's been seeing me."

Kiley slid a look at Collier, caught the same cautious optimism she felt. "How do we know you're not just saying this because you're mad at him?"

"Oh, I'm mad at him all right, but I'm mad at myself for letting the two-timing egomaniac convince me to lie for him." She shoved her long blond hair over her shoulder, her voice shaky as she continued, "I'm telling you the truth, but you don't have to believe me. What you said at my house the other night got me thinking. What if he *was* telling one lie to cover up another? What's so special about that night that he had to lie about it? He lied to his boss, and then to y'all, but why to me? Especially when I knew he *wasn't* with me that night."

"How did you find out he was with Ms. Sasser?" Kiley asked.

"He wouldn't answer my questions, so I followed him."

"And you're sure the woman you saw him with was Neva Sasser?" Collier asked.

She nodded, taking a deep breath. "I know who she is. I

saw her go into the motel with him and come out a couple of hours later. I'm pretty sure he was checking her circuits, if you know what I mean."

Kiley bit back a smile at the electrician reference. "If Neva can alibi him, why would he lie about being with her?"

"She's married. That's probably why." Angie's voice quivered and tears filled her eyes. "After y'all were at my house, I got real suspicious. He's cheated on me before and I forgave him. I thought we were trying to work things out, but now I see how things really are."

Kiley reached across her desk for a tissue and passed it to the other woman. "It's good you're seeing the pattern this early. It's a big warning sign about what's to come. You're smart to get out now."

She wondered if she should be telling herself the same thing about Collier.

Angie sniffled. "Thanks."

After Kiley and Collier walked their visitor back to the entrance, they made their way down a long corridor to the jail at the back of the building.

He glanced over. "I guess we've got a little surprise for Embry."

"Yeah, this should be interesting." The tension in her shoulders eased. He wasn't treating her any differently from the way he had yesterday, *before*. She just had to do the same.

After a long half hour of their suspect denying his girlfriend's claim that he was with another woman on the night of Lazano's murder, Embry finally admitted it was true. They sure weren't taking his word for it. Until Kiley and Collier talked to Neva Sasser, the jerk was staying in jail.

They found the woman at home. After much hand wringing and sidestepping, she confirmed Embry's alibi, but she begged them to keep quiet about her affair with Alan. Not only because of her marriage, but also because her husband was running for re-election to the school board. Kiley and Collier made no promises.

As they left Kiley gritted her teeth and called the station to have Embry released. Collier looked just as disgusted and frustrated as she felt. Just because Embry's last alibi finally checked out, it didn't mean he hadn't hired someone to kill his ex-wife and the other firefighters, but right now Kiley and Collier had zero proof.

While that fact tightened her shoulders, she felt reassured about the change in her relationship with Collier. From the way he was acting, he was of the same mind as she about keeping that information between only them, but Kiley wanted to be sure. As they climbed into his truck to return to the police station, she started to ask, then hesitated. Maybe she didn't need to bring it up.

He flicked her a concerned look. "What's going on?"

How could he read her so easily? Surprised, she glanced at him. "Why do you think something's going on?"

"It's all over your face, Blaze."

"Who are you?" she muttered. "A mind reader? I just wanted to say thanks for not giving away our—last night. I think it's better not to let on that there's something between us during our investigation. I wouldn't want Lt. Hager or anyone else to think it could be compromised."

He was silent for a long minute. "What about after we clear the case?"

She blinked and drew back. Where had that come from? "What do you mean?"

He shrugged. "I'd like to take you out, to dinner or a movie or whatever."

"But I thought…"

"What?"

Why was he acting as if he wanted something more than

what they had? "Let's not get ahead of ourselves. Just take it one day at a time."

"That sounds like one of my lines," he murmured.

So why aren't *you* saying it? she thought desperately.

He must've seen her panic. "Don't worry, Blaze. I won't ask for anything you don't want to give."

That was the problem. She wanted to give this man way too much.

"I hear what you're saying." Collier glanced in his side mirror as he changed lanes. "When we're at work, Blaze, we're partners only. But when we're alone, I plan to put my hands on you. All over you."

She couldn't control the delicious shiver that moved through her. The memory of that kiss he'd given her this morning had her nerves ticking like a time bomb.

Her emotions seesawed between pleasure and exasperation. It bothered her that she was so affected by their being together last night, but she liked him. He was funny and smart and she respected the way he did his job. If he'd been just another pretty face and rock-hard bod, she wouldn't have been tempted. But he was so much more.

He made her wonder how things might be if he could ever commit to one woman, to her. She squashed the thought. From the beginning, she'd known his rules about involvement. The only reason *Collier* and *future* were in the same thought was because he'd thrown her off balance with his question about continuing their relationship. That, and the fact that she couldn't stop thinking about tonight, had her muscles tightening.

If she was this rattled after one night, how was she going to be if they kept this up for a while? Refusing to examine that further, Kiley forced all her focus to their investigation.

Once back at the station, they wrote supplemental reports on their interviews with Angie Bearden and Alan Embry. The rest of their day was taken up with meetings. They updated their respective bosses, who then requested they both tag along to a sit-down at the mayor's office in case he had questions the chiefs couldn't answer. That was all kinds of fun.

By the time Kiley and Collier finished a short interview with the media, they looked at each other with the same tired frustration. Their last stop late that afternoon was at Terra and Jack Spencer's home. As the first investigator on the arson-murders, Terra wanted an update. Now they finally had time to give her one.

As they sat in Terra's kitchen, teased by the aroma of roasting meat, Kiley found herself impatient to wrap up the conversation with Presley's lead fire investigator. She was restless, edgy and not really sure why.

She wanted to be alone with Collier. And she didn't. She found it secretly thrilling that no one knew about them being lovers, but the sense that their affair was clandestine caused uncertainty as much as it did anticipation.

"So, now you know what we know, which isn't a lot," Collier said to Terra a half hour later. He shoved a hand through his hair. "We know Embry's a liar, but we can't prove he killed anybody. Or Vail, either."

"It's frustrating," the other investigator admitted, sitting at the end of the oblong table between him and Kiley who sat on opposite sides. "But I think the two of you are doing a great job."

He dragged a hand across his nape. "We're stalled out."

"It happens," Jack said from behind his wife's chair. "Something will break."

"We'll keep you posted, Terra." Kiley rose when Collier did and she started out of the kitchen. He looked tired. She found herself wanting to soothe the lines of fatigue from his face.

He hung back. "Hey, Kiley, give me a minute with Terra, okay?"

"Sure."

"I'll step out with you," Jack said to her.

She shot Collier a curious look and went into the living room with the other detective.

Kiley wondered if Collier wanted to speak to Terra alone because he was still concerned that she know he was doing the best job he could.

A baby's cry broke over the monitor sitting on an end table between the dark sofa and love seat, and Jack excused himself to go check on the infant.

Kiley and Collier had driven in separate cars so there was no need for her to wait. She would see him later, anyway. He'd made that clear this morning. As she started across the living room toward the front door, she admitted she wasn't sure how long she could keep things casual between them. Maybe she should break things off now, before she fell for him.

Just as she reached the far edge of the living room, Collier and Terra walked out of the kitchen to join her. The other woman smiled over at Kiley. "I'm glad you both came."

As they all walked together toward the front door, Terra said, "Let me know how things progress, all right?"

"You got it." Collier's cell phone rang, and he reached for it. Glancing at the readout, he held up a finger to Kiley, indicating he would take the call.

He moved closer to the door, standing several feet away. She could tell by the way his shoulders relaxed that the call didn't concern their investigation.

Terra touched her elbow and drew her back into the living room, asking in a low voice, "What's going on with you two?"

Kiley fought not to give away the shock that drove through her. "What do you mean?"

"Something's different." The other woman's green eyes were warm and curious. "Are you seeing each other?"

"Why would you think that?" Even though Terra was her friend and Kiley longed to confide in her, she wouldn't. How had Terra guessed? Kiley and Collier had been extremely careful about how they interacted today.

"I've never seen Collier look at anyone the way he looks at you."

"Terra," she protested with a laugh. "He's not looking at me. He's answering a phone call."

"I saw him. Twice," her friend whispered. "I can feel something between y'all right now."

Panic streaked through her, but Kiley managed to keep her tone teasing. "He's too far away for you to feel anything!"

Terra grinned, her gaze shifting to Collier. "I think it's great."

She shook her head, wishing desperately that the other woman would believe she was mistaken, but she could tell that Terra knew. Still, Kiley held her smile until she and Collier reached the curb outside. Under the yellow pool of a floodlight, they stopped between their two vehicles parked one behind the other.

"That was my brother on the phone." Collier jammed his hands in his coat pockets and hunched his shoulders against the biting cold. "He wanted to know if I had plans for dinner. I told him I definitely do."

If she was going to cool things, now was the time. She arched a brow. "You don't think *I'm* going to cook?"

A slow, wicked grin hitched up one corner of his mouth. "I wasn't thinking about food at all."

She suddenly didn't feel the frigid winter air. The thought of seeing him tonight had buzzed her nerves all day.

"Your house or mine, Blaze?"

She glanced back, making sure Terra's door was closed and that no one stood at the windows.

"You didn't forget what I said this morning." He took a step toward her. "We have a date."

"I didn't forget, but…I don't know, Collier."

He lowered his voice to a rough whisper. "I've been wanting to kiss you all day, and in exactly five seconds I'm going to whether we're standing here or somewhere else."

"Okay, my house." She would use the time to make a decision.

Her mind racing, she didn't remember the drive. As soon as they stepped inside her laundry room and he closed the door, she turned to him. "I'm not sure—"

Collier pulled her into him at the same time his mouth came down on hers. Her body responded immediately, even though she fought to hold on to some thread of reason.

Taking the kiss deeper, he laced his fingers with hers and backed her to the wall. He brought their hands up to her shoulder level and pinned her there as he pressed full into her. His mouth was hot and hungry and possessive, turning her body to liquid.

He lifted his head, his eyes glittering down at her in the shadows thrown by the light from her yard that streamed through the window.

"Collier." His name shuddered out.

He kissed her again, doing things with his tongue that had her knees turning to powder. He buried his hands in her hair and she gripped his biceps, trying to still him. There were reasons they should slow down. She had reasons.

Finally he dragged his lips from hers.

"I don't know if this—us—was such a good idea," she breathed.

"It was. Trust me."

"We need to talk."

"I'm listening." Nibbling his way down her neck, he pushed off her outer coat, then her deep-cranberry suit jacket. With a flick of his wrist, he tugged both her clip-on badge and holster from the waistband of her slacks, then reached back and laid both on the washer. His fingers moved down the buttons of her white tailored shirt.

Before her thoughts were overwhelmed by the feel of his hands on her, she said, "Terra knows there's something going on with us."

"Yeah, she said something to me about it, too." He got her shirt open and tugged it out of her slacks, spreading it wide. His jaw clenched as he stared down at her.

Her nipples tightened beneath the sheer lace of her bra. Before she completely lost her sanity, she asked breathlessly, "How could she tell?"

Her question was supposed to be important, but Kiley couldn't remember why.

He lightly trailed his index finger down the center of her chest, came back to tease one hard nipple. "Probably because you were looking at me like you couldn't wait to get me naked. Or maybe that's how I was looking at you."

She squeezed her eyes shut, trying to focus on what she wanted to say. "Did she have a problem with it? Is she worried about it affecting our jobs?"

"No." He slipped her shirtsleeve off one arm, slid down both bra straps with long fingers still a little cool from the winter air. He bent and pressed his hot, open mouth over the single freckle on the swell of her left breast. "She said she remembered how things were for her and Jack."

Kiley couldn't feel her legs any more. She could only feel Collier's hard strength, the heated silk of his mouth. "I'd forgotten…about that. Did you reassure her? What did…you tell her?"

"I told her we were having sex five times a day." He nudged down the lacy fabric of her bra and closed his mouth over her.

A ragged moan worked its way up her throat and she arched into him. Steadying herself, she slid her hands into his hair and held him close. "Collier, please."

"I'm trying to."

That wasn't what she meant. What *did* she mean? He

kissed his way to her other breast. Pulse pounding wildly in her throat, between her legs, she laid her head back against the wall. The shadowed room swirled.

Helpless to resist, she fought to keep from succumbing to the dark, seductive draw of his kisses, his hands. It was happening again. The connection she'd felt to him last night. She wanted to sink into it, wanted to find out if it was more than physical. And at the same time, she didn't. She couldn't.

Awash in sensation, Kiley couldn't draw a full breath. She wanted to drown in the dark male scent of him. His day-old beard rasped against her breast and the wet fire of his mouth had her humming in pleasure. The brush of his shirt against her bare flesh drew her belly tight. She liked him; she wanted him. She wasn't saying no.

This thing between them was temporary. She wasn't going to think past that. Her unsteady hands went to his slacks, unzipped them. "Five times a day?"

He lifted his head, eyes dark and fierce, reckless. "Okay," he said gruffly. "Five times a day might be an exaggeration."

She slid a hand down and found him, rigid and straining. "Or not."

He groaned, cupping her bottom and lifting her against him. "Can we do this standing up?"

"I can," she said silkily. "Can you?"

"Hell, yes."

"Let's go, cowboy."

Chapter 11

She'd gotten to him. Just like he was getting to her. Collier knew why Kiley was coming up with this let's-not-get-ahead-of-ourselves stuff, but he wasn't having it. He knew it spooked her. It should've spooked *him*. How much time had he spent telling himself he couldn't—wouldn't—be involved with her?

His asking about continuing their relationship after the investigation had caused her to withdraw. It was nothing blatant, but she'd raised her guard. And she was skittish, dodging any situation that might make them seem like a couple. Like the invitation from Walker for dinner. Collier had managed to get her to his house the last two nights, but she'd left before morning both times.

He couldn't escape the sense that she was counting the hours until he ended their personal relationship. Until *he* walked away. But he wasn't walking away. Knowing her background with her father, Collier understood, but he wanted her to know he wouldn't jump ship the way she thought he would.

He didn't want anyone but Kiley. He didn't want her with anyone else, either, which was why the thought of those extra toothbrushes at her house still gnawed at him.

She was the only woman who had ever held his interest outside of the bedroom as much as she did in it. She made him laugh. He liked the way her mind worked. He loved looking at her and knowing she wore sexy, nearly nothing underwear and a gun beneath her clothes. And she fired him up faster than any woman ever had. Whenever she walked into a room, it changed, seemed brighter. Bigger somehow.

They also worked well together, but even that couldn't help them dig leads out of thin air. After they'd confirmed Alan Embry's alibi for the Lazano murder, they spent the next four days going over all their interviews and their timelines. They reviewed Collier's photos and diagrams of each one. Still, they couldn't pinpoint the one crucial common denominator between the arson-murders.

When the sniper first hit, Kiley, Terra and Collier had restricted their focus to calls all the dead firefighters had responded to in the last year. No fire station ever responded alone, and because of that the victims had been on several of the same calls. Terra, Kiley and Collier had determined early in the investigation that the murdered firefighters had worked six of the same calls together. So had twenty-four other firefighters from three Presley station houses and one from Oklahoma City.

One call involved city workers and the collapse of a trench being dug for water lines. No one had died at that scene, but one man had been paralyzed for life. He had a lawsuit pending against the city, but after checking him out, Kiley and Collier decided he wasn't a good suspect for the murders. Two calls were house fires, one with a suicide. One was a pipe bomb thrown into a bowling alley. Another was a fire started behind the junior high school. And the other was a five-car accident on nearby I-35.

Two of the accident victims had died en route to Presley Medical Center. Kiley and Collier spoke to the victims' family members and came up with nothing that remotely hinted at revenge, bitterness or blame toward the fire department or the firefighters who'd worked those scenes.

Midmorning on Saturday, they were back at the Lazano murder scene. They had already revisited the others. As they started up the long, concrete drive of Rehn's Coffee Warehouse, Collier shoved a hand through his hair, knowing Kiley was as frustrated as he. They were racking their brains about what else they could do, where else they could look for something. Anything.

Her cell phone rang. As she answered, he continued up the drive, turning to eye the distance between Rehn's front door and the warehouse across the street where the shot had come from.

When she hung up, the huge smile on her face had him smiling, too. "What is it?" he asked.

"A break. I'll tell you on the way."

He followed her down the driveway. "Where are we going?"

"To OCPD headquarters." Excitement glittered in her eyes. "A patrol cop picked up a guy last night on a burglary charge and he says he has information on the Lazano murder. He wants to deal. His name's Bart Damler."

"We haven't heard of him before." Collier opened the passenger door of his truck for her.

"I know we've gotten excited about leads before that led us nowhere, but this is it, McClain. I can feel it in my gut."

He wanted her to be right, and he didn't. Because when they closed this case, things between them would change. "You sure you're not just coming down with something?"

She made a face. "I'm sure. Drive."

Forty-five minutes later they had a new lead. Damler, a small-time drug dealer and burglar, claimed he had been hired to bypass the security system at Rehn's warehouse and disable the sprinklers on the night Dan Lazano was murdered. And he had a tape recording to back it up.

Kiley and Collier found that awfully convenient. In response to their skepticism, Damler told them that his stint in prison had taught him to tape all his dealings with his less-than-desirable associates. He'd known it would one day help him get a pass on a return visit to jail.

Kiley and Collier wouldn't agree to speak to the D.A. about a deal until they had the tape in hand. He gave it to them along with the name of the person who'd hired him: Dominic Narr.

Not having heard of Narr before, they ran his name through OCPD's computer as well as the National Crime Information Center. He had an impressive number of arrests for possession of and fencing stolen property. He had done time for the same. They had no idea what connection he had to Dan Lazano or any of the Presley firefighters who'd been murdered, but they would find out.

The files also yielded the name of the detective who had worked Narr's most recent conviction and Kiley spoke with him by phone on the way to Narr's apartment. As she and Collier drove to a new complex on the west edge of Presley, she told him what she'd learned about their new lead. "Detective Stevens said Narr is cagey and calm."

"We've got the tape. Even though it's as scratchy as a screeching cat, let's try to catch him in a lie."

Kiley nodded. "Stevens also told me that Raye Ballinger was Narr's attorney on this case. Said she was a real piranha in the courtroom, which we already know."

"She must represent every skank in the state."

"She does attract them."

They found Dominic Narr at home. Easily six foot seven and three hundred pounds, the ex-con was massive. With his thick dark hair and droopy mustache, he reminded Collier of a woolly mammoth. Kiley and Collier both showed their badges, then explained what they were doing there.

The man was leery, but he let them inside his sparsely furnished, amply littered home. After Kiley read him his rights, Collier led with their questions.

"We looked at your record. You only served half of your three-year term on your last conviction."

"Yeah, I was released early for good behavior."

Collier noted that Kiley's gaze skipped around the small living area, over the take-out containers, pizza boxes and beer cans as she asked, "Do you know Bart Damler?"

"Never heard of him."

"Maybe you'll recognize him." Collier pulled out the Polaroid they'd taken when they had spoken to the burglar an hour ago. "He claims you hired him to break in and disable security at Rehn's warehouse."

Narr barely glanced at the picture. "Nope. Never seen the guy."

"He claims he knows you."

Narr folded his beefy arms and stared flatly at them. "Well, I claim he don't."

Kiley stepped up beside Collier, eyeing the ex-con. "Have you ever been to Rehn's Coffee Warehouse?"

"Is that on Benson? I've heard of it."

"Yes or no. Have you been there?"

"I could've been, at some point. I've lived here for almost ten years."

"You mean, when you weren't in prison." Kiley flashed a cold smile.

"Yeah."

Collier didn't like the way Narr's eyes narrowed on Kiley. He shifted, putting himself between her and the heavyweight.

"Burglar boy says that you hired him to bypass security and break in to disable the sprinkler system."

"He's lying."

"Really?"

"Really."

"That's funny," Collier said softly. "Because he's got a tape recording of you hiring him."

The big man's eyes hardened, but other than that his face didn't change.

Kiley brought out the minicassette recorder and punched the play button.

Narr said nothing until it was over. "That's not my voice. It don't even sound like me."

"Sounds like you to me." She slid a look at Collier. "What do you think, Investigator McClain?"

"Yeah, sounds just like him."

Narr folded his arms and rocked back on his heels. "It's not me."

"The police lab has voice-analysis software. We'll be able to prove it's you."

He smirked. "Don't try to con me. Even if you did have some software that could recognize my voice, you'd have to have a print of my voice and you don't. 'Cuz that ain't it."

Too bad Kiley's bluff hadn't worked. Collier knew she wouldn't follow up on trying to get a voice match between Narr and the man on the tape, at least not with the current quality of the recording. Besides having too much static, the conversation had been recorded over the phone. About the only part of the conversation they could understand clearly was the location of the warehouse Damler had been instructed to break into.

After exchanging a glance with Collier, Kiley said, "We might have more questions later. You'd better stay available."

The scumbag shrugged.

Once Kiley and Collier were back in his truck, she huddled into her coat. "Shoot, I really thought that punk Damler might've given us something besides a big fat zero. Are we ever going to get anywhere?"

"Eventually."

"Which right now feels like never. I don't know where else to look."

"Neither do I."

"Let's take this tape back to the police lab and see if the tech can clean it up at all. Maybe he can get us something helpful."

"All right," Collier said.

"You'd think we'd be closer to solving the case now, not spinning our wheels."

She didn't sound nearly as frustrated about the sorry lead as he'd thought she would. Maybe because she didn't want to call it quits with them yet, either? He knew she wasn't ready to discuss the possibility that there might be more than sex between them, but maybe he could convince her to see where things might lead.

He wouldn't bring it up now. Neither of them could afford to split their focus, and he didn't want her distracted by anything when he told her he was crazy about her. Convincing her would be a hard sell, but he'd do whatever it took to show her he wanted her and only her.

Things between her and Collier were changing, and Kiley fought the sense of being overtaken, swept under by some thrilling, frightening wave of emotion. She didn't like his asking questions that made her think he wanted to take things further with them. She wasn't even going to consider it. She knew where their relationship stood, what was going to happen.

She needed to focus on the investigation, keep her mind off Collier. Off *them*. Stop dwelling on the way he made her feel.

Back at the PD, they took the tape to the lab. Denny Larkin, the tech, told Kiley and Collier they could wait if they wanted. Putting the cassette tape into a black machine that looked like a shoebox sprouting wires, he went into a computer program and began working his techno-voodoo. After a few minutes he played the tape.

Kiley shook her head. "I think Damler's voice is more clear, but I can't tell anything about Narr."

"Neither can I," Collier said.

"There are a couple more things I can try," Larkin said. "Don't know if it'll make any difference."

"Go ahead," Kiley urged. The tape was all they had right now.

The tech rewound the tape and started again on the computer. A phone across his desk rang and he answered. He glanced at Kiley. "Yeah, she's here." He grabbed a sticky note and scribbled something on it. "I'll tell her."

He hung up and passed her the note. "Someone called Crime Stoppers with an anonymous tip about your case."

Kiley stood, hit with a jolt of adrenaline as she read, "Go talk to Raye Ballinger." Her gaze shot to Collier's as he also got to his feet. She looked at Larkin. "Did they say anything else?"

"No."

"Did Crime Stoppers say if the caller was a man or a woman?"

"A man."

She turned to Collier. "I want to run a general records search on Raye. Run her for any kind of record, traffic ticket, whatever."

"I'm with you."

Going to the squad room, they faxed a request to the OSBI for a general records search and received a call a few minutes later. The computers were down for maintenance and wouldn't be back on until after noon.

While they waited, they checked with the Oklahoma Bar

Association to see if anyone had lodged a complaint against Raye or if she had lodged one against someone. Kiley's on-line search of public records turned up one formal complaint, filed against the attorney a year ago. The charge that Raye had consistently failed to disclose certain information to a client had resulted in a private reprimand by the Oklahoma Supreme Court.

Collier ran a check through the police department's database, searching for traffic tickets or citations, anything outstanding, but found nothing. He eased down onto the corner of Kiley's scarred metal desk. "We don't have much on Raye, at least not yet. And we still don't have a connection between Alan Embry or Sherry Vail to someone they could've hired to do the murders."

"There's still the possibility that the arsonist-murderer acted independently." Kiley angled her chair to face him. "Embry or Vail could've managed to get into every murder scene except Rehn's Coffee Warehouse without special skills. Anyone could've cut the padlock on the high school gym door to start the fire where Gary Miller was murdered."

"Yeah, that would be easy enough. And a knock on the door could've gotten the killer into a hotel room, like the one where Rex Huffman was last seen alive with a blond woman."

"Same with Lisa Embry. Nothing except patience was required to wait outside her garage and shoot her when she pulled inside."

"Those reasons are good enough for me to keep Sherry Vail as a suspect," Collier said. "But Rehn's Coffee Warehouse was challenging. Someone would need electrical knowledge to by-pass both the sprinkler and security systems."

"Alan Embry has years of electrical training, but we have no proof of anything other than the fact that he's a liar and Sherry Vail is bitter."

"We don't have any information that gets them off our list either, though."

"And now there's Raye Ballinger. Weird getting that tip about her. I wonder what she knows."

"That's what we're going to find out," he said.

Since they had time while waiting for the OSBI's computers, he and Kiley decided to go over their notes on Raye from her first interview back in November. They had talked to her because of her suicidal brother's connection to the murdered firefighters. The man Raye had given as her alibi for the night of Dan Lazano's murder confirmed that he had, indeed, been with her all night. A phone call to the resort in Cancun backed up the lawyer's claim that she'd been there in October on the night of Gary Miller's murder.

The alibi she'd given for the night of Rex Huffman's murder, that she was at a city council meeting, was also solid, but the meeting let out at such a time that she still could have been the mystery blond who'd been the last person to be seen with him alive. That, and the fact that Kiley and Collier couldn't prove or disprove that Raye had been home alone the night of Lisa Embry's murder kept the attorney on their radar. She could've hired someone to do the killings for her just as easily as Alan Embry or Sherry Vail could have.

If he let himself, Collier could be completely distracted by Kiley, but he managed to keep his attention on the case just as she was doing. He e-mailed a copy of the PD's records check as well as the formal complaint on Raye to his computer at the Fire Investigator's office.

They took a break for a late lunch. When they returned to the squad room a little after two o'clock, Kiley checked the fax machine. Whipping a piece of paper from the machine's tray, she hurried over, eyes glowing with excitement. "Look at this! Guess who has a permit to carry a concealed weapon?"

He leaned closer, his shoulder brushing hers. "The counselor?"

She smiled, handing him the piece of paper and pointing

to the information about Raye. "So, the lawyer knows how to use a gun."

"Even so, that doesn't mean she pulled the trigger herself."

"I know, but it's a place to start. Her fingerprints are also on file. When she applied for her concealed carry permit, she was printed."

Collier glanced at the report. "This says she took the qualifying course for her permit at DRT Gun Range. Let's call and see if they can tell us anything before we go talk to her."

The owner-manager of the gun range informed Kiley and Collier that Raye was a regular long-time member and a crack shot. With both handguns and rifles.

Not sure where they'd find Raye Ballinger on a Saturday, they drove first to her home. She wasn't there, so they went to her law office, a bungalow-style building of buff-colored stucco and a wide front porch framed by twin white columns. It was late afternoon when Collier held the door and Kiley preceded him inside. A light buzz announced their arrival.

The interior was done in dark, elegant wood. Misty greens and blues in paintings, chairs and carpet kept the reception area from being too pretentious. It was understated and elegant, much like the woman whose name was on the door.

Pausing at Kiley's side, Collier reached over and tucked a loose curl behind her ear. Even that small touch had heat sliding under her skin and she gave him a look as Raye swept out of an office just behind a large reception counter. She stopped short at the sight of them, her welcoming smile fading.

Dressed more casually than Kiley had ever seen her, Raye still looked chic in a pale yellow sweater and slacks. Her blond hair was pulled back in a low ponytail.

"Collier, Detective," she said coolly, quickly masking the surprise in her dark eyes. "What brings you here?"

Kiley saw no reason for small talk. "We're following up on some information."

"Regarding?" Raye arched a brow.

"Our current investigation," she said smoothly. "I need to read you your rights. As a matter of SOP, you understand."

"Standard operating procedure. Of course." The other woman folded her arms and listened with a neutral look on her face.

When Raye said she understood what had been cited to her, Kiley reached inside the pocket of her black wool coat for her small notebook. "We got a tip that you might have information about these firefighter murders."

"Me? Ridiculous." She laughed. "Who told you that?"

"They didn't give a name." Collier shifted, not touching Kiley, but close enough that she could feel his warmth. It was both reassuring and disconcerting.

The other woman's gaze sharpened, slid from him to Kiley. "Whoever it was gave you wrong information. The only thing I know about those dead firefighters is that they're dead. And, of course, that you suspect one of my clients of killing them."

"All four of them worked the scene of your brother's suicide." Collier watched her closely.

Pain tightened her refined features. "I still don't know anything."

"We found out you have a conceal and carry permit," Kiley said.

"So what? Half the people in this state carry guns." The attorney skimmed her gaze slowly over Collier. "Besides, you've seen some of the people I represent. I feel better having one."

Not liking the flare of irritation she felt at the hungry look Raye had given Collier, Kiley made a note of the lawyer's statements. Everything needed to be on the record, by the book. "We spoke to the owner-manager of DRT Gun Range. According to him, you spend a lot of time there."

"Well, the two of you have been busy," Raye murmured. "So?"

Collier fixed Raye with a stare. "That makes us think you're more knowledgeable about guns than someone who just wants to be prepared in case of trouble."

Kiley studied the other woman. "You shoot in monthly rifle competitions, and you're a superior marksman."

"What are you implying, Detective Russell? I know how to shoot a gun. So what?"

"Those murdered firefighters were killed with a sniper rifle."

"I know that." The other woman stiffened. "Are you saying…you think I killed them? Because I know how to use a gun?"

"You know how to use a *rifle*," Kiley reminded.

"I'm an attorney. Why would I do anything that might get me disbarred? Or sent to prison?"

"Revenge makes people do things."

"Revenge?" Her gaze went from Collier to Kiley, then comprehension swept her features. "Oh, you mean for my brother's death."

"All the murdered firefighters did respond to that call."

"Well, I imagine some others did, too." She folded her arms, her eyes glittering as if she were enjoying every bit of this.

Which she probably was, Kiley thought. She did like to play games.

The attorney leaned back in her chair, resting her elbows on the thick arms and steepling her fingers beneath her chin. "You must be desperate for suspects if you're checking me out."

"We didn't say you were a suspect, Counselor," Collier pointed out silkily. "We're simply following up on a tip we got."

"Ah, yes, from some anonymous person." Her gaze flickered from him to Kiley, weighed them both as a sly smile curved her lips. "Take a *tip* from me. You should be more concerned with your own personal business. Last time I saw you, the two of you weren't nearly so…cozy."

"Meaning what?" Kiley really did not like this woman.

"You are supposed to be conducting a murder investigation, but it's apparent what kind of business you're really conducting. I'm sure the mayor, along with your bosses, would be very interested to learn that the two of you are involved."

Kiley gave the lawyer a flat stare, struggling to keep heat from rising in her cheeks and trying to breathe past the knot of alarm that coiled in her gut. She didn't look at Collier.

Raye folded her arms and studied them. "What other suspects do you have?"

"We're here to get information, Raye," he said evenly. "Not give it."

"Well, how about this for information? Whoever gave you that tip could be setting me up to look bad. Anyone who knows about my brother's death wouldn't be far off in assuming I have issues with the fire department."

"Why would someone set you up?" Kiley asked baldly.

"The same motive you just cited. Revenge."

"Who would want revenge against you?"

"There are plenty of people who hate me for doing my job, Detective, just as I'm sure there are those who hate you for the same reason."

Kiley arched a brow and stared expectantly at the blonde.

Raye shrugged. "Some of those people are my clients. Maybe I didn't get them the deal they wanted or a not-guilty verdict. Any one of them could be pissed at me. I've been threatened by my own clients before, as well as others."

"And you think one of them hates you enough to go to the trouble of framing you?"

Collier sounded as disbelieving as Kiley felt. Her gaze met his.

Raye shifted her attention to him. "I don't have to tell the two of you how revenge drives people. Some of my clients are pretty vicious, filled with hate. And any one of them could find out what happened to my brother. Killing the firefighters who let my brother die would be the perfect way to set me up."

Collier clenched a fist at the blame she assigned to the people who had tried to save Jamie Ballinger. As much as he hated to consider the possibility, he silently agreed that someone could use Raye's very well-known anger against the fire department to make it look as if she were the one killing these public servants.

"I do blame those firefighters for failing to catch my brother when he fell off the ladder, and that is why I've already filed a lawsuit against the fire department. Their public humiliation and a hefty settlement will be a sweet enough revenge for me."

Collier glanced at Kiley, noted her rigid posture, the cool disdain just beneath the surface. He knew she was too professional to let her personal dislike of Raye show; he just hoped the attorney didn't catch on.

"It's not that far-fetched, is it, Collier?" Raye asked softly. "Why don't you put the taxpayers' dollars to better use and find out if someone's trying to make me look bad?"

"Give us some names and we will," Kiley said quickly.

Good call, Collier thought. To put the burden on Raye. Although she certainly didn't act like a person who was guilty.

The attorney smiled. "I'll make some inquiries on my own first. I believe people are innocent until proven guilty, which is just the opposite of how you law enforcement types operate. If you don't have any other questions, I'm expected at my mother's."

Kiley nodded. "We'll let you know if anything comes of this."

"Thank you."

"We may have more questions, Raye," Collier said quietly. "Stay available."

"I'm an officer of the court, Collier." Her voice dripped sweetness. "Of course I will."

They stepped out into the frigid January air. Evening settled around them in a wash of pale blue and gray. Neither of them spoke until they were in Collier's truck. As he drove out of the parking lot, Kiley shifted toward him. "Do you think she's our suspect?"

"Hard to know." He could feel tension pulsing from her. "What do you think about her theory that she's being set up?"

"Someone would really have to hate her in order to go to all that trouble. And, brace yourself, it's not that hard for me to imagine that someone could hate her enough to do it."

He grinned. "I feel like it's a wild-goose chase, but we can't ignore it. Especially since we haven't found anything new on Embry or Vail."

"What do you think is the best way to find out the names of her clients? Asking Raye for a list would've been a waste of time." Kiley pushed her hair over her shoulder as she snapped her seat belt into place.

Collier wanted to sink his hands into the thick cloud of fire. And the urge to touch her that he'd felt since first seeing her this morning hadn't abated just because they'd been tending to business. "Would the D.A.'s office have a record of that? Files on cases they prosecuted that also give the names of opposing counsel?"

"I can check. If not, I think we'll have to go to the courthouse and dig through a load of records. By hand." She groaned. "That will take forever."

"Yeah. I don't know how high on our to-do list that should be, especially since we're only guessing that it was one of Raye's clients who called Crime Stoppers and snitched on her. We don't know she's involved at all or has any connection to the victims other than her brother's suicide call."

"Whatever we do, we can't do it until Monday."

He glanced over, found her staring intently out the window. He tickled a spot behind her ear. "Don't let her get to you, Blaze."

Could he read every thought in her head? How had Raye figured out that she and Collier were involved? It wasn't as if either of them were walking around panting after each other. Not in public, anyway. "How could she tell?"

"She couldn't." Collier stopped at a red light. "She was fishing, same as we were. She only made that insinuation to deflect our questions, get our focus off her. She does it in the courtroom, too."

Raye had questioned Kiley on the stand before, so she knew he was right. Still she was shaken. "I wish she *was* our murderer. Jail would be a good place for her."

"She doesn't know anything about us."

"We can't be sure." If Raye could tell the two of them had a personal relationship, couldn't everyone else? If not, they soon would. That would terrify Collier. It terrified Kiley.

"So what if she does know something? We're not breaking any laws. We are consenting adults, Blaze."

"You heard what she said. That sounded like a threat. What if she tells the Chief of Police? The Fire Chief? What if this case gets to court?"

He took her hand, his thumb stroking the sensitive skin between her thumb and index finger. "Don't be jumpy. Everything's gonna be all right."

"I wish I felt as sure as you do."

"Wanna grab some dinner? Or if you're feeling brave, I can make pancakes."

Something warm fluttered in her chest. She was afraid she was falling for him, and she was not going to let that happen. Talk about asking for heartbreak.

Their relationship had shifted in a huge way. A scary, meaningful way. Last night they hadn't even made love. They'd just fallen asleep together on her couch. That was too comfortable, too…intimate. "I…kind of need to see my sister tonight."

"Kiley—"

"I missed our weekly breakfast again this morning, plus I have things to catch up on. I'm sure you do, too."

He studied her, protest darkening his eyes.

"I need a little time to myself. Just for tonight, okay?"

"Okay," he finally said.

The understanding in his eyes caused her throat to tighten.

"I'll call you tomorrow."

"All right."

He leaned over and ran a knuckle along the line of her jaw. "I've got a safety inspection first thing Monday morning. I'll meet you at the D.A.'s office around nine-thirty. Maybe by then you'll have compiled a list of Raye's clients."

"Trying to get out of your share of the work, McClain?"

"You know it." She smiled and he cupped her nape, pulling her to him. "I want you to think about me tonight, because I'll be thinking about you."

His mouth covered hers, hot and sweet, melting her from the inside out. He hadn't kissed her like this before. Hungry but tender, causing her whole body to ache. He didn't stop until she was dizzy and breathing hard, trying to remember why she thought it was a good idea to go home without him.

He dropped her at the police station, and she got into her car, more confused than ever.

Chapter 12

Collier had missed her like crazy last night. He'd been reminded of life before her, and he didn't like it. If Terra's comments last week had made Kiley uncertain of continuing, Raye's remarks had probably spooked her.

He figured she'd spent the night thinking about calling things off between them. But Collier didn't want to call things off.

They weren't supposed to see each other until tomorrow, when they had agreed to meet at the D.A.'s. Telling himself to give her some space, he decided to wait until this evening to call her. They both had things they needed to do, at the office and around the house. Walker was coming over later to help Collier start tearing up the hallway floor in preparation for the new one.

Just before noon, as he was pulling in to get the oil in his truck changed, a call came over his radio about a fire at one of Presley's newest apartment complexes. The one where Dominic Narr lived. The apartment number was his.

It might be nothing, but Collier's instincts said go. He called Kiley and she agreed to meet him there. He drove west across town, reaching the complex in about ten minutes.

He maneuvered his truck through the parking lot to the affected building and parked behind an engine from Station One. The blaze was out, puffy white-gray smoke pluming over the complex.

Police cruisers blocked off every entrance to the complex. A news van from a nearby Oklahoma City station pulled up to the edge of the scene. Collier had initially responded to this call because of Narr, and now that he was here, he'd investigate. The chances were slim that a do-wrong implicated in their investigation would just happen to lose his home to fire so soon after coming to their attention.

The entire building was evacuated as were the ones on either side of it. If the flames had jumped, the close placement and position of the structures would have had them burning like a fuse. Dozens of people milled about.

Collier pulled on his boots and turnout coat, then closed his truck door. As he tugged on his heavy gloves, Kiley drove up and got out of her car. Her hair was down, the way he liked it best, and Collier wanted to bury his hands in it. Wanted to get his hands on *her.*

It was all he could do not to pull her into a dark corner somewhere and kiss her until they both gave out. Her warm cinnamon scent teased him. Beneath her long coat, she looked sleek and professional in a slim-fitting black pants suit. Her gun and badge were clipped to the waistband of her slacks. The pale green silk blouse she wore made her eyes more green than blue.

Her greeting was professional, no different from any other day since they'd gotten involved, but he saw a glimpse of something undefinable in her eyes. Regret? Whatever it was ratcheted up the restlessness he already felt.

He stuck to their agreement, partners only while on the job, and tried to narrow his focus to the blaze. Handing her a pair of steel-soled boots, he waited while she put them on. After speaking to the cop who was logging in personnel and learning that the apartment's resident, Dominic Narr, was at work, Kiley and Collier ducked under the crime-scene tape blocking off the affected area.

Each two-story structure was tan frame with colored shutters that varied from building to building. The ones on Narr's building were green. Flags of smoke and soot streamed black on the exterior walls.

Stations One, Two and Four had responded, as well as two engines from Oklahoma City. Some firefighters moved away from the building, pulling off their helmets and Nomex hoods. Others squished through ash-gray water, rolling up hoses.

Captain Sandusky from Station Two saw Collier and Kiley, and waved them over to where he stood next to the building. He shook hands with them both, then asked Collier, "Somebody call you?"

"I heard it over the radio. The guy who lives in that apartment is a suspect in our arson-murders."

The captain's flinty eyes narrowed. "I went through the scene. From what I saw, the iron was left on the high setting with no water in the fill port. The iron overheated and started the fire. It looks like an accident, but after what you've just told me, I gotta wonder. Let me know if you reach the same conclusion I did."

Collier nodded.

Sandusky stepped a few feet away and hollered up at the firefighters on the second floor. "Stop overhaul! McClain needs to get in there and take a look around."

Collier clapped the older man on the back. "Thanks, Cap."

"The origin is in the bedroom, if you want to start there. Let me know if you find something I missed."

"I imagine you're right about the cause, but I'll keep you posted."

As he and Kiley mounted the stairs to Narr's apartment, she glanced back at Sandusky. "Are the captains supposed to make determinations about how fires start?"

"It's okay as long as they back up their findings with reports and documentation. Sandusky's very thorough and he's rabid about documenting everything. I expect to find the fire was started by the iron being left on."

"But? I can hear a *but* in there." She followed him into Narr's apartment, speaking to the firefighters she recognized.

The apartment consisted of the small living area and attached kitchen, one bedroom and one bathroom. The blaze had been doused before it had traveled too far into the living area.

Collier tugged off one heavy glove and reached in his pocket to hand Kiley a pair of Latex ones. They stopped in the bedroom doorway and he scrutinized the room for a couple of minutes.

He looked at the ceiling that had been chewed through by flame, the charred wall behind the dresser. The glass in the window opposite him was heat-cracked as fine as a spiderweb. His gaze went to the iron, which sat on the corner of an old oak dresser.

Coning—the way a fire starts from a particular point then spreads in a fan- or conelike pattern—told him that the fire had started at the appliance. The dresser's surface was heavily blackened in the area immediately beneath and around the appliance. The dry iron had caught fire; flames latched on to the dresser then spread up the wall behind. He finally answered Kiley's question. "Just because the iron started this fire doesn't mean it was an accident."

"You mean Narr could've done this on purpose so it'd look like an accident?" She followed him farther into the room.

"I've seen it before."

"Maybe someone tried to kill Narr."

"Maybe so."

"We talked to him about Lazano's murder twenty-four hours ago, and today his place catches fire? That seems too coincidental to me."

"A woman after my own heart." Collier saw her stiffen at the phrase and he tried to dismiss it. "If Narr did start this fire on purpose, maybe it was to destroy something he didn't want found."

"That really makes me want to look around," she murmured.

"Even if he did deliberately leave on the iron, we may not be able to prove it. I fought a fire once where a man who owned a dry cleaners used his clothes steamer to set a blaze, but nothing could ever be proven. About three years later, the fire investigator at the time, Harris Vaughn, told me that the business owner was caught doing the same thing in another state."

"How did they prove it wasn't an accident? *Can* it be proved?"

"The fire department in Colorado Springs had a string of fires with the same cause. They investigated, talked to the business owner and did a background check to see if he was involved in any previous fires. He confessed to the one here and about a dozen others over a three-state area."

"How long did he keep pulling that stunt?"

"About ten years."

"I see your point about not being able to prove if a fire like this was an accident. People do leave appliances on all the time. Since we're here, 'responding to the scene,'" she said with a sly grin, "we should take a good look around."

"You're reading my mind. Maybe we'll find something that'll tie Narr to Lazano's murder."

He opened the closet door. An ironing board rested face-out against the wall to his right. Muddy work boots, a pair of scuffed tennis shoes and a clump of dirty clothes made a pile on the closet floor.

Kiley moved up beside him, the narrow doorway causing her to lean in from the side in order to see. Her body brushed his, and he fought the urge to slide an arm around her and pull her into him. He'd never had this much trouble concentrating at work. Forget seeing her tomorrow. He had to see her tonight.

When her body touched Collier's, Kiley knew it was time. She was way too aware of him and his big, warm body. Even beneath the smoke, she caught the blend of tang and man that was uniquely him. She had to break things off before she got in over her head. The way he'd kissed her last night had flashed WARNING in big neon letters. She'd wanted to melt into him, forget everything she'd learned in the past about guys who moved from woman to woman. But she couldn't forget.

She'd gotten involved with him knowing it would be temporary, *needing* it to be temporary. And that's what it was.

Collier glanced at the empty overhead shelf, then moved the ironing board away from the wall. A hollow clang sounded as something fell against the metal then into the corner.

"Look!" they said at the same time.

Kiley's jaw dropped as her gaze met Collier's. It was a rifle, like their murder weapon. Without touching anything, they both peered closer and found that it used the same caliber ammunition as had been used on their murder victims.

"Now, this is good."

Collier's breath fluttered against her ear, and his low, smooth drawl sent a shiver through her. She straightened when he did, trying to pretend she didn't want to get him alone somewhere and rip off his clothes.

"Finally a lead," she said, slightly breathless and a whole lot irritated about it. "Let's pay Narr a visit at work."

"Definitely." Collier's gaze roamed over her with enough heat to melt rock.

She stepped away, unclipped her cell phone from the waistband of her slacks and called for a crime scene investigator.

Collier indicated he was going out and she heard him move back toward the living area, telling the firefighters to hold off on further overhaul until the CSI arrived and had a chance to go over the scene. As she walked out to join him, she called to request that a black-and-white meet them at the fast-food joint where Narr worked.

Fifteen minutes later Dominic Narr strolled from the kitchen of his workplace. "I don't have nothing else to say to y'all."

"Thought we should tell you that your apartment just burned."

Shock wiped the smug look off his face. "What! Burned? How?"

"Looks like you left the iron on."

"I didn't iron nothing!"

"It doesn't matter to us if you did or didn't. What we care about is what we found in your bedroom closet."

"Is everything gone?" he snarled.

"Not the sniper rifle," Kiley said sweetly.

"Sniper—"

"You're under arrest for violating your parole. Having a firearm in your possession is a big no-no. Once the CSI goes over that gun, I imagine there will be other charges."

Narr's face changed from panic to fury as Kiley pulled one arm behind his back and snapped on one cuff then the other while she read him his rights.

The ex-con shook his head. "I don't have no rifle."

"And yet one has magically appeared, tucked in behind your ironing board. Sorta clever. If that gun's not yours, how did it get there?"

"I sure didn't put it there. And I didn't burn down my apartment, either. I wasn't even there! Ask my boss. I've been here since seven this morning."

If the iron had been purposely left on in order to start a fire, the appliance would have served as a timing device, giving the arsonist time to get away from the scene well before the fire started.

Collier stepped up and took the guy's beefy arm. "Hiding that rifle in your apartment was some kind of stupid, Narr."

"I'm a lot of things, but stupid ain't one of 'em! I'm sayin' that gun ain't mine. I don't know how it got here."

"Hmm." Kiley pretended to consider. "I think you're the first person to ever tell me that."

"I swear on my mother's grave."

"Never heard that one, either."

He let loose with a string of heated curses. When she turned the ex-con over to the two patrol cops she'd requested, Kiley told them that she had read the suspect his rights, but they should do it again, for good measure.

As the uniforms escorted him down the concrete steps, he tried one last time. "Detective, that's not my gun. Why would I violate my parole?"

"Maybe you like life better in the joint than out. You wouldn't be the first con to feel that way."

"No! I don't! I want to see my attorney, Raye Ballinger."

"Why am I not surprised he's one of her clients?" Kiley braced her hands on her hips as she and Collier watched Officer Hanson stuff the prisoner, still swearing, into the back seat of his cruiser.

Collier waited until the black-and-white left before turning to her. "That was way too easy."

"Yeah. And too neat. If Narr did set that fire, did he really think the gun would burn up?"

"Most people think flame destroys everything, but it doesn't."

For a moment she stared down at the concrete landing. "Play 'what if' with me. What if Raye is our murderer? Say she hired Narr, a client she's represented more than once, to get her an untraceable gun and take care of disabling the security system at Rehn's warehouse."

Collier nodded. "Say the only people who know about this are Narr and Ballinger. When we went to see her yesterday, maybe she figured that our anonymous tip came from him, which it could have."

"To get the focus of the investigation off her and back on him, she plants the rifle, leaves a dry iron on to catch fire and takes off."

"Great theory." Collier dragged a hand down his face. "Wish we could prove it. Right now we can't prove anything about anyone."

She punched in a number on her cell phone. "I want to ask the CSI to put a rush on the tests for that rifle and the ammunition. We need to know ASAP if we've got the right suspect."

A couple of hours later they still weren't sure, but they had booked Narr into custody. The entire time they'd taken his statement, he'd sworn to his innocence. Kiley actually believed the guy hadn't known about the gun, but without proof that he'd been set up, nothing could be done. Narr's having the weapon at all was a violation of his parole, so he was going back to prison, no matter what.

Judging from Collier's somberness, he wasn't convinced Narr was their guy, either. Still they wrote up their reports and filed them.

By the time they finished their paperwork, it was after seven o'clock. Unless the lab found something, she and Collier had nowhere else to go on the investigation. Or their relationship, either.

Her stomach was a mass of knots. It was best to just talk to Collier and get it over with. She probably never should've gotten involved with him, but she'd done so with her eyes wide-open. She didn't regret a minute of being with him, but it was time to let him move on before she got in way over her head.

They walked out of the police department into the brittle cold and stopped beside her car. She could see her breath on the air. A cloud scudded across a silver crescent moon. She felt him studying her and fought the urge to blurt out what she wanted to say. Anxious to have it done, her nerves were raw. He wouldn't make a big deal out of this, so neither would she.

"Let's go grab some dinner," he said.

"I'm not hungry."

His dusky green gaze locked on hers. "We need to talk."

"I know." Despite her best effort, her voice was unsteady. "We can talk right here if you want."

He glanced around at the other cars in the lot, frowning. "I don't. Your house or mine?"

She'd feel more in control on her own turf. "Mine."

"I'll meet you there."

Part of her wished things could be different. That he could, *would* commit to her, and only her. But she knew guys with his MO didn't do "forever." She'd learned that from her dad *and* from David.

She parked in her garage, and as Collier pulled into the driveway, she walked through the house and let him in the front door. "The lab tech called on the way here to tell me they found a cartridge in the gun, and there's a fingerprint on it. They're running it now."

"Good." As he moved past her into the living room, he shrugged out of his overcoat, then draped it over the back of her sofa.

She stayed at the edge of the carpet, fighting the urge to move closer, to touch him one last time.

His gaze settled on her, knowing and steady. It put a quiver in her belly. "Tell me what's on your mind, Blaze."

It's been great. See ya around. She couldn't bring herself to be so blasé. "I've been thinking about what Raye said last night. About us."

"I told you she was just blowing smoke."

"She was right, Collier. If this case goes to trial, which we both want, what if our affair comes out? It could look bad for both of us, for the city, too. It's not worth risking our jobs over."

He closed the distance between them, looking down at her. "I don't think it'll come to that."

"But we have to consider the possibility."

He searched her face. "Is that what this is really about? Or are you having second thoughts about us?"

"I haven't had any first thoughts about *us,* McClain. There is no *us.*" Her reaction was pure knee jerk. "It's been great. You've been great, but—"

"But you want to break things off."

"We agreed this was only temporary."

"No, Blaze. *We* didn't agree. You made that decision on your own, and that isn't what I want."

"What *do* you want, then?"

"Us, together." He cupped her shoulders but didn't try to draw her closer. "I like what we've got going. I don't want to end things."

"You mean, you don't want to end them right now?" Something hot and tight grabbed her throat. "This is the best time, Collier. Even though we don't believe this investigation is entirely finished, it's close."

"I don't care when the case is solved. I don't want to break things off at all."

How long would that last? "It was fun, but now it's over. It's time to move on. That's what you do."

"Not this time. This time, I want more."

A huge wave of alarm swamped her. Stepping away, she crossed her arms, as much to hide her shaking hands as to try and steady herself. "Then you've got the wrong girl."

"No, I don't." Collier had half expected her words, but her vehemence hit him with surprising force.

Her jaw dropped, then she recovered. "Don't change the rules on me."

"I'm telling you how I feel, Kiley. I thought women were supposed to like that."

"Not every time," she muttered.

"I'm just telling the truth. I'm nuts about you, Blaze."

She shook her head and walked past him with a doubtful look, shrugging out of her long coat and tossing it on the couch. "Then why haven't you said anything before now?"

"Look at you." He turned, hiding a smile. *Be patient,* he told himself. When she found out he was serious, she'd admit she didn't want this to end, either. "Any time I say a word about us being together for more than a day at a time, you get this look like I just poisoned you. I wanted to give you time to realize you feel the same way I do."

"It doesn't matter what I feel." She wrapped her arms around her waist, her eyes stormy and troubled. "What matters is what I know."

"Or what you think you do," he muttered, shoving a hand through his hair. "Do you think I'm going to hop out of your bed and straight into someone else's? I haven't looked at, much less thought about another woman since I met you. That was after our one dance at Christmas, before we even started working together."

"I thought we were on the same page. You don't want any strings. I don't want any strings."

"I do, Blaze. With you."

Looking completely baffled, she huffed out a breath. "What is it? Do you want to be the one to walk first like you always do? Fine."

"No! I don't want to be first. I don't want to walk at all."

"You'll get tired of me. One. Woman," she emphasized. "Think about that."

"I am thinking about it," he growled. "Look, I know my reputation. I did that on purpose after Gwen because I didn't want to get mowed down again, but who I am underneath hasn't changed. It took you to make me see that, to make me want to be that way again. I've only had three girlfriends in my whole life and I nearly married one of them. All long-term relationships, all monogamous. And I was never the one to leave. I'm not leaving this time, either."

"What we have is only physical. What you wanted."

"I never said that. You did."

"But…this wasn't the deal."

"What deal? I was gonna back off and *you* jumped *me*. I say all bets are off."

"We're not supposed to get this involved." She looked close to panic. "I don't want to."

"Kiley." Hesitantly, he reached out. When she didn't back away, he stroked her cheek. "I know it's hard to trust after what your dad did."

"It's not just him."

Collier frowned.

"You asked me that first night about my past relationships. I was in love once, with a guy named David." She stepped away, unclipping her holstered Taurus from her waistband as she walked to the bookcase-table along the wall behind the front door. "I dated him from our junior year in high school until our junior year in college. He was the school bad boy until we got together, then he settled down. Or so I thought."

Placing her gun and badge on the dark wood surface, she let out a sharp laugh. Collier could hear the pain beneath it.

"We were together almost five years. I believed he'd changed but I was wrong. I caught him with another woman and it nearly killed me. I was so proud of myself for falling in love with a man completely unlike my father," she said scornfully. "After being with David for so long, you'd think I would've known him better. I learned the hard way that even reformed bad boys like him, who seemed trustworthy, couldn't be trusted. I've never let myself forget."

"Kiley, I'm not him." Collier cupped her shoulders, his gaze searing into hers. "Have I ever led you to believe one thing and done another? Haven't I been up-front about what I want since the first day we started working together?"

"Yes," she answered hesitantly.

"I'm shooting straight now, too. I know what I want, Blaze. You. For tomorrow. And every tomorrow after that."

"David said things like that, too."

"This is about *you* and *me*," he practically growled. He didn't want her to talk about that other guy. He sure didn't like her comparing the two of them. He cautioned himself to play it cool. "I know you're not ready for this to end. Not yet. I see it in your eyes when we make love. Your heart beats every bit as hard as mine when we're together. I know you feel something for me."

"Even if I do, I can't trust it."

"You mean you can't trust *me*."

She hesitated, then nodded.

Hurt slashed deep. "You really believe I'll leave."

"You will."

He huffed out a breath and dragged a hand down his face. "You're deadly for a guy's ego, Blaze."

"I'm sorry." Her voice quavered; tears filled her eyes. "But I can't turn my back on what I know."

"Neither can I, and I know this." He slid a knuckle under her chin. "I'm crazy about you, Kiley Anne."

"For now, maybe."

"For always," he gritted out, trying not to lose patience. He understood her skittishness; he'd been the same way.

"We both know how this is going to end. You walk, I walk. It's better to do it now."

"I thought I'd never trust another woman, but I trust you. Am I wrong to do that?"

Her heart clenched. She recognized what it had cost him

to say that. Any other female would've melted at his feet, and Kiley wanted to. But she had to consider the source. Intentions didn't matter nearly as much as patterns did. And his pattern was just like her father's, just like David's.

Collier snagged her hand, folded it into his. "You've got the best BS detector of anybody I know. Look in my eyes. You'll see I'm telling the truth."

She searched his face. He *was* sincere. She didn't doubt that, but how did she know she wasn't seeing what she wanted? Seeing love rather than affection? "There are a lot of women out there, McClain. Waiting just for you. Tell me that isn't tempting."

"It isn't."

"Maybe not right now, today." She pulled away, her withdrawal causing his heart to clench. "How long will that last?"

"Forever. I was only with those women because I was waiting for you to catch up to me."

"Don't say sweet things to me."

"Why not?"

Her lips trembled. "Because you're all about moving from woman to woman."

"If I wanted to move on, wouldn't I be doing it right now? I've never known anyone like you, Blaze. Whatever we've got, whatever you do for me makes me want to keep it." He considered giving her an ultimatum, forcing her to admit the feelings he knew she had for him. But she needed to come to the realization on her own, not because he'd gotten in her face. "I don't want anyone else, and since I'm spilling my guts here, I don't want you to be with anyone else, either."

"What if you change your mind one day?"

The sadness in her voice made his chest ache. "What if *you* do? What if you're the one who decides to move on?"

He had every right to ask, to wonder after what Gwen had

done to him. Kiley stared hard at him. She wanted to believe him, but the doubt in her mind overruled her heart. "It won't work."

"You mean, you won't give it a chance," he said tightly, irritation flaring.

"It's only sex." She wondered when she had stopped believing that.

"Bull."

"It was great, but things are over. We should move on."

"I can't believe you're making this about sex." Anger slowly, steadily built inside him. "You know it's more than that."

"Not to me."

Now *that* hurt. Every muscle in his body clenched as he resisted the urge to grab her and kiss her until she couldn't deny what they both knew. "If it's only physical, then why is it so important that we end things now? I'm having a good time. You're having a good time. What's the big rush?"

"It isn't working for me anymore."

The frustration he'd held in check exploded. "What do I have to do to get through to you? You're scared. So am I. This turned into more than either of us expected. I'm overwhelmed, too. We can take things slow."

"I…don't want to see you again. I think you should go."

His temper snapped. "So do I. Because in about ten seconds, I'm gonna throw you on the floor, rip off your clothes and show you just how much we don't mean to each other."

"See, it *is* about sex!"

He wanted to shake her until her teeth rattled. Instead he snatched up his coat and turned to leave. "You are one stubborn woman—"

The front door exploded, shooting off its hinges, shattering into shards of wood raining down on them. Splinters, metal, sparks flew into his face. Fire leaped from the door's remains, caught the carpet, a table leg and headed straight for them.

Chapter 13

A ball of fire erupted at the same time Collier saw a flying piece of metal and recognized it as part of a gas can. The force of the blast, the rapid-hot fan of fire told him that some kind of explosive had been taped to the container. Flames hurtled up the wall, snaked across the carpet, eating their way through the room.

He grabbed Kiley and shoved her toward the nearest exit, away from the billowing smoke. "Go! Back door! Now!"

They tore across the living room, dodged a wall and headed for the French door leading to her deck. He kept her in front of him. Fire chased them, its whine building to a hissing crackle as it bore down.

She looked over her shoulder, slowing a bit.

"I'm right behind you! Go!"

Someone had placed that gas bomb in front of her door and lit it with either a fuse or a blasting cap. Heat surged at his back, stung one ear. Kiley reached the glass-paned door, struggled with the top latch, then the dead bolt. She was nearly out of danger. The tightness in Collier's chest eased slightly. She was okay.

She flung open the door and rushed outside. Everything happened in a blur, folded together in one frozen moment.

He saw a flash of blue-orange light in the darkness, heard a loud pop. The door's glass reflected the flames behind him. Beyond, the night was black and silver. Kiley turned toward him, yelling something. Then she stumbled, fell to the deck as though pushed.

Collier lunged out of the house, dragging in deep breaths of cold air. He reached her, went to his knees.

"Don't touch her!"

At the shouted order, his head jerked up. He looked into the barrel of a gun. And Raye Ballinger's hard glittering eyes.

Even as he tried to figure out an escape, his mind processed. Raye had shot Kiley. Now she was going to shoot him. The attorney had him dead center. "Bye-bye, lover."

Her eyes glittered as she pulled the trigger. The blast was deafening. Collier dove, rolling to his side. He scrambled to move again as Raye crumpled to the ground. And lay motionless.

He skidded on his knees, reaching across her to shove the gun away. The mix of moonlight and flame showed a wound in Raye's neck, a small hole, a trickle of blood. Her chest wasn't moving. He rushed back to Kiley, only now realizing she'd managed to pull her gun from her ankle holster and get off a round.

"That was one good shot, Russell." He leaned over her, his breath frosting the air.

Her hand fell limply to her side, her gun thudding to the deck.

"Kiley?" He saw now that the pale green of her blouse was dark—slick with blood. Gut shot.

He could hear the fire, engulfing everything in its path. Orange wisps of flame licked at the French door, growing larger as they slid around the frame with a hiss. Smoke rolled out in a cloud, choking him. He had to get her out of here. He snatched up his coat, lifted her in his arms and ran down the wooden steps, over to the far side of the neighbor's yard.

Sirens blared. Someone had called 911. He was vaguely aware of the neighbors rushing out of their homes. The sounds of ambulance sirens and fire truck horns moved closer.

Under the foamy glare of a street light, he laid her on his coat in the stiff, frozen grass. His hands shook as he pulled her blouse from her slacks, unzipped them so he could see her abdomen. The small entrance wound was just above her navel.

He compressed his hands firmly against the wound, desperately trying to stanch the blood flow. He watched her pale face, urging her silently to come to as he leaned down to listen to her heartbeat. Weak, fading to thready. "Blaze, I love you," he whispered. "Wake up."

Two hours later Collier stood in the surgical waiting area of Presley Medical Center. Where was the doctor? How long had the team of surgeons and nurses been in there? He and Kiley had gotten here about eight. The digital read-out on his watch showed 10:14 p.m.

His gaze skipped over the dozen or so people gathered round, all waiting for information. His mind raced. Kiley had shot Raye in the carotid artery, killing her instantly. It was too good for her as far as Collier was concerned, but what he really cared about was the redhead on that surgery table, fighting for her life.

The trauma team had been ready the instant Kiley arrived. In the ambulance the paramedics had started an IV of Lactated Ringers; upon seeing the E.R. doctor they had reported that Kiley's blood pressure was critically low and she wasn't responding to the replacement IV. A nurse had immediately run for a bag of blood.

Kiley had been deathly pale, so pale that Collier's entire body went numb. She'd needed B-negative blood. Her sister didn't match the fairly rare type; neither did Collier. And they couldn't wait for the five-day turnaround to screen a new donor. The nurse had quickly begun infusing the universal donor blood type, O negative.

A nurse from the operating room had come out about an hour ago and told Kiley's sister that the doctor had put her on a ventilator. She explained that it was in case complications developed and the staff needed to work on her in a hurry. Hearing Kiley was vented had panic squeezing Collier's chest until he couldn't breathe. He didn't let on to Kristin, but he wondered if something had gone bad.

He still wasn't breathing that well. At the other end of the room, Kristin talked to Clay Jessup, Kiley's friend and police academy buddy who'd offered to pick up her mother, JoAnn Russell Martin, at the airport. Collier had reached Kristin on the way to the hospital then offered to call their mom because Kiley's sister sounded too upset to string two words together.

The low drone and murmurs of conversation flayed his nerves. He hadn't been sure how Kiley's sister would hold up, but she was coping quietly. There were occasional tears, but no panic or hysterics.

He couldn't shake the picture of Kiley's bloodless face as he'd climbed into the ambulance with her. The paramedics knew him and didn't try to prevent his riding with her. If he didn't stop replaying that gunshot, he was going to hit something.

He thought through every detail of the case, so he didn't have to deal with what had been said before hell had literally rained down on them. He and Kiley believed Raye was the right suspect, and hopefully it would be her fingerprint that the CSI matched to the one on the rifle cartridge they'd found at Dominic Narr's apartment.

Now that they knew the identity of their arsonist-murderer,

they also knew the connection between the victims. The four dead firefighters had all tried to save Jamie Ballinger from the second story of the house he'd torched in an attempt to kill himself. They'd gotten him out of the house, but on the way down, he'd jumped from the ladder. No one had been able to grab him. And they couldn't resuscitate him after that fall. He'd died before they got him in the ambulance.

Collier speculated that it was the firefighters who physically touched Raye's brother during the rescue effort whom she held responsible for her brother's death. That group of firefighters consisted of two more men. If Narr hadn't put the focus on the attorney, she would've taken revenge on them, too.

Knowing that the Ballinger suicide was the link between the murders, Collier figured Raye had to be the mystery blonde seen with Rex Huffman at the motel on the night of his murder. He could also now discern that the dates of death formed a pattern. Raye's brother had died on the third day of the month. A firefighter had been murdered on days on either side of that number, though not in numerical order. The first, the fourth, the fifth, the second.

Collier had told Kiley all this in the ambulance on the way to the hospital. He had talked so she'd hear him if she regained consciousness, and so he wouldn't go insane with fear. She'd never opened her eyes, never responded at all.

His chest hurt as if it was splitting open. Rubbing it, he walked to the far end of the hall, away from everyone else. The quiet hum of the heating unit dimmed the voices from the waiting room. He stared blankly through the glass door leading to the recovery area.

"How's it going?"

"She's been in there two hours." Collier turned as his brother came toward him. "A while ago, I asked a surgical nurse and she told me that's probably typical, but much longer than that means major blood vessels are involved."

What damage had she sustained? How much longer would she be in there? He kept seeing himself push her in front of him, making sure she went out the door first.

"I know what you're doing, bro. Don't." Walker leaned a shoulder against the door so that he faced Collier, nailed him with a look. "It's not your fault she got shot."

"I practically pushed her out the door in front of me." Collier shoved a hand through his hair, holding on to his control by a thread. His eyes were gritty from lack of sleep and burning from smoke. "I put her right in Raye's sights."

"You were protecting her. The fire was the immediate threat. You had no way of knowing about that psycho lawyer outside."

He pinched the bridge of his nose. "I said some things…"

"And she'll hold it over you for a long time."

"No," he said hoarsely. "Just before that gas bomb exploded, she broke things off."

"Man, I'm sorry." Compassion flared in Walker's eyes. After a minute he asked, "How'd Ballinger know where y'all would be, anyway?"

"She knew we'd find that rifle she planted at Narr's apartment. She was probably watching us from that point." He closed his eyes for an instant. "I should've told her—"

"You still can. Kiley's going to come out of this."

He should've said it at her house, when they were hashing things out. But knowing she didn't want to hear the words, he'd kept quiet. Did it even matter now? She'd ended things between them with a finality that made Collier's gut clench. "Where's that doctor? I know Kiley had a lot of bleeding, but what about other damage?"

"Want me to go check?"

"It won't make 'em hurry any faster." Leaning against the wall, he laid his head back, staring blankly at the ceiling tiles. "Besides, I hounded that surgical nurse ten minutes ago as she was going back in. She didn't have any new information. I just want to know—"

"Collier?"

He straightened, turning toward Kristin who stood down the hall, her eyes huge with worry.

"Do you think it's a bad sign that we haven't heard anything else?"

He wanted to reassure her, but he had no idea. "I don't know."

The quiet swoosh of a nearby door had him looking over his shoulder at the slender woman striding toward them. Blood streaked her green scrubs. Tendrils of blond hair escaped her surgical cap. She pulled off her mask, and Collier recognized her as Dr. Meredith Boren, a good friend of Terra's.

Kristin moved quickly to meet the woman, motioning for Collier to join them. The doctor's blue eyes were kind, but she didn't waste time with preliminaries as she spoke to Kristin. "Your sister's fighting, but she's lost a lot of blood. A lot."

Kristin nodded. A hard knot formed in Collier's chest.

"Her liver was nicked. We removed the bullet and stopped the bleeding, but we had to take a small piece of her liver."

He knew the organ could operate fine with only a section left so that news brought relief. "Any other organs or major blood vessels hit?"

"One major blood vessel, and she's darn lucky it's only one. She'll go from recovery to ICU."

"And then?"

Her gaze met his, solemn and concerned. "We'll just have to wait and see."

On Tuesday Kiley was moved to a regular room, and by Thursday she was able to stay awake for small stretches at a time and think clearly. What she thought about squeezed her heart in a vise. Neither the gunshot wound nor the pain from her surgical incision hurt nearly as badly as her heart did over what she'd said to Collier. What if she'd convinced him she had no feelings for him? What if she'd killed anything they had between them?

Since waking in ICU, she'd been in and out of consciousness due to heavy drugs. Once she was moved to a regular room, the nurses got her up every few hours to walk around. She'd already been up twice today and it wasn't noon yet. Collier had been in here briefly yesterday, but she hadn't seen him today.

He'd talked to her even when she couldn't keep her eyes open. He had laid out the connection between the firefighter victims and told her how the dates of each murder bracketed the death of Raye's brother. Whenever Kiley thought about the attorney aiming that gun at Collier, she wasn't sorry for killing Raye.

Dominic Narr wouldn't be charged with a weapons violation because the sniper rifle found at his apartment had been planted, but he had procured a gun for Raye Ballinger and he had hired someone to disable security at Rehn's warehouse, actions that had directly contributed to murder. Collier had recommended Narr be charged as an accessory, but the ex-con's new attorney was trying to cut a deal with the D.A. Regardless of the deal struck, Narr had earned a trip back to the house of many doors.

A few minutes ago Kiley's mom and sister had helped her to the rest room so she could wash her face and brush her teeth. Finally she felt semi-human again.

She slid weakly back into the bed. Dr. Boren walked in just as Kristin finished brushing Kiley's hair and pulling it back with a clip.

As the doctor checked her vitals and her dressings, Kiley's thoughts were on the man she hoped would walk through the door, the man she hoped would give her a second chance.

Kristin had told her that Collier hadn't left the hospital since bringing her here.

He'd been a rock for her family, even being the one to inform her yesterday that most of her house was burned to the ground. The ache she felt over losing her home was nothing compared to the bone-deep fear that she'd done something irreparable to her and Collier.

Her close call with death had made her realize life was short, too short to do stupid things like walk away from the first man she'd cared about in years. He'd told her he trusted her not to hurt him and what had she done? Told him she didn't want to see him again.

Dr. Boren finished her exam and moved to the foot of the bed, pulling a chart from the slot there and flipping it open to make notes.

Until today Kiley hadn't been coherent enough to carry on her end of a conversation with anyone, let alone the conversation she needed to have with Collier. The one thought that the drugs hadn't been able to drown was that he had said he wanted to be with her. And she'd practically drop-kicked him.

She had tried to apologize yesterday, tried to say something lucid, but her mind had been liquid with painkillers. She couldn't keep a thought for more than two breaths, couldn't keep her eyes open for more than a minute at a time. Today was better. She would talk to him today.

She glanced at the door for what had to be the tenth time in five minutes.

Kristin noticed and shot a look at their mom.

Dr. Boren followed Kiley's gaze, too. "You ready to see that gorgeous hunk of man? The fire investigator who's been guarding you? You must be living right, girl. He seems like a real keeper."

He'd probably only stayed because he'd been there when she was shot. Out of a sense of obligation because they were partners. She wanted it to be more than that. It had to be more. "We're just co-workers."

The doctor laughed softly. "Let me note that on your chart. Patient is delusional."

Kiley smiled, nervous about seeing Collier, but ready. She couldn't let herself hope until she'd talked to him. "I love y'all," she said to her mom and sister. "But please get out and please send him in."

Kristin looked uncertainly at JoAnn, then said quietly, "He's not here."

Kiley's stomach took a dive. For an instant she couldn't breathe. She mumbled something to Dr. Boren as the doctor walked out of the room.

Kristin sat on the edge of the bed; their mom moved up beside Kiley.

An ache spread through her chest. "I shouldn't be surprised he left."

"Why?" JoAnn stroked her hair. "What happened, honey?"

"I told him I didn't want to see him anymore."

Her sister's mouth fell open. "You're worse than delusional! Why would you do that? Don't you care about him?"

"Yes."

"It's obvious he cares about you, too."

"I know."

"Then why did you tell him to get lost!"

At the time it had seemed the right decision to make. "You know his reputation. He moves from woman to woman. Mr. Love-'em-and-leave-'em."

"Isn't that what *you're* doing to him?" Kristin asked quietly.

"Huh? What are you talking—"

"Think about it. He walks in on his fiancée and his friend having sex. There goes his trust in women so he shifts into major rebound mode, playing the field like he's trying to win a medal in bed hopping. Then he meets you and whoa."

Kiley had never seen her sister look so fierce. "Take a breath. Sheesh."

"Then there's you. You thought David was Mr. Right. Turns out he wasn't. Instead of bed hopping, you put up a wall. You meet Collier and bam. The difference is, he's willing to take a chance. All you want to do is move on."

Her sister's rant drew Kiley up short. Was she doing exactly what she'd accused him of planning to do to her? It killed her that he'd taken her at her word and left, but why shouldn't he? She'd thought it out. Told him their ending things seemed like the thing to do. She'd been so sure. So why did she feel so empty?

"For what it's worth, Ki, a guy who looks at a girl the way he looks at you isn't playing around." Kristin shook her head. "He didn't go home until he made sure you were going to be all right. Before that, he took care of everything. Called me and mom to give us the news, had Clay pick her up at the airport, kept us from falling apart that first day you were in ICU and nobody was sure you'd make it. I don't think a man who does things like that is ready for anything less than permanent."

What he'd said the night she'd been wounded played through her mind. *I haven't looked at, much less thought about another woman since I met you. That was after our one dance at Christmas, before we even started working together.*

Since then he'd had plenty of opportunity to look at, think about, do whatever he wanted with other women. Kiley had seen that for herself. And yet he hadn't gone out with anyone.

"He was here for days, Kiley. He's got to be exhausted." Her mom patted her shoulder. "I'm sure once he gets some rest, he'll be back."

Kristin's gaze met hers. "If he isn't, what are you going to do about it?"

"I don't know."

Kiley was in the hospital a week. Collier didn't come back.

Chapter 14

On a Saturday, two weeks after being shot, Kiley stood on Collier's front porch, her chin huddled into her coat against the brutal winter air. The cold made her recovering body ache even more. She wasn't supposed to be here. She wasn't supposed to drive yet, either, but she had to see him. She'd been staying with Kristin. Once her mom and sister had left to go to the store, Kiley had gingerly made her way to her car and come here.

She wasn't sure how long her wobbly legs would hold her.

Her sister was right. Kiley had been so afraid of getting hurt that she'd walked away from the best thing to ever happen to her. She wouldn't blame Collier if he closed the door in her face, but she had to try. She would do whatever it took—beg, crawl, cry, bribe. She'd come to his house before checking the office. The garage door was down so she didn't know if he was here. She hoped he was.

Nerves raw, she rang the bell. When there was no answer

after a few seconds, she punched it again. The lock clicked and the door opened.

And there he was. Looking gorgeous and tired and sweaty in a pair of low-slung jeans. He was shirtless, shoeless, much like the first time she'd come to his house. His eyes flared hotly, and she couldn't tell if it was from pleasure or pain, but the way his face closed against her answered that.

"What are you doing here?"

"I need to talk to you."

"About the case?" he asked tightly. "I wrapped everything up. I told your lieutenant to let you know."

"No, not about the case. About…" *Us.* She wanted to say it, but she couldn't. He looked so good. She hadn't really seen him since that night, and she wanted to look at him forever. "I don't blame you for not wanting to see me, but could you give me just a minute?"

His face was unyielding until his eyes narrowed on her. He stepped out and saw her car, cursing. "Where's your sister? Did you drive yourself? Get in here."

She walked inside, soaking in the warmth as he shut the door behind her.

She turned. He stayed where he was, an awkward silence growing between them. Her teeth were chattering, but she figured that could have been due to nerves as easily as the frigid temperature. Unable to help herself, her gaze roamed over his broad chest, the thin ridges of muscle in his belly. "You working on the hallway floor?"

He nodded.

She closed her eyes briefly. She'd come here to beg, and that was what she was going to do. It would help if she didn't already feel winded.

He finally spoke, his voice indifferent. "What's going on? I know you're okay. I've been checking."

"Physically I'm okay. Mentally I'm a wreck."

There was a brief flare of emotion in his eyes, then nothing. "Getting shot can take a while to get over."

"That's not what I'm talking about." Slightly light-headed, she took a deep breath and tried to steady her rubbery legs. He had every right to kick her out. She'd been horrible to him. "I really hoped to see you again at the hospital."

"You look like you're about to fall down," he muttered. "Go sit on the couch."

"I'm okay." She didn't want there to be any more distance between them, physically or emotionally. Despite the remoteness in his eyes, she cut to the chase. "After I took that slug, I remember shooting Raye and waking up with you listening to my heartbeat. I thought I heard you say... Did I imagine it? Did you tell me you love me?"

A muscle flexed in his jaw. He looked away, said nothing.

"You did, didn't you?"

"You were really out of it," he said gruffly. "You'd lost a lot of blood."

She gave a self-deprecating laugh. "I'd have to be dead to miss that."

"You almost were," he said fiercely, his eyes tortured. "Don't joke about it."

Please, oh, please let that mean she hadn't killed all of whatever he felt for her. She moved closer, only a step, still so uncertain. "I was scared, Collier, but what really scares me is the thought that I've hurt you so badly you won't give me another chance. Give *us* another chance."

"*Us?* There is no *us*. I'm quoting you, Blaze."

"I was an idiot. I panicked." Her wound was throbbing now and her legs felt like wet string. This weakness irritated the fire out of her, but she wasn't stopping until things were resolved. "Telling you I didn't want to see you again was the stupidest thing I've ever done."

"You can't help the way you feel."

"That's right." Why had she ever thought she could walk away from this man? "And I didn't level with you about that."

He gave a harsh laugh. "You sounded pretty level to me. I got the message."

"The wrong message."

His gaze, skeptical and hard, lasered in on her.

"I misjudged you badly. Even when I knew I was wrong about you, I was too stubborn to let go of that image. I want—need— Can you forgive me?"

Surprise flared in his eyes, yet she still sensed a deep reserve in him. "There's nothing to forgive," he said gruffly. "You had a good reason. My past gave you *plenty* of reasons."

"After I learned what kind of man you really are, I had no reason except stubborn fear. I was wrong about you, and I hope it's not too late to tell you that I think you're pretty amazing. I'm sorry I acted like such a jerk that night. I didn't want to let myself believe you could be different because…"

"Because?"

He was still listening. That was a good sign, right? She took the first step to baring her soul. "Because if you do decide to move on, it will break my heart." *Maybe me, too.*

He didn't speak, the silence dragging out for so long that Kiley felt each second like a sting to her skin. "Collier, I'm afraid I've ruined everything. You laid your feelings on the line and I threw them back in your face. I regret that with everything in me. I thought if I walked away first, I wouldn't get attached, but I already was."

"You just got out of the hospital. I don't think now is the time to talk about this."

"These last two weeks of being without you have been awful." She continued, not wanting to give him a chance to stop her. "I regret everything about that night, especially that I didn't tell you how special you made me feel when you said you trusted me. That meant so much, and then I…I told you to leave."

She thumbed away tears she hadn't been aware of crying, following the urging of her heart rather than her head. She'd never been so scared in her life. "I don't want to spend the rest of my life wondering what could've been. It isn't fair to ask you to suffer through all the mistrust I've built over the years, but I'm asking, anyway. I love you, Collier McClain. Even if you don't feel the same way, I want you to know that. You're the best man I've ever known."

A muscle twitched in his jaw as his gaze searched hers. Long seconds passed. "Why, Blaze? Why now?"

"I could say it's the sex," she said with an attempt at humor, swallowing around the lump in her throat. "But it's because I nearly died. And because I thought about what you said the other night."

"Which was what?"

She wanted to touch him, but the guarded look on his face kept her from reaching out. Jamming her hands into her coat pockets, she clenched her fists, feeling shaky. "That you're taking as much of a chance that I won't hurt you as I am that you won't move on. You never asked me to prove anything to you, yet that's what I wanted from you. That was wrong. I know I hurt you and I am so, so sorry."

He was quiet for a long time, his green eyes bleak. "I can't take it again, Blaze."

The pain was so sharp, so piercing she thought she might fall down. She was too late. He couldn't forgive her. "I understand. I'll go. But I want you to know that I do trust you. I never would've gotten involved with you if I didn't. I couldn't admit that to myself until my sister pointed it out, and she was right."

Her control was slipping. She had to get out of here before she bawled like a baby. She started to move past him toward the door.

He gently snagged her elbow. "You don't think I'm letting you walk out, do you? Without having my say?"

Tears blurred her vision. She deserved whatever he said to her. "No. Go ahead."

His gaze settled on her face and she couldn't decide what emotion passed through his eyes. Very carefully he curled an arm around her waist and lifted her into his arms.

Stunned, she gripped his bare shoulder for balance. "Wh-what are you doing?"

He carried her into the living room, sinking down on the couch. She wanted to hope he would forgive her, but she was afraid to. "Collier?"

"I'm making sure you stay for this part."

"I'm staying."

He settled her on his lap, his arms warm and strong around her. His gaze locked on her face. "I want to know how much further you want us to go."

"Whatever you want."

"Hmm." His gaze settled on her lips, setting off sparks beneath her skin.

She wanted him to kiss her. *Now.*

"I meant everything I said the other night."

"I know."

He slid his free hand into her hair. "I want forever, Blaze. If you don't, that's gonna be a problem."

"Forever?" Had he really said that? Was he going to forgive her? "Are you sure? After what I said, what I did?"

"Forever," he said firmly. "When I tell you that, do you believe me?"

Staring into his eyes, she saw the truth. "Yes."

"Good, because the only way this is gonna work is if you trust me."

"I do."

"And if you love—"

"I do! I love you!" Finally, finally his lips touched hers. His tenderness brought tears to her eyes. She thought about how she'd hurt him, how she'd nearly lost him. Uncaring of the sharp twinge along her incision, she put her arms around his neck and held him close.

Long moments later he lifted his head. "You better be in this for the long haul."

"Yes, absolutely," she said breathlessly.

He peered closely at her. "Are you okay? You're not going to pass out on me, are you?"

"Not a chance."

He kissed her again, then hugged her tightly to his bare chest. "When I saw you shot, I wanted you to live more than anything, even if you didn't want me. But these last two weeks have been torture."

"For me, too."

"Here's the deal." He drew back to look at her. "Nobody leaves."

She smiled, cupping his raspy jaw. "Nobody leaves."

"Whatever we need to work out, we will."

"Yes. Kiss me."

He did, pulling away a minute later to rest his forehead against hers. "We've got to cool it. You're in no condition for what I want to do to you."

"You're such a big talker."

"Don't mess with me." He brushed a kiss across her hair, pressed her head to his shoulder. "About those toothbrushes…"

"Toothbrushes?" She let herself drop every guard she'd worked so hard to build. "What are you talking about?"

"That supply you have in your bathroom. Just how many of those do you have, anyway?"

He sounded…jealous? Collier McClain? The whole idea hit her as extremely funny and she laughed, wincing. "Don't make me laugh. It hurts."

"I'm serious. How many?"

She smiled, making him wait.

"Blaze," he growled against her temple.

"One."

"One?"

"Yeah."

"It better be for me."

She snuggled into him. "It is."

"That's how it's gonna stay, too."

* * * * *

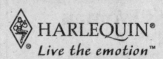